42 & Beyond

Volume II

Copyright © 2018 Hydra Productions
All copyright for all material within, remains with the authors:

> Kisonu Yuutatchi
> Iris Sweetwater
> Lilly Rayman
> Sondra Hicks
> Maggie Lowe
> Brian Hagan
> Joseph McGarry
> Philip K. Chase
> Marsha Black
> Paige Clendenin

All copyright for the cover art is held by the publisher and is not transferable.

> First Edition
> Printed in the United States of America.
> Published August 25, 2018
> All rights reserved.

This book is licensed for your personal enjoyment only. It may not be copied or re-distributed in any way. The authors hold all copyright.

This book is a work of fiction and does not represent any individual living or dead. Names, characters, places, and incidents either are products of the authors' imaginations, are used fictitiously or with permission.

> Cover design by Hydra Productions
> Editing by Hydra Productions
> Formatting by Lelene Designs

The unauthorized reproduction or distribution of a copyrighted work is illegal. Criminal copyright infringement, including infringement without monetary gain, is investigated by the FBI and is punishable by fines and federal imprisonment.

For permission to reproduce or distribute any part of this book, contact the publisher directly at:

Hydra Productions
Salt Lake City, UT
657-206-5360
https://www.hydraproductionsonline.com/

Table of Contents

Voided Dreams 5
A Change In His Stars 10
An Unexpected Space Story 29
Blood & Space 49
Darkness Lurking 82
Lucky's Books 94
From the Files of Operation Mermaid 109
Forbidden Home 127
Planetary Relics 150
Fifty Days Forced to Love A Space Conspiracy 178
Bonus 220
Intergalactic Bridal Market 221

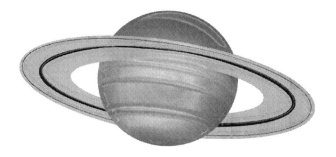

Void Dreams
Kisonu Yuutatchi

    At 42 years old Jeremiah believes the chance to live his dream or do anything exciting has come and gone. However, an odd day at work begins an adventure he never could have imagined.

Void Dreams

Jeremiah sighed as he opened the hatch of the Bazumat's cargo hold. He had always wanted to fly one of these beautifully streamlined, cargo ships, but now, at the age of 42, he felt that it was nothing more than a pipe-dream. He didn't feel old, but most cargo pilots nowadays were young guns with no ties and big aspirations.

As Jeremiah entered the hold he pulled out a hologram docket listing all of the cargo that was supposed to be aboard the ship. Beginning his pre-inspection checks, Jeremiah realized there was something odd about this cargo shuttle. Jeremiah exited the ship, and upon turning around, realized his suspicions were correct. The cargo hold seemed suspiciously small for this shuttle.

The Bazumat IC-4 was the fourth-generation shuttle of the line, and though it was meant for small interplanetary jumps, its hold was capable of holding up to 80 tonnes of cargo with ease. This hold seemed capable of holding maybe half of that.

Jeremiah re-entered the hold and pulled a small brass wrench from his tool belt. As he neared the back wall of the hold, tapping gently on the panels as he went, he became overwhelmed by the stench of rotting fish. As he continued, he heard a hollow sound as he tapped one of the panels. Using his wrench, he removed the bolts holding the panel on and discovered a secondary hatch filled with sealed barrels. He immediately contacted his supervisor on the holo-docket and began recording his progress through the hatch.

Jeremiah's supervisor, along with the Bazumat's captain, soon arrived, and the questioning process began. Jeremiah was dismissed, much to his dismay, upon the arrival of the station security and customs officials. As Jeremiah left the scene, he wondered how many more times this would happen today.

To Jeremiah's displeasure, the rest of the shift was uneventful, as it often was. So was the life of a dreamer sometimes. When you were a child, you thought you could do anything, and Jeremiah had been no exception. There seemed to be a million different ways to get to the end goal he wanted, but in reality, it had never happened. He had been practicing on flight simulators his whole life, and in fact, had even taken classes early on at the academy, but the license, well that was another story. It was a pricey piece of paper that he just couldn't afford, and he didn't dare ask his friends or family for such a thing. It just wasn't right.

So, he had instead found easy work and easy money right here and had been inspecting ships with cargo ever since. He knew everything about every ship that came through, which was at least nice, but he was never allowed in the commander's seat, never allowed to fly.

The last ship came in just before he was about to sign off, and Jeremiah yawned as the Valkyrie 1M-9 approached. It wasn't typically a cargo ship, and was in fact, a small vessel usually privately owned. However, the law said if they had over a certain poundage of baggage even they would have to stop for him to check. It was likely inconvenient to those aboard, but it kept everyone safe. It kept everything operating smoothly.

If he was honest with himself, he would admit his job was important, crucial even. It really was, but that didn't mean he always liked it.

Jeremiah stepped onto the ship, expecting to find some food supplies, medical kits, and clothing in the tiny cargo hold that would fit the family of three that he saw onboard as he waved at them with a smile. However, they said nothing back, and he was hit with that scent again; the smell of fish.

He crinkled his brow in concern and wondered for a moment if it was time to call his superior once more, but then his curiosity got the best of him. There was nothing locked or hidden here, just the typical hatch to the cargo hold that he opened with no issue. Just a peek and no one would ever know...

Looking inside, Jeremiah was in shock, finding three barrels again just as before in the larger ship. That was all it seemed to fit in this tiny space. What were the odds of encountering such an odd thing twice?

He stood up straight and turned to face the man that had been piloting the ship; likely the patriarch of the family. "Can you all tell me what is in those barrels and if you have the proper permits you can show me to carry those?" Jeremiah pointed towards the cargo hold, but the man just stared and smiled. In fact, the whole family looked that way, a little out of it, This was so bizarre, he couldn't even fathom what was in there.

Not knowing what else to do, Jeremiah instructed the family to step out as he went out to grab a crowbar, a flashlight, and his towel. He never worked without a towel. Cargo could get real messy sometimes, and with the smell of fish around, he was not risking that.

He stepped back inside and crawled into the cargo space, his head so tall he had to bend down not to touch the ceiling as he used the crowbar to pry open all three barrels, the smell of fish getting even stronger now. He covered his nose and grunted for a moment, trying to to get sick from it before finally getting the courage to step forward and peer into one of the barrels.

He was blinded for a moment by an aqua glow that was otherworldly, and he had to shield his eyes until he heard an angelic whisper. "Sorry, we did not mean to frighten you," it said. Startled, he looked down into the barrel to find the blue glow coming from a pair of eyes attached to a small child-like creature with long, fuschia hair and the hint of sparkling scales below the water. He had heard of them before. They were the origin of every myth about mermaids and sirens out there, and they were tricky creatures. They could be kind and peaceful or ruthless and controlling at a moment's notice. What were they doing on these ships?

"Why have you been locked into barrels on these ships?" Jeremiah questioned, hoping for a truthful answer as he was sure to look away, closing off their biggest link for temptation. Though, he knew sometimes just their voices could convince a man to do anything, even kill himself or his own family.

"Our home is being destroyed. We must find a new one," she told him. "But I fear that not all of us have trusted the right ship commanders," she said, her voice like a ghostly song. Jeremiah thought back to the ship earlier and how his superior had sent him away and said nothing else. The reason these creatures had such power was because they were so physically vulnerable.

"Our leader, we have lost her, she has been taken on a large ship with many of the others," a more tiny voice piped up, and Jeremiah looked into another barrel to find red eyes and golden hair looking back at him. Maybe it was their influence on him, he couldn't be sure, but he felt like he had to help them. He felt like his destiny was calling.

He stepped back out and scratched his head thoughtfully. His shift was over. The family was so out of it they were useless to these poor creatures. Flying a ship of this size, well, it shouldn't be this hard with all he knew, and surely there would be a manual.

Jeremiah's breathing picked up as he defiantly walked up to the controls and sat down, his hands on them and ready to leave, to leave behind the routine that he had known for so long and go on an adventure.

"Here goes nothing," he said to himself, not looking back even once to see if anyone would come after him.

To Be Continued…

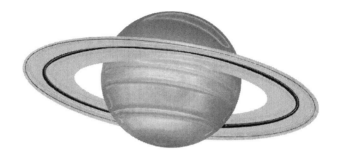

A Change In His Stars
Iris Sweetwater

     Nevin is one of a small population of pure humans left in the galaxy and a warrior of sorts. He has joined a group called The Galaxy Watchers with a righteous cause; to reestablish the rule of pure humans and take down those that they believe have been dirtied with mixed blood. But once he becomes a prisoner of war on a planet full of dirty bloods, Nevin learns a secret and meets a woman that changes his life and view forever.

A Change In His Stars

  I pulled out my sword, admiring the way the curve reminded me of the beauty of a woman's body. Though, the shining metal was much more trustworthy in my hands than the treachery of another being. I had been taught to trust only a few, and even then, sometimes, those few disappointed. It was an inevitability. This sword, though, would take its aim and hit the target as long as my hand was sure and steady and my cause righteous. As the ship descended, a smile came across my face, and I pulled my gray hood on. This was a large colony. If The Galaxy Watchers prevailed here, it would serve to send a message all around the universe; we are coming.

  A fellow comrade came by and slapped me on the shoulder. I was moving up in the ranks quickly. This was something I knew would make my family proud, if I ever found them again, to tell them. I doubted that I would. They were the reason for all of this; the reason that I had joined the ranks of the Galaxy Watchers. I had watched them suffer at the hands of those who are not human; of those who sought to mingle. mix, and take over humanity, in its entirety. With their technology and their knowledge, they all thought they were better than us. We were what was better. We had hearts. We had strength. We had morality. These creatures now breeding with us and spreading across the stars, were taking what was our right as human beings under God. They were nothing.

Today was my first day without Raul by my side. He was my leader, my trainer. He was our commander and was considered to be the greatest commander the Galaxy Watches had ever seen, able to expand us further than we have ever been before.

I had never seen so many humans until I was 13 and went to train with him.

Here, today, 13 years later, I still work proving myself. Everyone thinks I will be the next Commander. I will take Raul's place, but this is a big job. If I don't get this right; if I don't win this for us, then this is it. I am useless, and I have failed.

As a whole, we had too many victories for me to keep count. The Galaxy Watchers were a righteous group, and they would win every battle in the end because that was the way it was meant to be. When I joined them, I had dreams of grandeur. I waited so long for the moment when I would be a part of one of their sieges and witness firsthand how they were making the galaxy better. I wanted to be a part of making the galaxy a better place. Ever since humans had procured the ability to travel the links of the universe, instead of focusing on conquering, colonizing, and trading they had been crossbreeding with almost every race they found. Now, humans were the minority in the universe. But that was not something to put up with. Humans had the right to conquer, own, and rule, but only when they are pure of blood. It was our duty to make sure that humans became pure again and expand through the galaxy, as the rulers that we were.

I felt the jolting of the ship as it landed and knew that it was time. My comrades and I waited at the ship's entrance as the ramp began to descend. I was near the front of the line, one of the best warriors in the group. Several years of training had been worth it even though I hated waiting to be able to be a part of all of this.

I could feel the energy around me as everyone was ready with their swords, ready to wreak holy justice on the many dirty bloods that would be awaiting us on the outside.

We came out with a roar, ready to take this large utopia like colony by surprise. The place was overrun by dirty bloods. I could tell instantly as I begin to slash into the crowd with my sword, clean cuts coming off so that torsos, heads, and feet were severed all around me.

There were some that look so human except for markings or strange appendages. Some look like they might be a mixture of several races. It was absolutely disgusting to me. I had no problem slaughtering them all.

As I grunted, surrounded by severed flesh, it took me some time to notice that we were more than outnumbered. In fact, as I began to check out my surroundings, I could see that somehow they had been prepared. I didn't know if these dirty bloods suddenly formed some kind of army that was always at the ready, or fate somehow gotten word that we were coming. Either way, it did not make me happy as I saw many men fall. To make matters worse, they were being killed. They were being taken prisoner. A fate worse than death. I could only hope that I would be given the chance, if I got captured too, in my life as the way of the warrior, not be slave to these dirty bloods. I could never live with myself.

I let out a roar, a last-ditch effort to kill as many of them as possible has a new surge of dirty bloods came at us. Had we known that they were trained and ready we would've brought more men. But I soon found my sword taken from me, and my hands bound behind me. I was a prisoner of war. These creatures, because I would never insult myself by giving the name men or people, had me and there is no escaping. I was chained and taken to the city as a patch was slapped on my shoulder, over my great cloak. Number 42 was emblazoned on it. My existence had become no more than a number. I suddenly wanted to rip the thing off and put it on one of the men who had me. They were the numbers. They were the scum.

* * *

I woke up in a white room. That's all there was. I was completely surrounded by white on all sides. As I came to, it took me a moment to see if there is actually a bed in the corner, that I had been haphazardly laid on. It was white like everything else, little more than a makeshift mattress on the ground. I turned over, not showing any signs of pain. I was completely alone. I saw that there was a lone towel, also white, laying on the opposite side of the room. I couldn't fathom, at this moment, the reason for it. It was looking like a mighty fine thing to use, this tool, in order to end my misery. But something held me back. I still, for some reason had a will to live. Maybe it was the idea that if someone ever came to get me out of here, for any reason, maybe I'd get the chance to slaughter another dirty blood, maybe the three who brought me in here to begin with. Now that would be a true warrior's death.

I growled as I noticed that stupid 42 still sitting there on me. I would spit on the first one to try and call me that. And from the sounds of footsteps headed in my direction, it looks like I might get my chance pretty damn soon.

Despite my injuries, I stood up proud, my hands in front of me clasped, my head held high. I would greet my enemy with strength and pride. In a fair fight, we would have won. Clearly, there was some trial here, something to learn, something righteous; otherwise, why would I have lost.

In front of me, I soon found a female surrounded by three dirty bloods in armor, and I couldn't tell whether they were there to guard her or to do her bidding. I was literally taken aback by the loathsome idea that a woman had any kind of authority, but also by the fact that her blood was clearly the dirtiest of them all.

She stood before me, her skin the pale mask of the human woman. She was tall like one of the old warrior races. Her mouth, her body shape, and even her long golden hair belied the fact that someone had muddied up their genetics by breeding. So she was something lower than human. The barely visible, red markings that covered the sides of her face and likely much of her body made that clear. I cannot even tell what race or descent she was mixed with. It was a shame considering she would remain a stunning human woman. Instead, she was something worthy of death before she even made it on this planet, or wherever planet she was born on.

"Are you going to continue to stare at me? Were you going to kill me? I assure you that I'm ready to die. I also assure you, given the chance, that I will take down every single one of you on my way out."

The female creature gave an eerie grin before responding. I would be lying if I said I wasn't completely surprised by the fact that she was able to speak perfect English. "Actually, I came by to see the one that they labeled 42. I came by to learn his name as he is the last of his kind alive of our prisoners of war. It seems that the towel I gave each of you so that when you were awake and less wounded you were able to clean yourselves, has turned into a means to an end. So tell me, why you were the only member of the galaxy watchers who did not use it for such a purpose."

She came close to the white bars to sit between myself and them. I couldn't tell if she was being condescending or genuinely curious. The only reason that I supplied her with an answer was to show the strength of my people. Though, I bowed my head for a moment out of respect for those I had lost. "You do not deserve my name, so you get it for those who will never be able to give it to you. I am Nevin, a great warrior for the galaxy watchers. While I did contemplate doing what the others followed through with, I saw an opportunity if I did not die yet. As I have already explained to you what said opportunity is."

The strange woman gave a slow nod, backing up only a couple of inches before she gave some sort of silent order to the two behind her.

Turning back to me, she said," no, I don't think I'm going to kill you quite yet. I want to try and rehabilitate you first. I'm not the barbarian they would have you think."

I didn't quite know what to make of her words. Or the fact that I was being let out of the cell. In this case, rehabilitation sounded more like brainwashing. I didn't know what was to come. And then a calm came over me and told me not to even try to attack these creatures. I didn't understand it. But something I had been taught by my commander was to obey my gut feelings.

* * *

If I had counted right, I have now been imprisoned on this planet for five days. For five days I had been taken from my cell to get clean, eat, and to go to what they called classes. They were for rehabilitation. They felt a lot like what I had feared, which was brainwashing. I could feel something changing within myself, and I struggled to remain the same man with the same resolve I had before, about these creatures. I had to give it to them that they were intelligent. As intelligent as a human being. That was the unfortunate part, that when we humans decided to muddy up our blood, we became heinous aliens, we lent them things like that. They were really good at strategizing, and I could tell that they had, at least on this planet, modern sciences, and arts, and politics. For the most part, all I had seen were the various guards and other high-ranking officials. And of course, there was her.

I came to learn that her name was Kaia. Everyone seemed to completely respect her, and yet, she did not lord that over anyone in the same way that I was used to. Raul was a great commander. He was a great commander because he had ideals, he had combat skills, and he had intimidation. He put fear into the enemy by putting fear into his comrades, and to his inferiors. I didn't know what to make of this woman. I would've said she was too soft, but I could see a hardness there.

I didn't understand why I was noticing her at all. She was a disgusting mutt. I should've retched at her feet. But I couldn't. I just couldn't.

They must've seen some kind of improvement in me, though I couldn't exactly see that as a good sign considering I was trying to be loyal to Raul. I wanted to make my commander proud even if he never figured out that I was here and alive. Though, I did have hope that I would be back to fighting for him one day. And if I didn't, I would find my way out one way or the other.

Today, I was brought in to the only thing that I could describe it, was a cafeteria. It was a large place where many gathered to eat. I would guess they were all either prisoners or low ranking civilians. Some were humans like me, possibly that have been captured and brainwashed, and some more alien. But they did not wear the clothes of the military or upper class of this planet.

I sat down with the food I was given, a large and nutritious meal. Despite the fact that I was a prisoner, I still remain mostly strong. Though, the first few meals I had refused to eat much. I was afraid I was being poisoned with their alien food. My stomach had gotten used to it after the first couple of days. After I couldn't hold out anymore.

A sudden quiet came over the entire place. I looked up to see that Kaia herself was entering the cafeteria. Whether or not this was a usual occurrence, I couldn't be sure.

I was even more suspicious of the situation as I saw her make eye contact with me and walk over. She sat down across from me as if she was going to have a meal with me, and it made me shift in my seat.

"To what do I owe the pleasure?" I asked her bitterly. She smiled a genuine smile that made my skin crawl. I can make out that she has fangs... fangs like a vampire. It turned out the legends like that came from an actual species of creatures. There is an entire alien race that actually had to suck blood in order to survive. What human had bred with one, I wasn't sure. Though, I had to admit that her beauty was much like I would imagine that of the Sirens. Her eyes would often go from a frightening black to striking blue, and the red splotches on her face actually made it look more symmetrical and angular. Her perfectly pursed lips, pale skin, and silvery hair were exactly what any man would like to see after a long dry spell. Though, I'd never seen signs from her of actually being some kind of seductress. Not that you would need to be looking like that.

"I wanted to touch base with you and see how you are doing. You made some progress, but it seems you are still stuck in your own ways. I wanted to see why. Very little of your kind has survived this long."

I narrowed my eyes at her. I didn't quite like what she was insinuating, and I felt there was more to what she was saying; teaching me that they can survive that long because they had to kill us? Or does she mean something else entirely, like the fact that many would kill themselves rather than allow themselves to be brainwashed? I had hung my head low, at that thought. I was letting down my comrades and Raul who had trained me to be one of their best.

"You truly want to know what I feel about you and those like you? You really want to know why?" Kia nodded her head encouragingly. Then, part of me told myself that she would regret asking. But who was I to deny her to be aware of her own ugliness? "Humans, from what I can tell, have always been the most intelligent and advanced species in the universe. What other reason would there be for no one ever making it to earth? For the fact that we had to go out and find all of you? It is a shame that many humans have, instead of spreading throughout the stars with colonies, new technology, and using all of you for trade and work, decided to breed with all of you. They have mixed our blood, muddied our blood with many other species. Those that are the step between animal and human. And now it is all of you who are taking over; all of those who are mixed. It isn't right. It is disgusting, it makes me gag just the thought of it. What I want, no, what we want is the right for pure humans to do what we were meant to do in the first place."

I looked at her with curiosity to see that she wasn't angry, sad, or anything of the sort. She no longer held a smile upon her face, but she seemed to not be so swayed by the awful things I have said about her.

"From the look on your face, I think that you are surprised that I'm not reacting in a typical way to this information. While I have been mostly aware of what the galaxy watchers were after, I have never had the pleasure of talking with one face-to-face and asking them why; asking them what they believe. You see, I believe in something else entirely, but I can respect you having such a strong resolve. I see you are not so easily giving up on what you believe just because you are a prisoner or because you fear something. In fact, I would say you are one of the bravest humans to come to us."

"Brave?" I scoffed. "Raul would have my head for such betrayal, for such sniveling behavior as choosing my life over the cause. I should attack you just so that you will take my life now rather than continue this game that we are playing. I don't know why I haven't, but it is certainly not out of bravery."

Kia suddenly stood up, and two guards behind her stood as well, like there were magnets attached to the both of them. "Follow me."

I looked at the two guards and all the guards that surrounded me in this cafeteria of sorts. I knew that I was going whether or not I agreed. So, I decided to save a fight, for now.

I was shocked to be taken past my cell and down to a corridor I never seen, then taken down a set of stairs down, down, down. I didn't realize something we've gone down further than where they kept their prisoners. As a cold chill came over me, I saw that we were going deep down into the planet. Then, a noise assailed my ears. I looked around as a new worry enveloped me. They had some kind of heating element down here. That, and there were hundreds of muddy blooded creatures bustling about. There were some making weapons, some looking at maps, and others performing various tasks. Everyone was so busy no one even stopped to look at the human prisoner.

"What is this place?" I asked, confused.

"This is the resistance. These are the people who in one way or another are helping us. They are helping us to fight the galaxy watchers, to push them back, and to make sure that we maintain our rights. You see, I know I'm bringing the enemy in here. But I don't exactly see you as the enemy. I see you as a person with strong convictions. A person who is grown being taught something that I was not taught, that I do not believe in. But I can tell that you are a strong warrior with a strong will. You could do great things here. But even if you never do, even if you waste away here or do decide to end your life, I wanted you to know one thing in return for your answer. We do not fight because we feel it is our right to fight. I believe in fighting for everyone, for everyone's right to live their life. I believe we are all made for greatness in one way or another and that we should all deserve to survive and thrive. That is how I feel."

* * *

The freedom I was given after that was unprecedented. I was wary of it. I felt something must've been waiting in the wings for me, or that perhaps I was constantly being watched when I didn't know it. Were they waiting for me to off myself, waiting for me to make a wrong move so that they felt justified in taking my life? My brain and my heart were rocking against each other. I knew what I had been taught. I knew the gray robes I wore of the galaxy watchers were those of the righteous. Those who were in the right, those who deserve all things in the universe. Yet, I could not find any specific faults with these creatures. They were kind and in a way that I had not seen as a human. They were logical and that too, I did not expect. And despite being a prisoner, I'd much more freedom than I would expect considering the kind of damage I could cause, even as a minority on this planet. Kia knew the kind of warrior I was. She had me pegged. And that also was messing with me. She consumed my thoughts! I was afraid it was because I was beginning to worship her the way the others did. Though I shouldn't, all I saw was my commander instead of a woman. I had to do something about it, and either I would get my freedom because of it, or I would be free in death. But it had to end.

My access to the resistance and their supplies in their quarters meant that I had seen that they had advanced technology. Tech similar to humans. There is actually a computer that I could easily access. Maybe they would have a map of the planet. Maybe they would be information about a ship I could take to get out of here and get back to the galaxy watchers. Then and only then I could be a worthy and true hero. I could bring the vital information about the resistance so that we could finally end this planet and in these people. Look at me calling them people. They were party brainwashing me.

I smirked to myself when I realized I still had my gift of intelligence. I opened the computer and knew I had to be quick. I used the hacking skills that I learned a with the galaxy watchers, something only I and a few others were trained in, to get into their systems. I scanned through numerous amounts of information like weapon design, maps, and databases. Something caught my eye that was strange though, and I had to do a double take. They had a file on some of the galaxy watchers and their leaders. It looks like Raul and I have a file, though there was very little in it about me other than I had been put in prison with a number 42 on my chest. But Raul, he was there.

If I was going to go back to my commander, I needed to know what they had on him. I need to know is this how they figured out that we were coming and bombarded us. Also wanted to know if he was alive.

And it looked like he was. However, I couldn't believe my eyes as I read his file, especially when I looked at his race. "Half Arcadian?" I whispered to myself. That couldn't be correct, and yet, they had pictures of him, pictures of him without his gray cloak that he always wore. I tried to remember if I've ever seen him without it, and I had not. But the markings on the back of his head were plain as day. Unless they faked these, then my own commander that taught us to kill muddy bloods, that taught us to kill these creatures because humans had a right to rule the universe, is not even human himself.

I no longer cared if I was found as I fell to the ground ripping out my hair and screamed in English. I didn't know which way was up; what more to believe. I was a prisoner here being brainwashed to believe that these creatures deserve just as much as humans did, and I've been lied to back at home my whole life as I dedicated to fighting for somebody who was not who he said he was.

Guards came running, and I was almost certain this time that they were going to kill me. This is the end of my life. And suddenly I didn't want it to be. I wanted to fight for my life. I wanted answers, and I didn't want to die for a man who had lied to me to get me to fight for him. What was he even wanting? Why was he fighting against his own kind? I didn't pretend to know. I realize that I was nobody and I knew nothing.

I let myself be carried out of there by the guards picking my legs up and going numb. I was dropped on the ground and dared to look up to see I had been brought into what seemed to be the private chambers of their leader, Kaia.

"Leave us, motioning, she said with authority, making the guards leave. What? Left for her to kill me herself? I had my head bowed, sobs coming without permission. I cannot remember the last time I cried, but I knew it had been at least a decade. I was at the lowest of my lows. "What did you see?"

"I couldn't even begin to describe what I saw. The trail. Lies. And I don't know who is lying, but I don't know if I can live with myself if he is who I think he is."

There was a strained silence that passed between us before she said anything again. "I don't suppose you would believe me if I told you that those records were entirely accurate. Your leader, the current leader of the galaxy watchers, is not human. Well, at least not by your definition. We do not tell your people when they come here because they would not believe us. They follow him with loyalty, and blindly. Because he is a good commander. Because he is persuasive. Despite the disgust that I have for him, I can respect that in him. He's a formidable foe. Though, I see the rest of you as his little sheep, doing his bidding without understanding what they were fighting for."

I bit my lip and taste of the coppery blood that I drew because of it. It was myself I was angry at. Any other time, being compared to a sheep would've made me lash out, but I had no will to now. I could see now that she was right. Despite how wrong and horrible I had been, she had been kind to me. She had given me a place; offered me a home. Offered me a place where I could still fight, where I could still have a resolve even when I found out the truth. I looked up at her reverently and knew that the obsession I've been afraid that I had, because of being brainwashed, was not that it all. In the weeks that I had spent here, I've been falling in love with this woman. The only woman I ever met with the kind of authority that I could respect and a beauty that also enchanted me and yet didn't take away from her power. I would be honored to be killed by her.

"I accept whatever punishment you feel necessary. In my death, I hope that the Lord has mercy on my soul, for I have sinned in my beliefs. I have followed a man that I thought I knew but did not. For that I am sorry."

"Have you learned nothing from your time here?" She raged, and for the first time I heard pure anger in her voice and looked up. There was fire in her eyes as she stared that me. "I do not go around killing good people. I kill when I have to, in order not to be killed. I kill to protect my people that is it. You are no longer a threat. You haven't been a threat. That's why have been trying to give your freedom."

I could hear something, feel something in her rage that I didn't expect. Did she feel something for me too? Without even thinking I stood up and ran to her clasping her face in my hands even though her power was so much more than mine here. She was my commander, and as my lips landed on hers, I tasted that power. I tasted her sweetness, the salty, the good, and the bad. But I didn't dare let go now that I had a taste of what I had been missing. I'd been too busy following the wrong man.

I pulled back and knew that everything in me had changed on a cellular level. This was love. This was life. And I had wasted so many years in true ignorance, not living it.

"I want to fight," I said. I had been raised to believe one thing, but this beautiful creature in front of me had changed every cell in my body with her alien beauty. Now, I would fight to the death to defend that which I used to hate.

"And you shall."

* * *

For weeks, I had been training others, working with the resistance in order to bring them up to my skill level; the only skill level that could beat someone like Raul. My nights were plagued by nightmares of meeting my commander again, of going back to him; facing his wrath for my betrayal. Through it all, there was her.

Kaia was my rock. I was falling deeply for her, and she comforted me on those nights where I felt like I was suffocating. I was suffocating from the guilt, from the lies, and from the truth. And she surrounded me with her own oxygen. My love was something different. While her kisses were magical, it wasn't about that. The physical affection had not gone beyond their unit, but it didn't have to first to know that we were supposed to be with each other. We were one. At least, that's what I was feeling.

She had given me a purpose again, one that actually meant something. She made sure that my transition had been easy despite the fact that everyone on this planet had a reason to despise me. Instead, she helped me earn respect. In addition to the training of them, all would learn how we would defeat the galaxy watchers. We would do it with blood we would do with fairness. Everyone would get their chance to learn the truth and make a choice. That was the way to righteousness.

I stared at the black cloak on my bed, and my hands trembled as I approached it. It was part of who I now was, my possession now since I began training the others, but it felt wrong. I had donned my grey cloak for so many years that donning another didn't feel sane. I also didn't feel like I deserved to pretend to be one of them. Sometimes I thought I never would truly be one of them.

But as we prepared to leave to go to a local small base of the galaxy watchers, and convince them to either come to our side or will be lost souls, in the expansive universe, forever, I knew that I needed to wear what my comrades were wearing.

With my hands, I slipped on the black cloak and found it to be heavier in a way. Had more meaning to it. There was more that I had to accomplish wearing this than I ever did, that I was ever meant to with my grey cloak on.

"You look sexy in black." I turned around to see that Kaia was there, standing in the doorway and looking me over. The sideways smirk was on her face. I didn't like the way that she could sneak up on me and how vulnerable she made me, but her comment and the look in her eyes sent chills down my spine. I knew the day that we decided to consummate this love that it would be a heartbreaking pleasure.

"Are you sure you should come with us today?" I asked her, changing the subject. I kept thinking that a mission like this didn't need the leader. I was so used to Raul only coming out for those large important conquests. He always had someone else fight his battles. Before, I thought it was a good military strategy, but now I believed it to be the sign of a coward.

"I will be fine, if that's what you're worried about. Besides, I had to find something to sink these teeth into eventually." I try not to cringe as she showed her fangs and ran her tongue over them. I didn't have the heart to tell her that I was still sensitive about that even though I was falling in love with her. The idea of her having to drink blood from people just still didn't hit me the right way. But I didn't want to upset her.

I said little as I got myself prepared for the fight. A small group of galaxy watchers had gathered on a nearby planet, probably preparing for more to come, to get ready to strike us. We all wanted them vulnerable to infiltrate and possibly win them over before the others came. They would be our Trojan horses so to speak. It was funny how many centuries ago that story was written down, and yet, it was so so relevant today in combat. It was still one of the best strategies around. Nothing could replace the element of surprise, as I learned the hard way, when I arrived here.

By nightfall I was no longer in the place had been calling home now for a few months. Gathering in the shadows, coming off of our small ship, I can't believe that Kaia took the lead. She was female, meaning that the galaxy watchers could see her as a weaker link, not understanding the dynamics here, plus she was the commander. Generally, weren't they to be in the middle, being protected? But she insisted, so I chose to be right there with her. I couldn't believe my own thoughts as I knew that if it came down to me or her, I would make sure it was me that went. I had been prepared to die many times in my life, and to die for her, it would be completely worth it. I would only regret not having more time with her.

I was surprised when they were willing to hear us out and let us talk. Though, I had my eyes on them the whole time. I knew it was just a matter of time before at least one of them lashed out.

I was right. They all came out screaming at once with accusations of brainwashing and the doubt in themselves to survive that. What was said was his rule; strong minds, strong minds that can be used for something else. They fear the way to have peace, a way to have trade, a way to live in harmony. They could easily join the resistance, but most just resisted the truth. So, those who loved my comrades turned on me, and three men took me once. That was not something I was prepared for, and as I was distracted keeping my eyes on Kaia. I didn't notice until it was too late that a cut went straight to my stomach. There's almost no way to get there and not hit something vital. Infections are common, even in this age, when it came to cuts like this.

I fell to the ground as I heard Kaia call for a retreat. The wounded were dragged, others running back to their ship as they are being chased; the galaxy watchers crying out victoriously. I have failed again, and as my eyes flutter closed from the loss of blood, the last thing I saw was the tears of blood, running down her face.

I woke up in a bed, a bed that I was now familiar with. It had been given to me once I became a member of this community. I felt the pain, the sting of my injury. I dared to look down at my almost bare body, save for my briefs, a bandage wrapped around me many times to keep the wound safe and clean.

That's when my eyes met hers, and she was sobbing on the side of the bed. The minute our eyes met, though, the look turned to one of almost hatred. I went to cock my head to the side questioningly, but even that small movement caused me to scream due to the pain. "How dare you get hurt like that. How dare you get distracted and try to leave me behind. I've never felt this way about anyone. That's why I've fought so hard for you to find your place here, and the Nico squandered away because you're so worried about what's happening to me. I will be fine, dammit. Don't you see what you have done to me?" No matter the pain I pulled her near and with that, our lips meeting each other.

"I love you, and I want you, pain be damned."

* * *

I couldn't believe we were doing this, that we were about to actually meet Raul and his most trusted soldiers in order to end this once and for all. We would either die or he would die, and he would be exposed.

I glanced behind me as the ship landed, all of us pretending to be new recruits I gathered from prisoners on other planets. I had given them all the grey cloaks and donned the one I once wore when my beliefs had been influenced by a liar. I didn't like the way it felt anymore and wished to be in the black of the rebels, but this was for a good cause. We were luring the leader of The Galaxy Watchers right to a whole army of us that could bring him down once and for all. We would let those loyal to him know exactly who he had been the whole time.

Kaia was to my right side, insistent on leading this battle just like any other. I would not have expected any less from such a strong woman. I found it difficult to think that she might be in danger up here with me, that I could lose her today, and it would be all my fault for being so naive in the first place.

I braced myself and stood my ground as the hatch opened from the ship that had just landed; a ship I had once been on myself before I knew the truth of everything. I often thought about that day many times and my choice not to end my life in one way or another. The only explanation I had for it all was fate. I was meant for something, just as I had always thought, that something had just gotten a little twisted for a while.

But most importantly...I was meant for HER.

Raul stepped off the ship, his grey hood covering almost everything including most of his face. I had always thought it was because he had received some injury early on in his recruitment, but now I understood why. It was the same reason the woman I loved sunk into her own cloak now; to hide her true nature.

I pulled off my own hood, showing my face. It wasn't like he had word on exactly what had become of me. I was his best recruit as far as he was concerned, and I had brought more to The Galaxy Watchers. I had saved more pure humans from servitude and death by the hand of these dirty bloods that were taking over. There was no reason to hide. It made more sense to hide in plain sight.

"Nevin, I always knew that you would become something great for us. Tell everyone behind me why we are here today," Raul spoke in that fake, kind, leader voice of his, stepping too close to Nevin. So close that Nevin had to hide a smirk threatening to appear on his face. This was going to be much too easy.

"I am here with news, friends," I said, trying to have the same air of authority that Raul projected because that is what these men would react to, would believe, and respond to. They were soldiers and needed someone to follow until they were completely clean and severed from the cause.I opened arms to them as he spoke so they understood, even subconsciously, that they were going to be welcomed by us as long as they understood. As long as they listened. "I want to thank Raul here for coming here today and bringing all of you." I smiled and moved towards him, the smile on my face belying my rapid heartbeat and my breathing, I could hardly control. I would have to do this quickly, or he would know what I was up to, and it would all be over.

I went to pat his back but ripped his hood down instead, exposing red eyes and his bare skull which showed his signs of not being a pure human. In fact, below his thin skin rose some unusual ridges. I jumped back from him as Kaia and I both pulled out our weapons, and everyone dropped their hoods to show the truth. "You can all see now that you have been lied to," I said sternly, meeting each and every face and gauging the confusion and horror on each one. "He is telling you that humans should remain pure, that it is our job to lay down the law and justice by getting rid of dirty bloods, when his blood is just as dirty. He is nothing more than a false prophet. If you come to our side of things we will welcome you with open arms. We will create a true and powerful Galaxy Watchers that protects all of the universe from those like him. Turn your backs and walk away, come to our side, or choose to go down with him."

I was firm. I did not want to kill all of these people, but I would if that was what would bring peace and absolution. I watched as many came over to us or many got back on the ship to leave, possibly to be threats later or to scatter among the stars and stay quiet forevermore. A very select few stayed by Raul's side, still looking determined to believe the man that had practically raised them; who made them what they are. It wasn't something I could fault them for, but I would have to destroy them if they got in our way.

"Don't you see!" Raul hissed desperately, pacing around like a caged animal. "I started this cause because my own flesh and blood did this to me. They ruined me for life. I am disgusting!" Raul spat angrily, but I could see the fear behind his eyes. "I am a sniveling creature because my mother bread with an alien." His eyes were wild, and I couldn't let him go on anymore.

I nodded my head to give the signal, and those that were left with him chose to come at the army behind me. Kaia and I would work on Raul ourselves.

It was a dance, a dangerous one at that. Raul had trained me, had trained all of us, and I had never known a better swordsman in the universe. It made no difference that two of us were after him, but there was some kind of satisfaction being the one to kill him. I didn't want to ask for any more help, but I knew as I heard Kaia cry out that my pride had gotten the better of me. In desperation and anger, I landed my target, my sword sliding right through his black heart. I didn't wait to watch him drop or bleed out, I turned immediately to Kaia and fell to the ground as I saw her injuries were so great, I didn't know that she would make it.

I fell to my knees, a defeated man in front of her, pulling her head into my lap. "No," I sobbed. I had just gotten her, just finally found my place in the world. I couldn't lose her. "Is there something I can do to save you?" I whispered to her, and she managed to give a weak nod even as she was pailing. "What?" I begged to know. She shook her head. She wasn't going to tell me, but that gave me all the information I needed to know. She needed blood. She was a vampire of sorts after all. But she knew I hated that part of her, at least, I used to. There was nothing about her that could deter me anymore, that could push me away.

I pulled the sleeve of my robes up, exposing my wrist to her and placing it to her mouth where her teeth could bite. She shook her head again.

"Kaia, please, I love you, and I need you to live. I don't care anymore. I don't care about anything but you." I felt her sink those fangs into my skin, and I knew that we would both live to see another dawn.

The End

About the author

      Iris Sweetwater has been writing for most of her life, completing her first poems and short stories when she was only five years old. Writing has always been in her blood, and she also is a lover of reading. Her favorite genres to both read and write have always been fantasy and paranormal, having always been a huge fan of JK Rowling, Holly Black, and Cassandra Clare.
      She has worked in the writing industry in many capacities throughout her life including educating children in both journalism and Creative Writing. She hopes that she can inspire children the way she was inspired by her favorite authors and eventually become an author full time.

      http://irissweetrh.wixsite.com/irissweet-author
      https://www.facebook.com/irisissweet
      http://instagram.com/irisissweet1
      http://twitter.com/irisissweet1

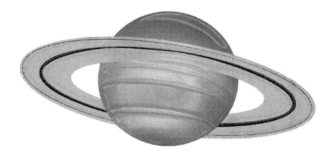

An Unexpected Space Story
Lilly Rayman

When you're a Romero, things rarely go to plan, and space is no exception. Nina knew this, yet jettisoned away without a moment's thought. She wanted to escape boredom, and a certain pirate captain stood ready, more than happy to oblige.

Dedication

To my loyal unexpected readers, you keep me on track and inspire me to write to the best of my ability.

To my "Captain" for pushing me out of my writers' comfort zone to actually write a story with a theme that I secretly enjoy reading or watching on TV.

And finally, to my family, who continue to love me when I am absorbed in my literary world.

To Rebecca for her editing input and to Angie of Novel Nurse Editing for her professional touch – I love you ladies!

Chapter One

"Space! The final frontier—and more boring than the last fracking millennium and a half on Earth!" grumbled Nina to the holographic image of her twin brother, Kade.

Kade howled out with laughter. "Well, you wanted to play Star Trek!"

Nina rolled her eyes, cycling her legs in the air as she lay on her back. "Yeah, well, twentieth-century TV made space look so much more fun than it actually is!"

"I told you that you'd be bored before you were halfway through your journey."

Nina rolled onto her belly, stabbing an accusing finger at her twin. "Ha! You were wrong! It was a quarter of the way."

Kade frowned and shook his head. "Tomato, Tom-art-toe. Have you tried meditation?"

Nina dropped her head onto the new age latex mattress. "Yup! Even my vamp is bored of the grousing of my hound wanting to run, and the faerie in me says 'good things are coming.' I swear, Kade, I want to rip myself in three! I've never felt more lost since Mom and Dad moved to the faerie realm."

Lifting her head, she placed her chin on her folded hands. "Life on the ranch seems so appealing right about now. What's been happening at Thunder Hollow lately?"

Kade moved out of his seat, leaving only his chair for Nina to stare at.

"Kade?"

He reappeared, a bundle in his arms. "Rosie gave me a beautiful baby boy," he beamed.

Nina crawled off the bed and kneeled before the hologram, all boredom forgotten as homesickness washed through her. "Lemme see the pup."

Pulling away the blanket, a tiny head covered in a shock of black hair, tipped with white, was revealed. The baby scrunched up his face in protest at being shifted out of his warm cocoon. Nina gritted her teeth, preparing for a wail that never came. Instead, the little one blinked before opening his shocking blue eyes and fixing them on his aunt.

"We named him Nate." Kade's voice was filled with pride as he spoke.

Nina dragged her gaze away from the blue eyes to settle on her brother's rich brown ones. "What did Mom say? Or Uncle Cash?"

"They appreciated the tribute to Nate's memory. Listen, Ni, talking Sloan's, I have a meeting with the Sloan Alpha at Murph's Place in twenty minutes. I have to go."

Rocking back on her heels, Nina smiled, trying to hide the pain she felt being light years away from her family. The isolation of space never felt more poignant. "Okay, bro. Talk to you again after your meeting?"

"Can't tonight, it's the first full moon of winter. We're having a combined bonfire in Eagle Downs this year since a few of the local humans have been claimed. That's what my meeting with Sloan is about. I love you, sis. I'll try to get Mom and Dad back from Faeria to talk to you next call, okay?" Kade looked away before Nina could answer, handing a now fretting Nate over to his mate, Rosie.

"Love you—" The hologram terminated with a quick wave from Kade, and Nina's head dropped. "Too."

With a low rumbling growl, Nina fell backwards against the carpeted floor. No matter how much technology the humans employed, Nina could pick up the minute tremors of the engine throughout the ship. It was half the reason she was never able to achieve the level of stillness required for the deepest level of meditation Roxana had taught her.

Nina had thought space offered the chance to break out of the doldrums she'd found herself in since her twin had found his mate nearly two years ago. Despite their differences in nature, the two had been inseparable since their birth over two thousand years ago. It got her through the desolation she felt after their parents moved to Faeria once their mother started ageing when Kade and Nina were about five hundred years old. It was just her and Kade against the world, even if he was alpha of the Remus pack.

Until Rosie came along.

Nina had no problem with her twin finding his mate. In fact, she couldn't be happier for him. The she-wolf was the perfect fit for him, but it just served to highlight Nina's loneliness. Kade had always been more wolf than a vampire, taking after their mother, Livia Romero, than Darius, their vampire father. It meant he was more comfortable in the pack, blending in effortlessly and making friends.

Nina had struggled with her vampiric nature and felt very little connection to her wolf. In fact, when they shifted at fifteen, Nina had been more hellhound than Kade, seeing as he was all wolf. She'd struggled with a surge of bloodlust, and her mother nearly hadn't been able to bring Nina's beast to submission. She'd been sent to Virginia then, fostered with Alpha White and his mate Roxana—the first ever hellhound and the only one for over two and a half thousand years. She'd taught Nina how to control her nature using Taoism.

The piercing wail of an alarm, accompanied by the red glow of warning, pulled Nina out of her reminiscing. She launched herself to her feet, silently moving across the small cabin to the doors. They opened automatically as she reached the threshold, allowing her to move into the wider, more brightly lit corridor. This was the first exciting thing to happen since she stepped foot aboard The Endeavour, the First Fleet ship to Centaurea Alpha.

The advertising for the first commercial flight to the other side of the known universe had promised a thrilling adventure from the moment you boarded the ship in space dock 42 within Earth's orbit. Nina had been disappointed from the moment she stepped aboard; she even contemplated demanding a refund of her uni-credits, since the advertisers had lied. Only, Kade had convinced her that since the humans were still unaware of the presence of Earth's supernatural community, they couldn't exactly cater to her personal needs.

Moving into the main thoroughfare of the communal areas of the ship, Nina found herself surrounded by a flurry of scents. There was a main flavour of fear that instantly fed her vampiric nature, yet accents of excitement and even confusion tamed her inner beast. Allowing herself to be swept into the crowd, she moved with the masses towards the main bar. Her ears pricked for any possible information as to what exactly was happening.

Chapter Two

"There's a large ship coming up on sensors, Captain."

Dakal opened one eye, capturing the ronarna fruit he had been tossing in the air. He pinned his eerie gaze on his sensors officer. "What breed is it?"

"It's an earthling; a First Fleet ship, Captain. Larger than their military vessels, minimal weapons registering on sensors, and primary defence shields. A substantial number of life signs detected."

"Deploy a warning volley, Karu, and enter stealth mode. Ping their communications with the G'Arutha identification. May as well let them know pirates are about," Dakal drawled, as he remained spread-eagled in his seat. The display flickered to life, bringing up an image of the large human vessel, and several red lights shot into view, exploding against the shielding on the ship with a scattering of sparks.

"They have increased engine speed, Captain."

Dakal grinned, his sharp teeth gleaming in the artificial lighting of his bridge. Both eyes now fixed on his prey. "Match their speed. Keep us on their tail. Deploy another volley." Excitement began stirring within his gut; he always felt a rush when their prey tried to outrun them, even more when they engaged in battle with them. However, unless a ship was a military class vessel, most targets weren't equipped to deal with the savage firepower of a demonis ship. The G'Arutha was the fiercest of all pirate ships. They had the weaponry and defences to take on almost any vessel in space. The G'Arutha itself had been commissioned by the

Demonis Empire to be used by the Emperor himself. Dakal had prided himself on his own audacity when he had stolen the ship straight out of its construction dock before the emperor had ever set foot aboard the craft. The few guards and remaining workers had been jettisoned as a warning to any who would dare follow him.

As was the Demonis nature, Dakal had proven himself superior, and the emperor had recalled his fighters, allowing the space pirate this one victory. His men had rendezvoused with him on the edge of the Demonis system, transported aboard with their possessions, and left their crippled Anaryian class frigate right where it was.

"Captain, they're preparing to launch a torpedo at us."

"Disarm it within their shields' immediate vicinity. Then ping their communications to prepare for boarding. I want on that ship."

Dakal left the bridge to a chorus of "Yes, Captain." He felt a nervous energy building within him as he used the motion tubes to reach the transportation dock. He'd always followed his instinct as to which ships were worth pursuing and what treasures he needed. The increasing excitement within him told him there was a precious treasure aboard the Earth vessel, and he didn't just want to get his hands on it; he needed it.

The transportation dock was a hive of activity as he stepped into the cavernous room. His men, all a variety of species and each one as vicious as the next, were arming themselves.

"My instincts tell me this is a passenger ship, let's not kill any innocents, only armed men." Dakal grinned at the sound of disgruntled acknowledgement. "I never said we couldn't terrorise the passengers, men. Let's just shake them up a bit, see what treasures we can find."

The room cheered a bit with the orders. Dakal ran a tight ship, everyone had their jobs to do, and every job got done. He also had a strict moral code, somewhat surprising for a Demonis pirate. If his quarry wasn't Demonis, only military were fair game for a kill shot. The reputation of the G'Arutha was such, that unless a ship and its crew fought back particularly hard, most times they would be relieved of 75 percent of their cargo, with minor injuries. After the first few who fought back were blown to smithereens, most vessels heeded the warning volleys and handed over their cargo.

"Captain." The intercom crackled briefly before the computer automatically fixed the connection. Silence descended within the transportation dock to listen to the word from the bridge. "The First Fleet ship sustained minor hull damage from their own torpedo. They've stilled their engines and have indicated they are awaiting our arrival."

A cheer rose to echo around the room, and Dakal felt his excitement ratchet up another notch. "Makon, bring the banking tablet, something tells me we'll be adding several zeros to our Uni-Credit balance today. Come on, men. Let's go fleece the First Fleet."

Laughter followed the nearly seven-foot captain as he made his way to the docking bay, ready for transportation. His eyes roved over his crew as they bounded up to join him.

He ran his thumb over the ring on his left middle finger, satisfied his personal force field was ready. The device had got him out of some tight situations, emitting an oscillating frequency shield that bounced laser fire away from him. He carried an energy stick on his hip, wielding it like the ancient titanium forged blade weapons of his homeworld.

With a sharp nod to the transportation officer, he indicated he and his boarding party should be transported onto the largest deck of his quarry's ship.

The energy began to whir above their heads, a golden glow lowered like a watery curtain around them, and then Dakal felt the familiar sensation of sensory deprivation as the scene before him changed.

Multiple containers stacked around the edges of the enormous cargo deck, yet it was the row of heavily armed men on the mezzanine layer three decks up that captured Dakal's attention. His crew spotted them, too, instantly darting away. Some used their species traits to bound up onto crates and crawl up walls, removing themselves from the line of fire. Dakal laughed evilly as he activated his personal shield, striding through the bright rain of red tracer fire. They were always more fun when they fought back face-to-face instead of hiding behind their ship's shields or simply rolling over onto their backs.

Chapter Three

Nina heard the F.F. Endeavour's crew run in the opposite direction to the ship's passengers. Deciding more action would come following them, she slipped out of the crowd and ducked down a side hallway. It was then the ship rumbled and rocked. Frowning, Nina wondered what was happening.

The side hallway spilt into a crew access corridor, one that was teaming with uniformed men, all armed with short rifles that used tracer fire. Drawing on her natural magic, Nina hid in plain sight with a little blanket of faerie misdirection. Falling in line with the tail end of the security detail, she heard the internal communication.

"They somehow detonated our own torpedo within our shields. We've sustained minor hull damage. The G'Arutha has advised they intend to board us. From intelligence we have, they will land on the largest open space. Security team, please report to the cargo hold. Permission to fire at will."

During one of her most dull moments, Nina had hacked into the ship's computer, reading anything and everything of interest. She found it amusing that there were actually pirates in space or that humans felt the need to explore the stars to find contact with races other than their own. There were three races of supernatural right under their noses, for frack's sake.

Her blood lust spiked as she sensed the excitement racing through the human security team as she moved with them through the staff corridors of the ship. Her fangs pushed at her gums in response, making her ache to sink them into a warm, living vein. Her doldrums finally seemed to be coming to an end.

Keeping her faerie magic surrounding her, Nina slipped into the cargo bay with the crew, settling out of the way, crouched on the railings that overlooked the cargo bay at least three decks below. She listened with interest as the crew stirred each other up with the stories they had heard about the pirate crew of the G'Arutha and their Demonis captain. A spike of interest shot through Nina when she heard the name Dakal.

She felt the air shift, the electricity prickling the atmosphere as a large group of aliens transported into the cargo bay below them. Instantly, she found her attention riveted by the tallest of the pirates. His form was massive, muscular, and humanoid in appearance. His skin, glistening under the artificial light, held a dark red sheen, offset by rich black hair swept back into a ponytail, reminding Nina of the pirates of old. Two glossy black horns curled out from the thickness of his hair just above his forehead.

Nina found her inspection of him cut short as the Endeavour crew opened fire on the pirates. As if with a sixth sense, the pirates peeled away, launching themselves onto containers and darting behind them. All except the Demonis. His face twisted with an exultant grin as he erected a personal force field, tracer fire bouncing harmlessly around him.

A feeling she couldn't explain moved through her, making her stand tall on the railings. Her misdirection dropped, allowing her to appear. As she threw her magic across, everyone gathered.

"Stop!" Her voice echoed over the ruckus of weapons' fire, stalling everyone present. All eyes landed on her, yet Nina couldn't peel her gaze away from the Demonis. He had tawny eyes, not a single bit of white stared at her, the iris split in half by a widening line of black, so alien, yet so perfect. She felt her own eyes shift, feeling the inner hellfire of her hound stirring within her.

"Ma'am?" hissed one of the crewmen nearest to her. "You shouldn't be here."

Nina snorted, she shouldn't be anywhere but here.

"You don't have to kill each other, you know." Nina addressed everyone, yet didn't take her eyes from the Demonis.

His black boots encased his muscled calf like a second skin, yet the material of his pants covered the rest of his legs loosely. A wide band of red silk cinched his waist, and a white shirt clung to his torso, leaving his arms bare.

His voice reached her then, the tone dark and gravelly. Her body heated instantly in response. "And what, my lady, would you suggest as an alternative to everyone killing each other?"

Nina grinned at the flash of his sharp fangs from the winning smile he directed at her, his head bowing towards her at a flirtatious angle. Running her tongue across her own fangs she tasted the telltale tang of her venom, bleeding from the sharpest points in anticipation of a good fight.

Hands tried the grasp at her from behind, yet she moved away, stalking agilely along the two-inch-thick pipe as though she walked the deck. "One-on-one combat."

The pirates laughed from their multitude of locations. A voice called out from the cargo containers. "We might as well offload their cargo now. There's not a single human I've ever met that could withstand a fight with a Demonis child, let alone a warrior like the captain."

Nina scowled in the direction of the voice, her head moving with the sharpness of a predator. Dropping her magic over the humans, she left them deaf, dumb, and blind to the proceedings.

"There are far more dangerous things to be found on Earth than mere humans." She growled, her head snapping back to the captain. She continued to saunter across the mezzanine railings until she stood front and centre. The humans were unmoving behind her.

"What's wrong with them?" he asked with a jerk of his head.

Her grin felt wicked as she let her fangs drop. "Let's just say, there's a reason humanity has been blind to what lives under their noses. The supernatural are as old as time itself, yet even to this day, the existence of our races remains shrouded in the mystery of myths and legends."

"So you have a little witchcraft, illuna. But what more have you to offer?"

Chapter Four

Excitement curled in Dakal's gut. He'd been confused when he first spotted the woman appear out of nowhere, perched on the railings like a bird. Her words elicited a physical reaction from him, making his eyes widen in response. He could feel the power radiating off her as she moved with such elegant grace across the railings. The humans were spellbound by her.

He barely heard her speak, his eyes raking over her body, her bare feet white as they rested easily on the railings. Her long legs encased in fabric so old to his sharp sight, he could see the pants were threadbare at her knees, and although almost white, he was sure they were once darker. Her taut midriff was highlighted by henna in a swirling of tribal patterns that disappeared under the bright red-and-white print of an open-collared shirt, knotted a hand span below her breasts.

"So you have a little witchcraft, illuna. What more do you have to offer?" The words fell from his lips unbidden as his mind conjured images of them naked together.

She lowered into a crouch, her elbows leaning on her knees. Her mouth pursed, the deep pink of her lips seemed to be begging for his attention. "Tut-tut-tut, Captain. Such dangerously naughty thoughts you have."

His eyes snapped to hers, unable to pinpoint a colour from this distance. He was mesmerised by the fire that seemed to flicker within them as he wondered how she could read his thoughts.

She moved, her body falling forward, curving into a graceful arc before she landed lightly on her feet. His eyes caught hers, trapped by her seductive allure as she moved towards him, her body undulating like the hollo-vids he had seen of the ancient cats that had once been apex predators on Earth.

"I can smell you, Captain. Your arousal, floods from your body in waves, even now peaking as you watch me. Tell me—" She stopped, almost standing on his toes with her head barely reaching his shoulder, head tipped back, and nose flared as she sucked in a deep breath. "Dakal, how good is the warrior when his body is filled with lust?"

His name fell from her lips in the most intimate of whispers, making him growl from deep within. No longer able to articulate with words, he moved to grab her, intent on hauling her up against his hard body and tasting her lips.

Only air seemed to whizz past his ear before being expelled with force out of his body as he landed on his back. He blinked, unsure of what had happened. He heard her sigh from behind him, making him shake his head to clear it.

"I'm disappointed. Here I thought this would be the most exciting encounter of the last millennium, and yet you're on your back already. What happened to the feared Demonis warrior I've heard so much about?"

Dakal curled his lip into a snarl, the warrior breaking out of his haze of lust. With a well-executed manoeuvre, he was back on his feet, spinning on his heel to face her.

She grinned, her eyes flashing with fire as her teeth elongated to fangs that rivalled his own. He clenched his hand into a fist, bent his elbow, making himself ready. She cocked one shapely eyebrow at him, daring him to move as she stepped silently to one side.

He moved, darting at her with every ounce of speed he held. But unable to strike at such a beautiful woman, he opened his hand. She thwarted his attempt to grab her, blocking his arm with her own and knocking him aside. It was the start of the most frustrating fight of his life.

They danced together, a flurry of arms, both attacking and defending as he fought to get a purchase of her and she tried to strike him. They moved around each other, using the space to move and trying to bring the other down with a sweeping of legs. They seemed to move in unison, neither taking the upper hand, every action anticipated as though they had fought this dance together for a lifetime.

She growled in frustration as yet again he blocked the high kick she'd aimed at his head. Capturing her foot, he locked her in place. Her legs were spread with one foot planted on the deck, the other held at his shoulder with one hand secured around her ankle. Her body was taut, fists held tight at her shoulders in a prepared stance. She watched him, unmoving, the long rope of braided black hair hanging straight down almost to the floor from its anchor high on her head.

"Are we at an impasse, my lady?" he cooed, his free hand teasing as it trailed along her leg, feeling the muscles tighten in reaction the higher he moved.

"No," she grumbled before twisting in his grasp. The grounded foot came up, striking him in the shoulder as her body twisted, the braid of her hair curling around her body like a ribbon following the dancer.

Dakal stumbled into his own body-spinning flip as he fought to keep his footing. One body slam on the deck was enough for him. He gained his feet again quickly and turned to face her, eyes widening in disbelief as he watched her transforming before him.

"She wants to sink her teeth into you, Dakal. Do you want that? I'm done toying with you. Take your men and leave this ship. Go while you are still in one piece." She growled as her face shifted. Large pointed ears became prominent, and her hair shrunk back into her head. Her jaw elongated, becoming a dangerous-looking muzzle. Her body grew taller, distorting as a layer of fine black fur replaced her skin, her limbs becoming more animal-like.

"No!" he yelled as he felt the telltale sensation of the transporter.

Chapter Five

Nina's hound let out a mournful howl as he disappeared. She stalked the area they had fought, his scent coating the back of her nose and throat. She wanted him. Needed him.

Confusion had ruled Nina's mind when he had traced intimately along her leg. Her hound instantly wanted to sink her teeth into his shoulder and fought for release from the confines of her mind. Her vampiric nature had craved his touch while her faerie essence had bloomed under his heated gaze.

Her beast had fought for freedom, and although she had slowed the change, it was inevitable. Only, where she thought the hound wanted to maul him, all her hound really wanted to do was run her body against his.

Nina growled. Closing her eyes, she concentrated on what she could sense of him, bringing all three elements of herself together in harmony. They agreed for the first time in her two-thousand-year-long life.

He was her mate.

She could sense him, his frustration at not being beside her, and his confusion at not understanding why. She'd never been able to move through space like her mother or brother, her faerie power lying more in subterfuge and manipulation. But as she centred on him, she felt her surroundings shift. The hold she had on the humans slipped away as she left the Endeavour.

After opening her eyes, Nina's hound looked around the busy location she found herself in. It was a bridge, if the large display screen fixed on the F.F. Endeavour was anything to go by. They hadn't spotted her. Which was surprising, considering she stood nearly as tall as their captain at the shoulder—her body long and sinewy, looking somewhat like a cross between a Great Dane and a greyhound. Her black coat was in stark contrast to the clinically bright white of the bridge.

A small, almost-humanoid alien walked towards her, head down, gaze fixed on a tablet in his hand. "Captain, I'm only finding passenger lists there's nothing—" He bumped into her shoulder. His pink skin took on a grey hue, and as Nina rumbled a warning growl, she spotted gills widening on the side of his neck.

Silence descended on the bridge as everyone turned to face the hound. Dakal's tawny eyes found her fiery ones then, his slit pupils widening to a thick black line as his gaze roved over her. Her muzzle opened, revealing wickedly sharp white teeth as she tasted his scent.

He moved closer, his hands open at his hips, his long-tapered fingers inviting her as he tried to maintain a submissive posture with his approach. Everyone else seemed to move away, the smell of their fear tormenting her, almost as much as Dakal's aroused her.

"Hi," he rumbled at her, his hand outstretched.

She stepped towards him then, her tongue darting out to wrap around his fingers, tasting the warmth of his essence on his skin.

He shuddered at the touch before gliding his hand across the top of her silken head. It was all her hound needed to release her hold on Nina. The hound jumped a little to rest her front paws on his shoulders. He staggered slightly to adjust and take her weight, hands settling over her rib cage below her shoulders. The shift came then, almost agonisingly slow in its reversal of her shift to hound.

His thumbs shifted to sweep across the edge of her full bust as his hands adjusted his hold on her. His eyes widened as they dropped down to take in her naked body now inches from his.

"You're naked?" His exclamation hissed around the bridge, and all eyes burned against her. He pulled her in close then, his hand dropping to shield her while he yelled out at the crew, "Someone grab me a towel! No, better yet, everyone eyes closed!"

Nina laughed, rubbing against the hard planes of his body in contentment before he lifted her off her feet and powered over to the motion tube behind her.

The door slid closed, cocooning them in privacy. He allowed her to slide down his body to rest on the balls of her feet.

"How? Why?"

She smiled. "Both simply answered by the fact that this is meant to be. I didn't understand my hound at first, mistaking her desire to claim you as bloodlust."

"Claim me?"

Nina lifted a hand from his shoulder, skimming it along the hard edge of his jaw. "Yes. Claim you. You are my mate, the perfect match to every element of me."

His eyes half closed, his expression heating as he dropped his head until his nose edged across her forehead. "Every element of you?"

She nodded. "The vampire, the faerie, and the hellhound. I'm the daughter of a vampire father and a wolf mother with faerie heritage. I've waited a very long time to find my mate."

His fingers skimmed across her silky soft skin, teasing her with every sweep. He laughed, the sound a deep rumble that only heightened her awareness of him. "A long time? You're barely twenty."

Her brow arched. "I stopped ageing at twenty-two. That was around two thousand years ago."

His hands stilled. "Unbelievable."

"Nope. It's the vampire. My dad is over eight thousand years old."

His laughter vibrated through her as he pulled her closer. "And I thought I was old at five hundred. So just what does it mean, being your mate?"

Her smile turned sultry as she pushed herself up, pulling his head towards her as she settled her mouth against his. Molten energy surged through her as they connected, drawing them together and binding their souls. He broke the kiss on a harsh breath and looked down at her in shock.

"Nina?"

She nodded, grinning at the incredulous look on his face.

"I heard your name in my mind. Raneenia, daughter of Livia Romero and Darius, son of the sun god Ra."

"Yeah, baby! I'm descended from a deity."

About the author

First and foremost, Lilly describes herself as a wife and mother. She was born in England where she had a dream at the age of fourteen. That dream was to chase cattle on horseback across the Australian Outback.

In 2008, Lilly had the opportunity to follow that dream and found herself travelling to Australia on an Outback working holiday, and she's chased cattle, on horseback, across the Outback. Lilly met her soul mate, while on her working holiday, married him, and now they have two beautiful daughters, and she is still in love with life in Australia.

Lilly loves to read, much to her husband's dismay sometimes when she has her head metaphorically buried in the pages of a book (after all, how can that be literal since the dawn of e-books?)!

Lilly love's fantasy; she used to take herself away from her nasty world of bullies and appear in some beautiful land of dragons and magic! Pern was her all-time favourite hide out world, and Lilly is often heard saying "God bless Anne and Todd MacCaffery".

Whenever Lilly immersed herself in her fantasy worlds, she would re-write the plots in her head, starring herself as some great, sword drawn character who wouldn't give two hoots what the local bully thought! That eventuated in Lilly's first foray into writing down her stories at the age of fourteen.

More recently Lilly was inspired to start writing again, and picked up on the whole craze of werewolf and vampire. She has had the most enjoyment writing AN UNEXPECTED BONDING, the first book of An Unexpected Trilogy.

Website: http://www.lillyrayman0007.wix.com/lillyrayman

Facebook: http://www.facebook.com/lillyrayman0007
Twitter: http://www.twitter.com/lillyrayman0007
Goodreads: http://www.goodreads.com/lillyrayman0007

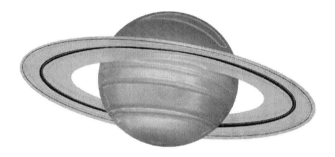

Blood and Space
Sondra Hicks

Erik Yukson is a vampire who leads a double life like most vampires posing as human and using his gifts to his advantage. He is hired security for a music label and has a beautiful girlfriend Gabby (Gabriel) Lindsey and he has special plans for Gabby's 21st birthday but during a night of food, presents and dancing when two alien men whisk her away. Now Erik must trust a space pirate his mother used to date to track down his girlfriend. He will make friends along the way that will aid in his battle and he will uncover secrets about his families past that will determine the future for all involved.

Chapter One
Erik

    Erik Yukson gazed at the beauty before him; an easy ten on any rating scale, even though she denied it. She had soft brown hair that fell down her back, beautiful hazel eyes, pouty lips, a trim body with perky breasts, and a small cute ass. Yeah, Gabriel Lindsey was a knockout, well for a human. He loved watching her try on clothes especially swimsuits. He spoiled her as rotten as he could, with the money he made with his business. Being a vampire had its perks. You could do things others couldn't. Like being a bodyguard for him, getting shot, and coming to work the next day was a normal day. The guys had nicknamed him 'The Lucky Saint', but he just told them it was the body armor he was wearing no explanation truly needed. They all thought he was the luckiest man alive, though. He was the bodyguard at the Gem-Gold Label for important talent; well bodyguard was a glorified term more like the babysitter.

    Erik glanced at his watch, realizing he would need to get to work soon. Damn singers were a pain in the butt if you were a moment late and didn't have their coffee or tea. "Gabby darling, I hate to cut this short. I do have to get to work shortly. Have you picked a dress out? Something that shows those long, tan legs off. I do hope." Erik playfully hinted waiting for her reply.

"Well actually, I have three of them I like and it's so hard to choose" came Gabriel's pouty voice from the changing room. He knew this all too well. She had found three dresses and wanted them all. He smiled and got up walking to the dressing room door.

"Well, Gabby darling, you're just going to have to choose. I know I am just a monster for making you do such a thing." He purred from outside the door. He heard her sigh and he leaned against the wall by the door. He saw the knob turn and she emerged a few moments later holding one dress. He smiled wrapping an arm around her waist pulling her close and they headed for the register. He handed the young cashier, with brown hair cut just above her chin and fascinating purple eyes, his visa platinum card. The cashier grinned at him and when she handed him the card back made sure to touch his hand with hers. Gabby saw this and frowned, putting a possessive hand on Erik's arm. The cashier smiled smugly at Gabby; but Erik patted Gabby's hand picking it up to kiss it gently.

"I have to say Miss that your treatment of me is borderline sexually harassing and disrespectful to my girlfriend. You see her here, but you flirt and touch me as though you know me, and I should know you. Next time I will speak to your boss and you will be looking for a new job. Regardless of how I look, sound, or act, NEVER disrespect the Lady I am with. Understood? Shall we go, my dear," he asked Gabriel not even giving this cashier another glance. It was always a pity when women wasted beauty on such negative and ugly personalities. He saw the look of glee on his Gabby's face, knowing she had enjoyed the affection, and the reaction of the cashier; which had no doubt been of surprise at his tongue lashing for her behavior. He and Gabby walked out of the store with their purchase and walked to the valet, who went to fetch his car.

* * *

"Penny for your thoughts?" Erik asked looking at Gabriel who was gazing out the window with a glazed look over eyes, as though lost in thought or the scenery. He didn't know which. At moments such as this, he wished he had the gift of mind reading so he could know how her brain worked. She didn't reply though so he tried to get her attention again but placing his hand on hers. She looked over at his hand and then smiled.

"There you are, I was wondering if you were still in there." Erik grinned squeezing her hand. She smiled over at him with her hazel eyes staring into his dark eyes for a moment; then reached out to change the station on the radio. A pop song she liked came over the radio and she turned it up and began singing to it. He never understood her moods at times. One minute she was talkative and then she was lost. Then this side of her came out where she was singing and... was she dancing in her seat now? That was his Gabby, though, unpredictable and he loved every part of her complicated personality. He pulled up to the house that she rented with two other female friends. He knew their names; Cassie & Megan, both worked in the entertainment industry, as they put it. In other words, aspiring actresses who took whatever bit part they could get. He admired them for chasing their dreams. As long as they were good to Gabby he had no problem with them. He parked the car and waited for his usual quick kiss and goodbye.

"Thank you for today, Erik, it means the world to me. I just know our date will be amazing. I only turn 21 years old once!" Gabriel hugged him and kissed him passionately on the lips, lingering for a moment, smiling and looking into his eyes. Then she grabbed her bag and got out of the car, skipped to the house. He shook his head and smiled; that girl was something else. She was turning 21 and she was skipping like a kid up the walkway. He gunned the engine on his sports car and took off. He had to get to work.

* * *

The freeway had proven to be a disaster and he had pulled into his parking spot in the garage with seconds to spare. He rushed into the building at Gem-Gold to clock in a minute late. He hated not being able to run at his normal speed but with humans around, he had to appear human as well. If they became aware of vampires, lord knows what would happen to his species. He took the private elevator up to the floor where the executive bodyguards would meet and get their assignments for each week. He just prayed he didn't get that new tween brat Sofia Glory again. She actually made him pick up her dog's poop last time. She had no respect for anyone. She thought everyone lived to serve her spoiled brat of a talented behind. The girl had raw talent and millions of records sold but a horrible personality. She was so fake with her fans, acting like she loved them, but as soon as she was in the car, she was making fun of them.

"Did you see that girl with the blue hat? She was way too fat for that dress. I swear all they want are selfies and autographs. They all want to be me; sometimes I swear they are so pathetic." Sofia had rudely laughed in the back of her limo as I sat quietly that day. I had wanted to rip her vocal chords out.

I walked into the room of the elevator and went to the board. I looked at my name and followed it over to see I was thankfully not with that brat this week, but instead with the new up and comer Michael James. I had remembered seeing him on that video site uploading his home videos of himself, singing covers of other's songs. He had a great voice and others had said he was a good kid. I guess this week I would find out just how great he was.

"The Lucky Saint strikes again I see. Michael James that's a good detail, I got stuck with Sofia Glory. Sure you don't want to trade?" Rick a 40 something ex-navy seal and one of my good friends asked laughing.

"Rick there is no way I am trading with you. You can suffer this week being that I asked you the same when I had her not too long ago. What is it you said to me? Ah, I remember, good freaking luck. Yeah, cheers mate," I told him giving him my best Australian accent which made him laugh because it was a horrible attempt.

"I'll just remember that when you need a favor one day, buddy." Rick laughed as he headed out to meet his brat of a client. Now that we had our assignments, we got the job of grabbing our SUVs, throwing our bags in them in case it was an overnight trip, and going to pick up our clients. We took precautions to prepare for emergencies as sometimes our clients required overnight protection in some situations. Knowing my luck, I would be relieved tonight, with no problems. Only once had my relief guy called in and I had to work through the night. Gem-Gold took their artists protection seriously. Well ever since their rapper Mac Man had been shot at a concert, things had been tight. I assumed the added security was paid for by the artists, but who knew.

I made my way to my SUV and thought about my date with my Gabby later that night. I was taking her out to eat at "Sebastian's", a fine dining experience. Well, they served amazing food, mostly seafood and steak in small portions, for larger prices, to be honest. The service and feel of the restaurant were amazing. Then we would do some dancing at the hottest club "Gheto La", a club you had to grease the palm of the bouncer at the door to get in quickly. Then we would go to the beach where we would walk along the water. I had decided this would be the night I would tell her my secret. I just hoped she wouldn't think I was crazy. I'd never told anyone I was a vampire, but I loved this woman more than anything.

I almost missed my turn for Michael James house because I was thinking about tonight, so deeply. I pulled up to the gate, hit the buzzer, and a voice came over the intercom.

"Yeah can I help you?" a female voice asked.

"Yes, I am Erik Yukson from Gem-Gold. I am his security detail for today" I informed her politely

"Flash your badge to the camera," she asked.

I sighed pulling my badge from my shirt, showing it to the camera. Than gate opened and I pulled inside and drove inside. I parked and got out walking to the front door, letting myself in. No one batted an eye, but an older woman soon greeted me. She had grey hair highlights in her brown hair, that ran to her shoulders. She had a trim build and she was maybe 5'7" and looked to be in charge, judging by the way she ordered a maid to fetch her coffee.

"Mr. Yukson, I am Mrs. James, Michael's mother. It is a pleasure to meet you. My son has a session at the recording studio today and an interview with Bop Magazine. I expect you to make sure he gets to these with no issue and safely. I want no delay and he tends to like to meet his fans so please watch them. After so much violence in the news, I don't need my son being a statistic." Mrs. James smiled sweetly but I had no doubt in my mind she loved to micromanage her son's career. That wasn't my job, though, to think about her motives. I was just here to protect the kid.

"No problem Mrs. James. Where is Michael?" I asked smiling at her hoping she wasn't one of those ladies who would swoon over me. The mothers tended to read into my smiles and think I was flirting when I was being polite; it got annoying. This time I was lucky. She seemed distracted and ignored my polite gesture and called out to a servant.

"Megan! Where is Michael?" she called out

The maid I assume stopped and looked at her. "Miss; he is getting dressed," she told her, standing still, till Mrs. James turned back to me and hurried to take off.

"You can wait here, he will be down shortly," Mrs. James told me and wandered off. I leaned against the wall to my left and waited patiently. I didn't have to wait long as I glanced at the stairs. A teenager with blond curls came hurrying down the stairs. with a backpack over one shoulder. He saw me and hurried over and smiled sticking his hand out to shake mine. This surprised me as most artists just walked past me and expected me to follow.

"Hi, I'm Michael, what's your name?" he asked politely looking genuinely interested in my response, making eye contact with his light blue eyes. I reached out and shook his hand. "I'm Erik. I'll be your bodyguard for the day. I'll keep the crazies off you, so you can get what you need to be done and get back home safe and sound kid." I smiled at him.

"I don't mind meeting fans honestly, they just get a little grabby sometimes." He told me running his hand through his hair. I turned my head to the sound of clicking heels. His mother was heading in our direction. I stood to watch as she walked up and began fussing over her son.

"Michael you are wearing that?" she looked disgusted with his black t-shirt, blue jeans, and black Nike's. Honestly, he looked like a normal kid to me; nothing wrong with it in my opinion. "Go change and put a dress shirt on and a pair of slacks. Your shoes were shined up earlier, so put those on. They will be photographing you and you need to look professional not like a public school hoodlum." She frowned at him.

"Mom I am wearing this, I am not going to pose as something I am not. We have been over this before. Erik let's go before I am late for my interview." Michael shook his head and walked towards the door. I couldn't help but grin, the kid had moxy. Nice to see someone who was normal and not pretending to be something he wasn't. We walked outside to my SUV and I opened the back door for him to get in, but he put his backpack in and walked to the front passenger seat. He opened the door and got inside and shut the door. I shook my head and walked around to the driver's seat. This was going to be an interesting day and I had a feeling I was going to like this kid.
***

I sat on the side of the set as the Bop Magazine photographed Michael. They had props they handed him, like a guitar for the 'country' look. He looked uncomfortable judging by the way his eyes looked around nervously, he kept shifting his weight from foot to foot. Then I heard the photographer ask a question, which was inappropriate for a kid his age.

"Can you take the shirt off?"

I stepped forward on that question and blocked the camera. "You are aware he is underage and that would be pornographic?" he sneered at him. The photographer frowned at me.

"We have people of all ages do it all the time and if he is 16 or older it is perfectly legal." He told placing his hands on his hips. "You need to get off my set before I have thrown out" he snapped at me.

"Buddy, if I leave so does the kid. I'm his bodyguard, so I am here to protect him. Take the pictures clothes on or we leave; got it!" I stared the man straight in the eyes and held my ground.

"Fine, I think I got what I need." The photograph proceeded to take his camera off the stand and walk off stomping. Michael walked up behind and cleared his throat.

"Hey, thanks for stepping in there. I was starting to feel uncomfortable" Michael said rubbing his hand on his neck.

"No problem. I protect my clients from crazy fans and crazy photographers," I grinned. We walked off the photo set and towards the office where they would conduct his interview. I knocked on the door and a young woman in 20s answered and smiled. "Come in please." She shook Michael's hand and looked at me. I walked past her and leaned against the wall. The questions were easy and it wasn't long till we were on our way. The studio time went fast and then we grabbed lunch. I returned him home and a few hours later my relief came. I headed back to the label and clocked out, then headed home, to get ready for Gabby's and I's date.

* * *

I straightened my tie in the mirror and did a once over in the mirror. I looked like a million bucks in this suit. Tonight had to be perfect and I was nervous because I was taking a big step with Gabby telling her the truth. I just prayed she believed me and I wouldn't have to prove what I was.

"You look amazing son." Came my mother's voice from the doorway to my room. Salli Yukson looked pale and I frowned, I knew she hadn't been feeding and I could swear she looked older than she had a year ago. Vampires don't age so I knew it was my mind playing tricks. "Thank you, mother. Have you eaten today?" I asked looking in the mirror one last time and then glancing back at her. Her eyes became distant then snapped back and looked at me. I will have something tonight while you are out. I promise," she smiled sweetly at me.

"Okay, I will be back later so don't wait up for me" I kissed her cheek as I moved past her, in the doorway. I took her word that she would feed, even though I worried it seemed she was feeding less than normal lately. I knew vampires couldn't get sick so there was no cause for my worry, but I still did; after all, she was my mother.

* * *

I pulled up outside of Gabby's house and got out. I walked up the path to the door and pressed the doorbell. I waited hearing voices and movement inside. The door opened and Cassie stood with a grin.

"Well don't you look handsome? Here to take my girl out for her 21st birthday? So what do you have planned?" Cassie asked leaning on the doorframe.

"Cassie! Let Erik in for god's sake!" Megan yelled at her from inside the house. I had to grin; Megan was more polite to me than Cassie was, on any given day. Cassie sighed and stepped aside. I moved past her into the house. I walked over to the brown recliner and sat down, knowing Gabby would be a moment. A few minutes later she emerged in the black spaghetti strap short designer dress I bought her earlier and black heels. Her hair was loose curls that framed her face. She applied makeup that did un-gentleman like things to me inside. God, she was beautiful. I stood and crossed the room taking her hand and kissing it.

"You are a radiating light of beauty, my Gabriel." I grinned at her. She smiled and blushed, looking down for a moment her lashes hiding her eyes from me. Putting my hand gently under her chin, I raised her face back up to mine looking into her eyes and then kissed her gently on the lips. When we parted I heard her sigh gently.

"Eww PDA, go get a room like away from this house." Cassie gaged.

"Shut up Cassie!" Gabby and Megan said in unison and laughed. I shook my head and extended my arm to Gabby. "Shall we go love?"

"Yes," she smiled sweetly.

* * *

Dinner was canceled as the restaurant had a fire in the kitchen, so we went to a sit-down diner at Gabby's request. We were very overdressed, and people gave us odd looks when they passed by. From there we went to Gheto La, the club that Gabby always talked about spending her 21st birthday in. I greased the bouncer's palm with a couple hundred and we were let in right away, amidst the grumbles of others in line. Inside dance music filled the air and I had no idea who or what it was. There were glowing light blue lights lining the bar and back glass. There were barstools that had many women lined up on them and men standing behind them. Most of the men trying to get the ladies attention; while they were trying to ignore them. Everyone was well dressed in mostly designer clothing. There were comfy looking plush booths located in different areas and some tables for people to stand at.

I led Gabby to a booth and sat down. A waitress in a short blue dress came over and took our drink order, then, looking at Gabby, she requested her identification. Gabby smiled opening her purse and fished it out, handing it to the waitress. She looked it over and handed it back.

The waitress smiled at us and grinned at me. I showed no interest of course so she hurried off to fill our drink order. She came back 5 minutes later and set our drinks down.

"Would you like to run a tab or pay for your drinks individually?" the waitress asked.

I grabbed my wallet from my inside pocket and fished out my credit card and smiled "Run a tab please" then I picked up my brandy and sipped at it. Gabby picked up her margarita taking a drink and smiled. "This is so good!" she smiled taking another larger drink this time. "I'm glad you like it, there are other drinks you can try, you know," I explained hoping she would explore more for her first experience. Your first drink is nice but one should defiantly sample the bar. We drank a few more rounds and she tried Jagermeister and Pina Colada.

"Okay I need to use the bathroom and when I get back we are doing tequila shots," Gabby warned me before heading to the back of the club. A few moments turned into a longer time. I got up and walked to the back near the bathrooms. I noticed there was a line but Gabby wasn't in it. I walked up to a girl in line with red hair and a green dress. "Excuse me but have you seen this girl," I asked showing a picture of Gabby on my phone to her. The girl looked at it then shook her head but the blonde behind her spoke up. "Yeah, two tall guys took her out the back door. I figured they were bouncers" she told me pointing to the door marked exit above it. I rushed to the door opening it looking around. It opened behind the club, to an employee parking lot. I stopped and stood still and listened with my vampire sensitive hearing. I heard muffled screams and shoes scuffling. I turned my head till I could pinpoint the direction and opened my eyes. I started running. As I came upon Gabby, the two men I saw had a shimmer over their skin and they turned orange with black swirls and symbols. They wore no tops, just pants and they looked surprised to see me. They began talking but in a language, I didn't understand.

"Let my girlfriend go now!" I ordered walking closer to them. Then one of them extended his arm towards me and opened his palm and it was like being struck by a force I couldn't explain, that sent me flying backward. When I landed I shook my head and sat up. This time I move at speeds not seen by man but when I got up to where they were and I went to grab my girlfriend there was a bright light and I shielded my eyes. When it stopped, I looked, and the two orange men and Gabby were gone. What had just happened? Where was Gabby? I stood there in confusion not knowing what do.

"GABBY!!" I screamed out but no answer came back to me. Then I looked up and there was nothing there. I collapsed onto the ground and couldn't think. Nothing made sense to me. I don't know how long I sat there until I eventually got up and drove to Gabby's house. Sitting outside though, I thought for a moment if I showed up without her and told them they would call the police. I left and headed home I needed to think.

Chapter Two
Erik

When I walked in I saw my mother on the couch and empty blood bags on the table. I walked over to the couch and looked at her. She looked up and frowned at me. "What is it Erik? I can sense your turmoil." she asked standing up moving over to me.

"I lost Gabby. Two men who can change their skin color from caucasian to orange, took her and I don't know where." I told her tears building in my eyes. My mother grabbed my arm pulling me to the couch sitting me down and then sat beside me.

"Erik, I need you to tell me what exactly they looked like." She said in a serious tone. Looking at her I thought back "They had a shimmer and they had orange skin, there were black swirls and symbols like tattoos. One of them propelled me with the move of his hand." Tears slid down my cheeks "I got up and tried to grab her but there was a bright light and then she was gone with them."

"Erik there is still hope, those men were Ancient Ballic Aliens and they have been known to kidnap women for marriage to their royal family. It's time you met a friend of mine and I think we can get Gabby back." Mother rushed off and I sat there waiting. She came back, phone in hand, and sat down. "He'll be in here a few moments luckily he was on earth." I looked at her oddly on that note.

A knock came at the door and my mother answered. In walked a man in leather pants, boots with buckles mid-calf, and a white shirt with a leather jacket, and spiked green hair. He was on the thin side and he smiled at my mother with a sense of fondness and familiarity. I did not like this at all.

"Erik this is Captain Seven James, he is a space pirate and a close friend of mine. He will get you to Kolopu, the Ballic Aliens home planet, to get Gabby back. I have already paid for your travel and he will have blood stocked aboard the ship. It is being taken care of as we speak. When you get back we need to discuss a few things. I think it is time." My mother informed me. I sat there trying to take in this sudden burst of information. What on earth; space pirate? Alien home planet? Yeah, I could say my mother had a lot to explain to me starting with how she knew a space pirate!

"Look, Erik is it, I will get you there and back if you want. However, no biting my crew and you listen to me. Also, no judging what happens on my ship either. You interfere you will be dropped at the nearest planet. Pack a bag and let's go." Captain Seven James informed me rather abruptly. I couldn't help but respect the man, or was he an alien too?

I packed and kissed my mom goodbye. I went to the door when the captain grabbed my arm. Before I could protest, I got a sick feeling, and everything felt out of place. The world faded from view and I was floating higher through the air, but I had no body. Then I was suddenly in a room made of metal or steel, not sure. There were cargo containers. I fell to my knees and the captain laughed. "Yay that happens the first time to everyone. Welcome aboard let's get ya to your room"

I stood up and composed myself. I followed him to a doorway that opened, as we got closer. Well, that's convenient I don't have to touch it or press anything. As we walked down a corridor, we passed a window and I got my first glimpse of space. There were stars that twinkled, black sky, and the earth below just a ball, a huge ball of the color blue, white; so many so beautiful colors. The Captain stopped in front of a door and rushed to join him not bothering to hide my speed.

"This is your room for the trip. Drop your bag and get comfy," he motioned to the door in front of him.

I did just that, in the small room with a window to the stars. I looked out and set my bag on the bed on top of the silver comforter.

"Gabby, I'm coming baby; don't give up," I whispered to the stars; wishing she could hear me.

I couldn't get there fast enough to kick some alien butt for taking my girl from me. If they bled red I would make sure their rivers ran with it. I just hoped she was okay and they hadn't harmed her.

I was snapped from my thinking as my door opened and there stood a man, well an alien I suppose, judging by his coloring. He was a bright blue with two things; I didn't know what to call them actually, they were just there. It was like someone had colored outside the lines. He saw my eyes looking and he grinned. "They are feelers and hearers mate. I can also shoot lasers from them." He laughed at me and I knew he was lying to me on the laser aspect.

"What can I do for you since you have chosen to barge into my room?" I asked him raising an eyebrow

"Testy little lad aren't ya? I am here to tell you that your blood, vampire, is stocked in the slop hall in the cold unit B. Didn't want that near our food; that's for sure," he grimaced at the idea, scrunching up his face as though it was disgusting.

"Listen I don't know your name but blood is not all I can digest. I can eat other foods so don't go putting me in a category." I told him sternly turning away hoping he would get the clue, he was dismissed. However, he didn't and he walked into the room further and chose to walk over by the window and lean on the wall.

"So vampire what's your deal? The captain says we are rescuing a human female from the Ballic's. Is that true?" he looked at me questioningly, waiting for an answer.

I sighed and sat on the bed looking at my hands then at him. "My girlfriend Gabriel and I were celebrating her 21st birthday when she was kidnapped by two Ballic I don't know henchmen or whatever they were. I love her and I will do anything in my power to get her back. She is the one I want to spend my eternal life with. I won't let anyone take that from me. I don't know if you understand that, but rarely does someone of my species find a gem like that."

He stood up and looked at me "You do know the Ballic species. They take women from other planets to be their brides and carry their young? I don't know how they choose them but you can't just walk in and demand her back. You will need a plan or you will never see her again." He explained to me.

"Why are you telling me this?" I asked suspiciously, wondering what his motives were. After all, this was a pirate ship and there had to be something in it for him.

He walked to the door and pressed a keypad on the door, I hadn't seen, and the door shut. He walked back over to me, grabbing a chair, he turned it backward and sat down across from me. "Between you and me I had a girlfriend once on my planet before I was a pirate and the Ballic jerks kidnapped her also. I wasn't like you I gave up because at the time I was too scared to go against them. That was 5 years ago and I still wonder what happened to her. I am willing to help you rescue your girlfriend; maybe it will give me some peace maybe it won't." He extended his hand to me and I reached and shook it. I had an ally and it felt good. I was one step closer to rescuing the girl I loved. I couldn't imagine the hell she might be going through.

Chapter Three
Gabriel

  I opened my eyes only to feel a sharp pain in my skull. I grabbed my skull and winced at the pain. Something was shoved to my lips "Drink, you'll feel better, the transport leaves you feeling a bit out of sorts." A female voice told me. I opened my eyes to see a clear cup of blue liquid. I looked at it and then at the green woman, the voice came from. "I'm not trying to poison you; just drink it." I downed the drink and looked at her again thinking maybe it was the lighting in the room that made her skin look green. Then it hit me, the parking lot and the two green men with the black ink. OMG Erik! Where was Erik? I looked around frantically seeing beds of other women, some who looked human, and others I couldn't begin to describe. Was this some joke? Aliens weren't real.

  "Calm down or I will have to sedate you, Gabriel." The blue woman told me sternly. She wore a lab coat with pink thick hair that ran down her back and she had bright blue eyes. She was slender and had a confidence about her and an authority.

  "Where am I?" I asked her afraid of the answer, I might receive.

  "You are aboard a Ballic cruiser headed for the home planet. You are to be presented to the Prince for selection among the others for potential marriage & breeding. If you behave, you will be allowed in potentials area of the ship. If you don't, you will be locked in the cage, after the tests are complete." She explained, not even looking at me as she went about her work on the computer, with weird symbols on the screen.

"Testing? What am I being tested for and why did you choose me to abduct?" I didn't understand why they had chosen me.

"We scanned your world for a variety of things and had access to medical records through sources. You were the ideal age; your body is of breeding compatibility and we are just monitoring the injections we made to make sure your body is ready should our Prince chose you. If not, you will be sold on the market to a different suitor, on our world. We do not waste the female stock we acquire." She stopped and looked at me as if this was common knowledge. I sat there stunned. I was being forced into an alien marriage and breeding. If I fought back I would be treated like a slave and placed in a cage. I suddenly became very scared and wished Erik was here to protect me and take me home. I hung my head knowing I would never see the man I loved ever again.

"Cheer up child. It is an honor to be chosen for selection, for the Prince. Not just anyone gets chosen; only the best do. It appears your body is adapting well to the injections. You are cleared to be taken to the potentials area unless you'd rather go to the cage?" she looked at me and I sighed. "I will go to the potentials area. I won't fight" I felt helpless as another blue female joined us wearing black pants and a brown shirt. The fabric was strange, it was form fitting and seemed to shimmer with moving symbols. She walked me out of the medical bay and took me down a corridor made of metal. We stopped outside two doors that opened in a circle and she motioned for me to step through; but didn't follow, shutting it behind me.

I stood confused on where on to go. I started walking forward noticing doors of copper lining the hall corridor that were closed. I walked up to them, but they didn't open so I kept walking trying each door I found. I finally came to an open doorway and walked in to what looked like a dining area, judging by the many women who were eating at tables. I saw human women like me, but when she turned, I saw she gills in her neck. There were others that had to be aliens, there, too. I mean they had skin colors of purple, pink, and some were multi-colored. Some had 4 arms, some had horns coming from their head, and others had tails. It was like being at comic con, yet, no one was in costume. It was a lot to take in for me; but no one looked twice at me.

"You new?" a girl with pink skin, one eye, and a slender build, asked me. I hadn't seen her walk up to me and I turned to her. "Umm yea they just left me on the other side of the door," I explained to her trying to not stare at her, as I didn't want to be rude.

"Your human, right, from earth? I'm Kala. I am a Gulopian," she asked extending her hand to me. I reached out and shook her hand and she smiled. At least she was nice and right now I appreciated that in this new environment.

"I'm Gabriel but you can call me Gabby and yeah I am human from Earth." I smiled back at her.

"Well if you're hungry I'll show you how to get something to eat. Have you found a place to sleep yet?" Kala asked as we walked further into the dining area. I followed her up to a wall with a control panel.

"Put your hand here" Kala pointed to a flat computer screen. I placed my hand on it and a green line scanned up and down the screen then the control panel converted from symbols into English. "Now just pick what you want to eat" she smiled at me. I looked at the menu pressing a down arrow until I found enchiladas and rice. Then I chose a glass of water to go with it. Then on the tray below the screen, a plate of food materialized. My eyes got wide in disbelief. I reached out to touch it and it was solid. Then a glass filled with water materialized and I smiled at Kala. This was so Star Trek! I never thought I would ever see this happen.

Kala laughed and handed me a fork and a napkin. I accepted, and we went and sat down at a table on the opposite end from some other women. I was anxious to try the food to see how it tasted. I cut a piece off the enchiladas on my plate and picked it on my fork and took a bite. My eyes became wide again as the flavors danced on my tongue. It tasted so authentic like my gran used to make. You could taste the shredded beef, the seasoning, the cheese, and the sauces. It melted together like butter and tasted amazing. The water tasted pure, not like the tap water, that had come straight from the pipe or fluoride taste in it. I noticed Kala was watching, smirking at me.

"What?" I asked looking at her confused.

"Nothing; it's just interesting to watch someone taste the food here for the first time," Kala explained to her.

"You talk like you have been here for a long time," Gabriel said between bites. Only stopping for a drink of water or to wipe her mouth with the grey colored cloth napkin.

"Well considering I was among the first batch of women taken, I have been here for a long time as you put it. Six months to be exact, actually." Kala's gaze became sad for a moment which made Gabriel set her fork down and reach for her hand. Kala put it in her lap. "Nothing to worry about though, most would consider it an honor to be chosen on my planet for the Prince of Ballic race."

"Then why are you sad?" Gabriel asked searching Kala's eye for some sign of emotion or tell. Kala was back in chipper mode, smiling and not giving anything away to her new friend.

"Gabby are you done eating? If you are, I will give you the tour and show you where your room is." Kala offered politely nodding towards Gabriel's plate.

"Yes, I think I am done, and I would love that because this place is confusing. I don't want to be sleeping in the corridor tonight." Gabriel laughed standing up, reaching for her plate and cup. Kala snatched them up, taking them to a hole in the wall, dropping them inside. She walked back over and grabbed Gabriel's arm. "Let's go"

Chapter Four
Gabriel

Gabriel walked down the mental corridor past many copper doors that apparently belonged to other women. Her legs were becoming tired; she could feel her calves starting to hurt & tighten, in fatigue. She had no idea how far they had walked. They stopped suddenly in front of one of the copper doors with a screen pad on the right side of the door. Kala placed her hand on the screen and the door slid open.

"Come on in these are my quarters," Kala explained as they walked into a room with two beds that appeared to be full size with silver comforters and matching pillows. The room had a desk that was metal and seemed to be coming out of the wall and was thin with a metal chair in front of it. Off to the side was a door that was open. Since it wasn't her room, she didn't explore further. She was curious as to where a closet or dresser was for a change of clothes, though.

"So, you may have noticed two beds and no I don't have a roommate yet and I was going to ask if you wanted to room with me till we get to Kolopu, the Ballic's home planet?" Kala asked looking at Gabriel, while holding her hands in front of her, fidgeting slightly, waiting for her answer.

"Sure, I don't see why not, my life is over when we get to that planet anyways; might as well enjoy my time on this ship." Gabriel smiled at Kala who was smiling so happily it lit up her face. "So which bed is mine?" Gabriel asked looking at the two beds.

"You get the one on the right side of the room. Also, the beds are quite comfortable. If you want to come and go you need to do as I did to get in with the hand scan. Come over here so I can get you added to the system in here." Kala pointed the computer on the wall near the door. Gabriel walked over to the wall with Kala. A screen appeared and Kala began typing on the screen.

"Put your hand on the screen here" Kala instructed, pointed to the left side of the computer screen that had a handprint outline on it. Gabriel placed her hand on it and it scanned her hand just as the one in the dining room hand.

"Okay, now you can access this room. So do you want to rest or explore the rest of this area of the ship?" Kala asked her.

"Honestly, I would love to rest for a few hours, if that's alright." Gabriel yawned covering her mouth. She glanced at the bed and then back at Kala.

"That's fine. I wouldn't mind catching a nap myself. See you in a few hours." Kala told her walking over to her bed pulling back the covers. Taking her shoes off, she got into bed, covering herself up, laying down. Gabriel did the same in her bed, noticing it was pretty soft. As soon as she laid her head on the pillow, she was out like a light.

Chapter Five
Erik

I was laying in my bed staring at the ceiling, wondering how I was going to storm the Prince's palace and get Gabriel back. I also knew, I now had an ally aboard this ship. I would make it a point to get to know this man. I had a feeling I would need his help. I swung my legs over the side of the bed and sat up. I sat there for a moment then stood up. It was time I explored this ship and found where they were keeping my blood supply. I should have asked directions to the cold unit B. I went to my door and stood there but it didn't open so l looked at the keypad and pressed the red button the screen, the door opened. I walked through and the door closed behind me. Well, that was nice. I looked left and right and decided on left; turning and walking down the corridor. I saw closed doors that were similar to mine, so I left them alone, figuring them to be sleeping quarters.

   After looking and exploring down the corridor for at least a half hour, I came to a set of double doors. Curiously I went up to the computer pad by the door. It was different from the one in my room. It was as big as my hand and had no red button, so, on a whim, I placed my hand on it. There was a green bar moving up and down the pad under my hand. When it stopped, there was a clicking sound from the doors and the doors opened. Inside were a few tables and a small group of, well I'd say, people but it was clear they were aliens by their skin color of orange and another of green. I walked in and they glanced at me. As I was looking around, someone placed a hand on my shoulder. I turned in defense mode unsure of who or what it was.

"Hey, vampire chill it's just me." My bright blue friend, I had met earlier stood before me. I relaxed and looked around and no one was giving us a second glance.

"Where am I?" I asked him looking at him

"This is the mess hall and your blood supply is through the door on the right, over there," he informed me, pointing to a door on the far wall. "It's in the cold unit with a B on it, can't miss it." he informed me. He, then, walked away from me, towards the wall that had a computer with a compartment on it. He pushed some buttons and a plate of food materialized. I stood there in awe, as this was something I had never seen before, and never thought possible. I had seen sci-fi movies with this concept, but to see it, in reality, was something completely different.

I walked up beside him and looked at his food. He saw my look of curiosity and smiled at me. Yeah, I bet you don't have this on Earth, huh," he laughed at me shaking his head. "Does it taste like the real thing?" I asked looking at it with curious eyes.

"Yes, actually the flavors are quite amazing and authentic. Would you like to try something?" he asked me taking his plate of food.

"Actually that sounds good, I would love to see if it can do a rare steak with Brussels sprouts and mashed potatoes with butter and bacon bits." I looked at the computer curious if it would come out as good as Earth food.

"Okay but what kind of steak? It's asking if you want a T-Bone, Filet Minion, Round Steak, or New York?" he looked at me waiting for my response. I stood there thinking about which I wanted. For once in my life, I could have whatever I liked and not worry about the bill.

"I will take T-Bone and a Filet Minion. I am curious to see how the computer does." I smiled smugly because I doubted the computer could compare to Earth's steak selection and cooking methods.

"Grilled or Pan fried?" he asked

"Grilled" I replied starting to think this computer was rather thorough. I stood there as the food began to materialize in front of me. I was surprised to see how appetizing it looked. So far it looked amazing, but the true test was the taste test. Some think vampires had no taste or couldn't eat normal food, which was odd. I could as well as my mother, but other vampires on earth avoided it. I drank blood and ate food. I don't know why I was so different, but I didn't mind.

I picked up the plate and he handed me a grey thin napkin, a knife, and a fork. We walked to a table and we sat down and he started eating. I grabbed my knife and fork and cut a piece of the T-Bone and checked the steak. It was indeed rare. I bit into the piece and the flavor was amazing; it was as though a chef at a fine dining restaurant had prepared it. The steak tasted heavenly and the rareness of the steak appealed to the vampire side of me; there was a slight bloody juice if you touched it gently. I cut into the filet minion and took a bite and sighed. It was utterly delicious, juicy and orgasmic. The filet was like cutting into butter, so tender.

"Dude are you making love to your food or eating it?" my blue friend asked me, looking at me with a look of concern.

"Sorry I just haven't tasted food this good in a while. I am surprised that the computer could make this out of thin air and it's so amazing and the flavor; my god." I grinned like a fool.

"You'll get used to it. I'd be surprised, when we rescue your lady, if you both don't stay on. Most that board this ship, don't leave. We all come from different backgrounds and have our reasons for joining the crew. I think it would be interesting to have a vampire and an actual human aboard." He grinned at me and for the first time I noticed how sharp his teeth were and stained yellow. Maybe they were yellow to start with; all I knew is that was something I wasn't asking about.

"So, what do I call you since you are the only one talking to me so far, on this ship?" I asked him finally after pondering the question in my mind. I took a bite of the Brussel Sprout on my plate.

"I was wondering when you would ask my name is Greg and I am a Longetar and my homeworld is a sore subject so let's not discuss that." He informed me as he ate his food.

"Well, Greg it's nice to meet you" I grinned and shook my head as he grunted and continued eating. This man took his eating seriously. I finished up the food on my plate just after Greg finished his. I stood up and followed him as he went and placed his plate and silverware in a bin connected to the wall. The napkins we placed in a hole in the wall marked trash. We walked out of the mess hall and I made a mental note to come back later to get some blood.

We walked down the hallway in the opposite direction of my room. He pointed out a rec room that had weights, a TV that got all the galactic channels including earth, and a swimming pool. I found this odd as we were in space wouldn't the water float. When I asked Greg, he laughed at me and tried to explain the gravity of the ship versus space to me. I tried to keep up but it was a bit confusing. We walked past what looked to be a storage bay and the doors were open. I stopped to look but Greg shut the doors. He ushered me to move along I made a mental note to check out that area, should I get a chance. I know the captain told me to not judge but he didn't say not look.

"This is the engine room, all the engineers hang out in here and this is the only place you will see them. They tend to stay away from us pretty much." Greg spoke loudly. A pretty blonde, with yellow skin turned around and glared at Greg and looked at me sizing me up. "We stay away from you because you are nothing but trouble Greg!" she shot back at him.

"Aww come on Loku you know you want some of this sexiness in your bed." Greg smiled and winked at her.

Loku scoffed at his advance "I am more likely to sleep with your friend before I ever sleep with you. What are you by the way?" Loku asked turning to me with a curious gaze.

"I am a vampire and the names Erik. It is a pleasure to meet you Loku and while your compliment is appreciated, I am a one woman type of man," I told her politely. "A vampire huh I don't think we ever had one of those on this ship. To bad you're taken we could have had some fun. Do me a favor get Greg out of here." She smiled at me and went back to her work.

"Greg I think that's our cue to leave my friend" I smiled walking back to the door we came in at. "Yeah hold up vampire. Loku why you sleep with him and not me?" Greg huffed. Oh, dear god, was Greg really going to whine about this, to this girl?

"Greg I have work to do and I don't have time to listen to you whine because I rejected you for the 100th time. This is a major part of the reason I am not interested, you have no respect for my choices. Please leave me alone or I will have you removed." She glared at him with her hands on her hips. It wasn't until this moment that I saw she had a tail and it was sloshing around like a cat annoyed. At this point, I walked up behind Greg and put my hand on his shoulder. He dropped his shoulders in defeat and turned around and we walked out.

Once we were outside the engine room and the door shut behind us, I turned around to face him. "You want to tell me what happened in there?" I asked him crossing my arms over my chest. When I looked into his eyes I swear he was on the verge of tears. He choked them back, though, and composed himself.

"I haven't liked anyone since my… well, the one I told you about who was kidnapped. Loku is beautiful, smart, and sexy. I just want to have dinner with her and have a conversation where she doesn't tell me to get out." Greg explained with sad eyes. He sighed heavily and leaned on the wall.

"I can understand this, but it appears you may need a wingman. Since you are going to help me on my mission, then I will help you get the girl, as well. However, we will let her calm down a bit before we attempt a conversation again." I nudged him and he grinned at me. He stood up and we continued down the corridor.

Chapter Six
Gabriel

I awoke to a gentle snoring sound coming from across the room, I was in. I rubbed my eyes and sat up forgetting for a moment where I was. Then it sank back in, I was on my way to an alien planet after being abducted by an alien race called the Ballic, to be presented to an Alien Prince, among other women who were abducted. If I wasn't chosen, then I would be sold to the highest bidder. I was 21 years old and this was a life that had started out as a celebration and had turned into a nightmare. The man I loved was so far away. I remembered him trying and failing to rescue me in that parking lot. I had never felt so alone in my life. Even though I had made a friend, it was different. My homeworld was probably so far away; I just couldn't help wondering why me. I sighed and threw back the covers and sat on the side of the bed. I slipped my shoes back on and made my way to the bathroom, hoping things weren't too different.

      I breathed a sigh of relief at seeing a silver-colored Earth toilet but looking around for the toilet paper I didn't find any. There was a silver sink basin just above waist high hovering, attached to nothing, with a facet extending from the wall. An oval-shaped silver trimmed mirror was above the sink. The wall was a metal substance and the shower had a nozzle in the center ceiling pointing down, but there was no shower curtain. There seemed to be no hot or cold handles in the shower either, just a keypad. I would have to ask Kala about that because I needed a shower, right now I needed to use the toilet. All the alcohol from the club was screaming to be let go. Honestly, I hated to not have toilet paper; but you had to sometimes do what you had to do. I pulled my dress up and panties down and sat on the toilet, which was surprisingly warm. I began peeing and when I was done I tried to get up but couldn't. It was like I was suctioned to the seat. Then I felt the warm water splashing my private neather regions, and then a warm breeze. Then the suction let go and I stumbled off the toilet. What had the heck, just happened? Was that why there was no toilet paper? I left the bathroom quickly to wake Kala.

As I entered the bedroom I noticed Kala sitting on her bed stretching. "I see you have discovered the toilet, judging by the look on your face. It is a bit different than your Earth toilets, I take it?" Kala laughed, as her eye twinkled with joy.

"You would find joy in my bewilderment. Hey, Kala how does that shower work and is there a change of clothes around here for us?" I asked looking around the room.

Kala stood up walking to the computer on the wall. She tapped the screen a couple times then looked at me. "What are your measurements?" she asked me waiting for my reply. "umm I am a size 6 on earth and a size 36 B according to my bra," I informed her watching curiously. She tapped the screen a few more times. "Do you want another dress or pants?" she asked me, waiting for my reply.

"Pants would be nice, thanks. A size medium shirt would be nice, pink if they have it." I smiled. She tapped the screen again and smiled at me. A drawer appeared out of the wall and I approached it looking inside to find clothing inside. I reached in cautiously and pulled the clothing out. The door closed after I pulled the clothing out and I walked back to my bed and set the clothing down. I picked up a pair of silver-colored pants. What was it with this ship and silver? The shirt was a metallic colored pink but soft. The bra was black and not flattering at all. That's when I noticed I forgot underwear I sighed and turned to Kala.

"I forgot to mention underwear," I informed her shaking my head. She looked at me confused. "What is underwear?" she asked me tilting her head to one side looking at me.

"We wear them under pants to well keep our pants clean from our genitals. Sometimes we wear our bra and underwear to bed. It's a cleanliness thing for humans." I explained to her, but she still looked confused.

"No one on this ship wears anything like that. We just wear pants and dresses with stretchy pants underneath." Kala explained. Oh, dear lord, the galaxy didn't believe in underwear. You had to be kidding me. Looks like I had to go commando from here out. Not something I was looking forward to at all. Erik would be laughing so hard at this if he knew. "Please tell me you have towels for the shower and shampoo?" I asked her hoping that the answer would be yes. She laughed and stood up.

"The shower has an auto dry feature and what is shampoo?" she asked looking at me again with confusion. I sighed and sat on the bed I was discouraged to ask my next question. "How do you wash your body in the shower? Also, shampoo is what we use to wash our hair on Earth."

"The shower has features for cleansing your body, and if you have hair it will cleanse that, too. It will take some getting used to. I am sorry this is discouraging for you. I am sure things are very different on Earth." Kala explained and gave an apologetic smile.

I sighed and picked up my clothes and walked back into the alien bathroom. I looked for the keypad to shut the door but saw none. I don't know why I didn't look when I used the toilet but after a moment I gave up and set my clothes on the back on the toilet and stripped my dress, bra, and underwear off. I stepped into the shower and looked at the computer pad. I pressed a glowing red button and the water began to pour down and I jumped at the coldness and shrunk to the side of the shower where the computer pad was and hit another button and I stuck my hand out into the water it began to warm up. I cautiously stepped into the water and sighed at the warmth letting it warm my body and wet my hair. I was enjoying it when a few moments later a jet behind shot out and began shooting up from my feet, up my body. I jumped in shock and went to move from the shower when I noticed a force field had been erected around the shower. Well, that explained the lack of curtain.

"Please turn around" came a computer voice in the shower.

I turned around and the jet started at the bottom again and moved up and stopped at my shoulders. "Please close your eyes," the computer voice asked

I closed them and felt water but it smelled different like there was something in it. I couldn't place my finger on it and probably never would, being I was on an alien ship. "Please keep your eyes closed as we have detected you have hair and have determined the best washing method." The computer explained to me. Oh god, I thought to myself as I stood there. I heard a hiss, the water had stopped and then a warm wind and my hair was blowing upwards. I smelt something that reminded me of roses blooming, then the water turned back on and it was gone. A few minutes later I heard further instructions "Please place your feet on the marks on the shower floor and raise your arms outward." I did as asked and it caused me to stand with my legs slightly open and then I felt a strong warm wind. It took only a minute, but I was dry, even my hair. Then I stood there for a moment waiting for further instructions. "You may exit"

I stepped out of the shower touching my hair. It was, indeed, dry and smelled like roses blooming. I guess in space they don't take showers for pleasure and relaxation. Maybe they had to conserve water or something. I went about getting dressed slipping the bra on though it looked like a mom bra; it was very comfortable. The shirt was soft and the pants were soft on the inside but slick like track pants on the outside. I looked down at my bare feet and wondered if they had socks or if they had special shoes because the heels I came in wouldn't be comfortable to walk in, forever.

I walked to the sink and touched the mirror to see if it was like a medicine cabinet. At my touch, it shimmered and the mirror disappeared there was a cabinet space in its place with two shelves. The top space had a shimmer over it and when I touched it there was an invisible barrier and access denied came across it. I assumed this was Kala's shelf. I looked on the bottom shelf and saw a brush with a pink metallic hand. I reached to pick it up my hand coming against a barrier again this time it said access granted. I grabbed the brush taking it out. Seconds later the mirror reappeared in a shimmer.

I gently brushed my hair working any tangles out, that were present. I touched the mirror again and the shelves reappeared and I set the brush back on the bottom shelf and the mirror appeared again. I looked at myself and walked back into the room.

"You done?" Kala asked sitting with her legs crossed on her bed looking in my direction. I noticed looking at her, as my eyes drifted to her feet, she had 3 little toes and a bigger toe on each foot. I wondered what I looked like to her and just how alien I was, in her thoughts.

"Actually I have a thought" bending over to pick up my heels and showing them to her. "There is no way I am walking in these. Does that thing make shoes and socks?" I asked hoping this ship believed in socks" she looked at my feet for a moment then got up and went to the computer.

"What's your Earth size?" Kala asked not looking from the screen. "Umm size 7" I quickly told her dropping the heels on my bed remembering the dress and underwear on the bathroom floor and quickly ran in and picked them up and brought them out to my bed folding the dress and putting the heels next to it. The panties, however, I didn't know what to do with them. I set them on the floor by my bed.

"Okay, so you can get your shoes in pink if you want." Kala laughed looking at me for a moment. I grinned at her and then saw a different drawer open on the wall then where it had last time. I walked over and looked inside and pulled the shoes out they looked like a pair of Nike's without the laces.

"Where are the socks?" I asked looking in the drawer and seeing none. I groaned and looked at Kala who seemed to find humor in my discomfort at that moment. "First underwear now socks. What else is this galaxy going to be primitive about?" I walked over to my bed and plopped on it, dropping my new shoes on the floor. I put my face in my hands propping my elbows on my legs and sighed. I moved my hands to the sides of my face and breathed. I had been pretty accepting of a lot since I had been here. Basically, I had no choice. Everything was different, and I felt like I was in the Twilight Zone, where everything was strange and different.

"Gabby are you okay? I am sorry if my laughing upset you. Can you explain socks to me?" She came and sat down next to me. I sighed and sat up looking over at her. "Socks are like clothing for your feet they keep them warm and dry. You can also wear them with shoes." I explained to her sighing. I knew it wouldn't do any good.

"Umm Gabby that sounds like Gibbles," Kala told me getting up quickly crossing the room to the computer typing on the screen. A door opened in the wall and Kala fished out a pair of pink looking socks. My face lite up, thank god they had socks! I took them from her hand and gave her a hug. Kala stood there as I hugged her and when I stepped back she looked at me oddly.

"Why did you grab me and hold me so tightly?" she asked looking confused "Is that customary on your planet?"

"Kala, it's called a hug, it's affectionate. You know friendly?" I tried to explain. "I was thanking you for the Gibbles, but we call them socks on my planet," I explained further hoping she would understand. Kala walked over to me and grabbed me in a crushing hug she was actually quite strong and was making it hard to breathe. I tried to pat her on the back to get her attention. When she let me go I was grateful for the returned air in my lungs.

"Kala you are strong, you might want to be a little more gentle with those hugs." I coughed trying to giggle.

"I was not trying to stop you from breathing I was just returning your gesture of an Earth hug," Kala explained looking at me, her forehead wrinkling and looking concerned.

"Don't worry about it I am fine. So, besides eating, is there anything to do on this ship before we get to this planet and my life, as I know it, is over?" I asked feeling a pit in my stomach, thinking about where we were going.

To Be Continued...

Look for Blood & Space the novel to see the rest of this adventure of vampires, space pirates, alien princes and one very lost earth girl caught up in it all coming soon!

About the author

Author of Paris Moon and London Moon, the first two books in the Kloe & Gavin Adventures Series. Also soon to be released Edge of Night Trilogy. She is a paranormal/supernatural, romance/thriller and sci-fi author.

Currently living in the rainy state, Washington State, when not spending time with her family and friends, you can find her writing, or contributing to the indie author community. She is known to be deeply immersed in helping new authors, also making book teasers, book covers or just giving helpful.

Website:
http://sondrahicks.com
Facebook :
http://facebook.com/sondradhicks
Email:
contact@sondrahicks.com
Twitter:
https://twitter.com/midnightmomma
Instagram:
http://instagram.com/sondrahicksbooks

Darkness Lurking
Maggie Lowe

Deadly mission, love left behind, past encounters. The crew of 42 set out on another fatal mission. To save a planet. Halfway to the planet things get dangerously chaotic. Who's after them and who will make it home alive? Find out in this fatal tale of a crew of heroics.

Dedication

I dedicate all my works to my parents for without them I wouldn't have made it this far. I miss them each and every day. To Shawn, my husband, who has supported me since the day we got together. To Hydra Productions, for without y'all I'd be nothing. And to my readers, thank you for believing in me.

Darkness Lurking

I was in my office going through my email and deleting the junk when I came across the one I'd been dreading; the mission to save the Usahna race. The Admiral was sending my crew on a very dangerous mission, one I wasn't really looking forward to.

I married my high school sweetheart, Celeste, just a few months ago, and we had yet to have our honeymoon. We were planning our future together, complete with the white picket fence and little ones running around.

This mission was going to disrupt all of those plans.

The mission would take well over a year to complete, and there was a good chance that we may not make it back alive. My crew, the crew of the 42, was the best of the best. We were called upon for missions such as this often, and because of that, we didn't have the option of turning them down. We just had to return safely. And so far, we had managed it.

I breathed out a heavy sigh as I pushed away from my desk, dreading the talk I'd have to have with my wife. To say I wasn't looking forward to it or the look that I know would be on her beautiful features would be the understatement of the century. It always was.

I locked up my office tight and rushed home to my Celeste.

"Honey, I'm home," I announced as I entered our home.

"I'm in the kitchen," came her beautiful and soft voice.

"Babe, could you come in here please?" I tried to keep the pain of the departure out of my voice.

She saw past it, though, as she walked slowly into the living room with a distressed look on her face. "You got the email." It was a statement, not a question. She had known the risky job I held and that the mission was on the table. She'd dreaded it just as much as I.

We'd been together for ten years now. There was no way to hide this from her even if I wanted to.

I nodded slowly as my heart broke at the well-known look on her face and the tremble in her voice.

"When, and how long will you be gone this time?"

"We depart the base tonight and will be gone for a couple of years at least," I told her, the pain of leaving my wife behind obvious in my voice.

"Seriously, Shawn? Do they not care that we still haven't even gotten our honeymoon because of the last mission you were on? Do they not care that we're going to be parents?" Celeste fumed as her heart broke. "I know it's your job as the captain, I know you can't turn this down since it's in your contract, but it doesn't mean I have to like it one single bit."

I wrapped my arms around her as I pulled her in for an embrace and rubbed her stomach that soon would be growing with my offspring.

And then I began humming as I looked into my beautiful wife's eyes as I spoke my heart to her.

> "My love, my beautiful angel,
> you're perfect in my eyes.
>
> You're the light of my life,
> the apple of my eye.
>
> You're the voice of reason,
> when things in life get too hectic.
>
> My love, my beautiful angel,
> you're everything I need.
>
> I may be leaving on a spaceship,
> we may be parting.
>
> But we'll always be together,

together in my thoughts.

Not a day would go by
without you on my mind.
You've always been in my heart,
and always will.

I know this is terrifying,
we know this is true.

I know it kills you,
because it kills me too.

But my love you know it's without saying,
my heart is with you for all of eternity.

Our deaths won't separate us,
not even a million light years apart.

My love, my beautiful angel,
you are the only one for me.

No one will ever take your place in my life,
it's always been you for me.

My love, my beautiful angel,
it's now time to part.

The ship is fired up,
the crew is on board.

The mission must be done,
and done it will.

My love, my beautiful angel,
it's time we say goodbye.

Not a forever goodbye,
just a see you later.

Not a final goodbye,

I will make it home to you.

My love, my beautiful angel,
I love you always and for eternity!"

As I spoke the final words to my beautiful wife, kissed her perfect lips, and her stomach, I grabbed my bag and walked out the door before I changed my mind and went AWOL.
***
We were on our way to the ship, destination beyond our solar system. Our crew was chosen for this specific mission because, according to the admiral, we were the best team they had in the fleet. The hardest thing about leaving for this mission, though was leaving my wife and unborn child behind while I ran off to captain this massive machine.

"Captain, it's time to get this show on the road," my commander announced, effectively bringing me out of my thoughts.

I nodded to him as I instructed Bryan, the pilot, to take her out slow and steady.

"Aye Sir!" He saluted before doing as instructed.

I took my seat next to my commander and flicked on the radio as I anticipated our mission.

My favorite artist, Nelly, was blaring through the speakers as we exited the launch pad and went to warp.

Once we were on our way I rose from my seat and informed the crew that I'd be in my ready room if they needed me. After the strained conversation with my wife and a long shift at the command center, I needed to rest my eyes and my brain. It was a must if I was going to be of any use when we reached the Usahna Solar System.

Inside my room, I undressed and took a long shower. Letting the heat from the water wash over my tense muscles, I realized that I needed to sleep more, or I'd be dead by the time I was thirty. I sighed as I turned off the water and stepped out, drying off with one of the white fluffy towels my wife made sure to pack for me, and got dressed as I climbed under the blankets.

Once my head hit the pillow, I was out….drifting off to dreamland...

I was in my sonic shower before bed, letting the heat drift over my tense muscles when in walked this beautiful woman. A redhead with a perfect body. Curves in all the right places, a body that would give a virgin a heart attack, but she wasn't my wife.

She shoved me up against the wall of the shower and drove her tongue down my throat. I went with it at first, but when I couldn't breathe, I panicked and tried pushing her away, but she wouldn't budge. She tugged on my hair as she continued the assault. I felt like I was going to faint.

I bolted upright as the red alert was blaring throughout the ship. It took me a moment to realize where I was, but when I got my bearings I jumped out of bed, yanked on my Captain's uniform, and darted to the bridge.

"What in Sam Hell is going on?" I barked at commander as I came to a stop in front of him.

"There's a hull breach. We were at light speed when out of nowhere something rammed us, sir," he replied quickly.

"Could it be debris from an erupted star or another ship? Maybe it's the light stream?" I asked.

"Possibly," he answered, quickly.

"Have you tried the sensor sweep?" I was feeling agitated. I hated this feeling, but knew it all too well.

At his nod I knew something wasn't right, a bad feeling crept over me as time seemed to stand still. The alarms stopped blaring, and everything went quiet. This wasn't right, something or someone was messing with us.

"Captain, oh captain," a female's voice was calling to me.

I found it odd since we didn't have any female officers on board. When I took over this ship that was one rule that I put into effect. Not that there was anything wrong with having female officers because let's face it women can do the job just as well as any man. But I didn't want female officers on a ship full of horny men, especially with how long the missions usually lasted.

The female giggled as she spoke again, "It's fun messing with you. All work and no play, though! Maybe I should pilot the ship, and take you to Hell with me."

My internal alarm system began to blare. I started checking the screens to tell me where the firing was coming from, but it didn't show anything. Then I check out the sensors, and still nothing. I finally checked the main systems to make sure it wasn't one of them malfunctioning, but they were in perfect working order.

The conduit near Bryan's position exploded, knocking him out of his chair as another one went off at the weapons station. In moments things went from bad to worse. I sent the commander to the infirmary with the pilot as the lieutenant followed behind. I had the repair teams hard at work fixing both units, and since there wasn't much else to do and things seemed to calm down for the most part, I headed back to my ready room to think of our next move, and to keep the crew from thinking I'm off my rocker, with a female voice in my head.

I closed my door before yelling a demand at the voice, "Who the hell are you?"

"Wouldn't you like to know?" she giggled again.

"I wouldn't have asked otherwise," I snapped.

"You'll see soon enough," she said with a cackle.

This infuriating woman! I was not going to let her ruin my ship or take control without a fight!

"I know what you're thinking, and it won't work," she stated. "You can't stop me."

"Watch me," I declared.

She laughed, "You think you can overpower me a second time? Not likely."

"I will be taking back control of my ship, you won't win," I growled. "I won't let you win!"

"I have already won and will be keeping the victory, and do you know why?" she questioned sinisterly.

I stayed silent, having enough with this mentality.

"Because you're not leaving this sector," was her threatening promise as her voice disappeared and the noise of the chaos came back with a force.

I ran out of my ready room and was blasted by a cloud of smoke as one of the main conduit systems was on fire. "How the hell did this happen?" I was beyond frustrated. "And who the hell is messing with my ship!"

We were traveling at a much slower pace as we were making our way to our destination all the while 42 was being attacked and we were getting closer. We will make it there if it kills us, I thought, determinedly.

I was hoping I wouldn't have doomed us to death with that thought, but alas, things got worse. The Lieutenant was back at his station firing at nothing when his station exploded, throwing him across the bridge. With the third degree burns he sustained and slamming his head on the metal railing it was enough to kill him instantly. To confirm my fears, I placed my two fingers on his neck at his pulse point to check, but he was no longer.

I instructed Ensign Smith and Ensign Jackson to take Lieutenant Alex to the infirmary to ready him for the impending funeral that would be scheduled for later tonight once things calmed down a bit.

I hated losing my crew, even though over the years I've lost many great men. Alex's death hit me harder than most because not only did he leave behind a wife and two kids but an unborn child as well as being my brother in every way that really mattered.

Alex, Michael, and I had been friends all our lives. When I joined the fleet and became captain I had the task of choosing my crew. I had informed the Admiral that I didn't care who he wanted to put on my team as long as Alex was my Lieutenant and Michael was my Commander. If I was going into danger I wanted both my brothers at my side.

Alex, Michael, and I had been through everything together; horrible exes, asshole parents, tragedies, college, the academy, and weddings.

"Commander, can I have a word with you in my ready room?" I stated, eyeing my brother for any reaction. He followed me as I headed into my quarters.

"What's up, Captain?" he inquired.

"Mike, you know when we're away from the crew you can drop the formalities," I deadpanned.

He stayed quiet as he watched me.

"Anyway, what are we supposed to tell Alex's wife? Sarah's going to be so devastated," I asked, trying to keep my emotions in check.

"It won't be easy breaking the news to her that's for sure." Mike looked close to tears himself. "But, I think it should be both of us who inform her."

"I agree," I nodded. "I knew something bad was going to happen, but I was hoping to whatever deity was out there that it wouldn't be this bad. Alex wasn't supposed to go out like this." Tears slipped down my cheek. "He was better than this!" I slammed my fist on the desk. My temper was flaring as reality set in.

"Man, you need to buck up. I miss Alex too, but you can't let his death affect you like this. He would want you to continue the fight, and if the crew see you in this shape they aren't going to take it too well," Mike reminded me of my position as he gave me a man hug.

I nodded as I swiped at my cheeks, went over to the sink and splashed cold water on my face, "Mike, you're right. We need to get back in this fight and try to get the rest of this crew home in one piece."

"Now that's the captain I know. Welcome back," Mike joked as he left the room.

I stayed behind for a bit longer to think of a way out of this mess.

"Captain, I told ya you weren't going to make it out of our solar system," cackled the female voice.

"For one, we aren't in your solar system. And two I will get us all home," I snapped.

"Cap, take a look outside, you are in our solar system. It's too late to turn around and flee," she said sarcastically.

I looked out the window as she instructed, and sure enough, we were in a different solar system than our own.

I blew out a heavy sigh, "You won't get away with this."

"I already have," were her final words as more explosions were heard outside my door.

I stormed out of my room and noticed that the pilot's station was engulfed in flames, and Bryan's body was slumped over the chair and his back was still on fire while the smoke was getting thicker as I tried to scan the bridge.

The only station that wasn't on fire was the captain and commander seats where Mike was sitting, a panicked look on his face. There were bodies lying all around the bridge with burns and different positions.

"Mike, what are we going to do? We have no bridge crew left!" I said in a panic.

"Cap, remember to stay calm. But we need to abandon ship," he stated as calmly as he could manage. "There's no way we can continue to stay here when this place is on fire."

"Dude, I can't abandon the 42. She is our ship, our crew. Besides, haven't you heard, the captain goes down with the ship?" I tried making a joke so it'd calm me some.

"Dude, that is not funny," he glared at me.

I just hardened my lips as I stayed quiet. Captains do go down with their ship, and I was going to do just that.

Mike shook his head sadly as he realized I was serious.

"What are we going to do?" he asked, unsure of our next move. "The ship is in shambles, and the crew is gone."

"We're going to crash land on the closest planet we can find and try our damnedest to survive," I replied in a confident voice.

He nodded slowly as he got to work fixing one of the sensors so we could find a planet that wouldn't kill us on impact.

I brushed off my captain's chair and relaxed into the leather and thought over what has happened to lead to this point as Mike searched for the perfect planet but then explosions were heard somewhere on the ship.

"Mike, find a planet, any planet! We need to get off this ship quickly, we don't have time to search for a planet that won't kill us. This ship will do the job if we don't land in the next few minutes!" I barked at my friend and commander. "We are running out of time!"

He nodded in agreement as he set to searching the solar system for any planet to land on. "I found one, but according to the sensor data, it's full of poisonous creatures."

"We have no choice," I stated as we descended upon the poisonous planet.

We held onto whatever we could so we didn't get thrown around the bridge as the ship crash-landed on the planet, but that didn't save us. Mike and I both were flown to the floor. My head hit hard on something rough and my vision faded.

A teenage boy was digging through his locker in a rush to get to class when a beautiful girl with fire red hair and legs for miles approached.

"Hey there sexy pants," she smirked as the boy turned around.

"I'm late to class," he tried rushing around her, but she put her hand on his to stop him.

She nodded, "So am I. Why don't we ditch this period and have a little fun?" She wiggled her eyes suggestively.

The boy thought for a moment, a smirk appearing on his handsome features a moment later, "Let's ditch."

He pulled her along the hallway, across the back of the school and to a nearby field and didn't stop until they were in the middle and away from prying eyes.

He looked the girl up and down hungrily as their lips crashed together.

She pushed him away playfully then pulled him back up against her body, craving more of him. Teasing his body with her eager touch, she slowly fell to her knees and began to unbutton his jeans. He leaned up against a tree as she continued exploring. He moaned at her touch and begged for more. She eagerly complied.

A few moments after they finished up, he got up to head back to campus.

"Baby, where you going?" Cinja asked, seductively.

"Back to class, the day is almost over, and I need my book bag," the boy replied as he smirked at her.

"We should stay here," she whispered with a look of concentration on her beautiful face.

He walked over and sat next to her, complying with her every word, which to him, was odd as I noticed the boy had been me. I never skipped class or played hanky. I wasn't a virgin, I've had my share, but I never jeopardized my schooling to get it.

"Shawny Poo, wakey, wakey," said a familiar female voice. Too loud for a dream, too real as well, and very close.

I slowly pried my eyes open and stared up into the eyes of my past. The eyes of her.

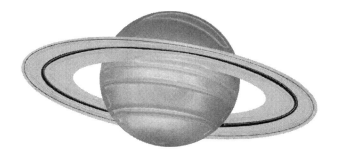

Lucky's Books
Brian Hagan

When Cho and Eric are rescued by Lucky, they all discover how powerful words can be.

Lucky's Books

Cho pressed his carapace against the window to get a better view of the robotic arm as it reached down from the open cargo bay of the Alexandria and grasped the floating capsule which was spinning below it. "Below" was relative, of course. From the perspective of Cho, sitting in the capsule, the Alexandria was upside down. The vessel was a cream color and looked like somebody took a bunch of bubbles and stuck them together in a vaguely symmetrical, elongated shape. At one end a single interstellar thruster jutted out, and at the other end Cho could see the long line of the bridge window and above it two huge floodlights. He groomed an antenna. It really was too easy to spot the human-made spaceships. All you had to do was look for their face.

Typical human, he thought. Always so self-centered, even without meaning too. Always ignoring the Orientation Convention of Khakl. It wasn't a huge problem, as long as Cho was able to position himself to be ready for the Alexandria's artificial gravity before it actually kicked in. He hated falling. Floating was okay, but falling was extremely unpleasant, particularly the bit at the end. The slightest dent in his exoskeleton would take forever to go away, depending on when his next molt would be.

He tapped his six limbs anxiously on the brown box he was carrying as the claw closed around them. Next to Cho, Eric wobbled. Eric was one of the aforementioned Khaklians, a species of green, globular beings about half a meter round, who had a terrible time telling up from down, and didn't usually bother designing their buildings or spaceships in a manner that was friendly to other species who enjoyed such things. Khaklians communicated through a complex combination of body movements and liquid-related sounds. Following his wobble, Eric gave a curious burp.

"It's a human ship," Cho replied. "I know because human ships all look the same, just like humans. They're not a very creative bunch."

Wobble slurp.

"Oh, I believe you," Cho said, "but you'll get some sympathy from me. I've met a few humans who were afraid of 'bugs,' as they call us, and they're impossible to deal with. I hate being compared to those minuscule things on Earth. At least you can just pretend to not be alive. Humans usually ignore not living things. As long as they're not shiny, anyway."

Eric gurgled. He wasn't shiny.

"If you don't like humans, why did you take a human name?" Cho asked quizzically. It was normal for Khaklians to adopt a name usable in normal speech. Eric made a slight slurping noise, but was interrupted by a sudden jerk of the robotic arm as it pulled their pod towards the larger ship's cargo bay.

Eric finished his thought as they watched the Alexandria get larger in the window.

"Humans aren't the only ones who love to make their computers talk," Cho reminded him. "Some of my own people will do that, from time to time. And—" Eric interjected a long fart, and Cho groomed his antenna a bit more. "Yes, you're right. Humans always have computers that can talk it seems. Well, we all have our quirks."

Their capsule was entering the cargo bay finally, and Cho scurried to the downward facing end of the capsule and prepared for gravity to kick in. The bay doors closed and slowly Cho felt his downward pull increase as the Alexandria's gravity began to take effect. Eric fell with a splat, but thankfully was able to keep himself together.

Cho exited the capsule into the cargo bay, leaving Eric behind for the moment, and carrying the small box. The cargo bay was an airless vacuum, as dictated by the Interspecies Convention of Being Nice to Each Other. The members who wrote that particular convention weren't very good at naming things, but they were excellent of thinking of ways they could inadvertently cause harm, or just as importantly, be extremely rude to each other.

One of the early realizations by the convention authors was that exposure to unexpected gases, which may be used by one species to breathe, could be fatal to another species. It was good manners to avoid gassing your guests to death, and it was expected that, if you know who your visitors were and what they breathe, you should either provide the necessary gas or the visitor should arrange for their own. In cases where the guest was unknown, such as Cho's own situation, a vacuum devoid of gases but without the pressures of the vacuum of space, would be provided until the guest could communicate which gas or, in some cases, fluid, they needed.

Cho's species could survive on any number of gases, which they breathed through the soft joints in their carapace. At the moment, he simply held his breath as he exited the pod and scurried across the floor, through the vacuum, to the courtesy panel on the way to the cargo bay. While Eric was capable of breathing an even greater breadth of gases (and fluids) than Cho, he didn't do so well in vacuums and was counting on Cho with his solid exoskeleton to take care of this task.

At the courtesy panel, Cho read the welcome message as it rapidly scrolled down the screen in dozens of languages, stating instructions to pick their air of choice. At the bottom, several buttons showed the available options and Cho picked 'oxygen/nitrogen' from the list. It wasn't his favorite gas to breathe, but their human host was doing them a favor by saving them from a slow death adrift in deep space. In Cho's opinion, he felt the least he could do is not inconvenience their host.

The cargo bay flooded with gas, and Eric rolled out of the capsule and onto the ground.

"Hello! Thank you for saving us," Cho said loudly, uncertain of how well he could be heard as the gas filled the room. "As you can tell, I speak Human. We mean you no harm." That last bit was a phrase he learned early on in his career. Besides being the truth, it seemed that humans just really liked hearing that phrase, so Cho always included it when he was meeting humans in an uncertain circumstance.

A moment passed by in relative silence before a nearby door opened. A human dressed in blue stepped through. As it walked in and looked to Cho, it made the happy human expression on its face: mouth curved upwards and showing its teeth.

Cho tried to tell if the human was male or female, but he was never very good at guessing when they had clothes on, which was nearly always. He knew that humans with thick hair on their face were male, but every other trick he'd learned to tell the gender of humans always had an exception. The length and color of their hair, the lumpiness of their bodies, their height, the tenor of their voice, the style of their clothes, the color of their skin, the symmetry of their body, and presence of a companion animal, all had exceptions or were outright irrelevant, as he'd found out. The only rule that seemed to hold fast was hair on the face, but even that wasn't infallible. Humans with hair on their face were always male, but humans without hair, such as the specimen in front of him now, might be male or female. It was very frustrating, because humans got touchy about that sort of thing sometimes.

At least this one didn't seem to mind Cho being a 'bug.'

It dipped its head in a standard greeting used by beings with heads before speaking.

"Hello! My name is Lucky. You're fortunate I picked up on your signal; this is really far out. Come on in, I bet you're hungry. I have a food printer that should be able to make you something to eat."

"Thank you," Cho said, dipping his head as well. "I am Cho, and this one is called Eric." He gestured behind him and toward the pod, pointing directly to the green ooze that was pulling itself back together. "We would enjoy a meal very much."

As they followed the human back through the door and down a hallway, Lucky chatted the whole way.

"I imagine you were on your way somewhere, but I hope you don't mind a short detour in addition to whatever caused your already unfortunate delay. I don't keep a lot of supply matter for the printer, just a bit more than enough for my trip. There should be plenty for the three of us until I reach my destination, but not enough for me to take you elsewhere without a resupply."

"You must be going to the Smov system?" Cho held his box tightly, hopefully.

"Yes, that's correct," Lucky said cheerfully. Cho and Eric exchanged meaningful glances that were a bit less cheerful.

Inside the meal-room of the human's ship, they each ordered a dish from the food printer. It was a modestly large, well-lit room with a single table with space for about eight humans. As Eric had trouble making himself understood to the food printer, Cho took care of the ordering for the two of them. They sat at the table while the printer whirred and buzzed. Cho set his box next to himself, and Eric slipped up on top of it.

As they ate, their conversation wandered over the usual topics discussed when spacefarers met: where you're from, do you have family, how long you've been in space, did you hear the latest gossip. Generally, questions about why one finds themselves in space were considered impolite, and small talk had evolved to avoid it. Nobody wanted to find out that their guest was banished from their homeworld for high crimes, or gleefully gallivanting about the galaxy marauding and pirating, or that they should be quarantined. Some questions were best left unanswered, and everyone more or less minded their own business as much as possible.

Lucky looked at the box under Eric before his next question.

"What's in the box?"

The question skirted the edge of social acceptability, but Cho figured the topic was going to come up, and rightfully so. It was the only thing the two of them had brought on the escape capsule when they were forced to abandon their ship. It was the most important thing in their possession.

"A book," Cho answered. "A very important book, which we were delivering to Smov 3."

Lucky's face became excited and changed from the kind and polite human expression it had been using during the conversation back to the happy human expression from earlier.

"Oh! I love books!" Lucky's happy human expression only grew with this excited outburst.

"You do?"

"I do! In fact," Lucky got up from the table and walked over to a door, a different one than where they'd come in, and opened it. The room beyond was a warm, golden brown space filled with gentle, but bright, light. The floor was soft and inviting, and on the far side of the room, a series of shelves constructed of wood stood. To either side were lamps, directing light as happy as sunshine, onto the books that were shelved there.

"Oh, no," Cho whispered.

"I'm a librarian, you see," Lucky said. "I travel from star system to star system in the Alexandria with my library."

"Oh, no," Cho said again. Beside him, and under Eric, came a quiet but deep laugh. It grew in volume quickly, and the three of them stared at the box as it began to rattle and shake.

"Quick, Eric!" Cho grabbed his friend and leapt away from the table just as the box came apart at the seams, bits flung across the meal-room. From the debris floated the book, thick and black, rotating slowly as it resisted gravity. The laughter, growing dark and menacing, was deafening now. Suddenly, it flew across the room and through the door, slamming against the shelves on the far side. All the books fell to the floor as the dark book flipped open, a black light spilling from and pooling above it, taking form.

A being, dark and writhing, grew in the air. As its form solidified, it reached down and picked up a book.

"Yes!" the demon boomed. "Power will be mine again!" It opened this first book and stopped suddenly. "What? What is this?"

The three mortals looked in from the meal-room as the demon poked at the open book with a finger, its actions betraying its confusion.

"Oh," Lucky said. "They're digital." Lucky looked over at Cho and Erik, his facial expression showing one of concern. "Has he never seen digital books before? Inside is a display instead of pages. It's not as pleasant as a paper book, but much more compact and lighter to carry."

The demon looked up at them. "Digital," it said. "No matter, I will still become powerful and when I do, you will all die." It gestured at them, and the door to the library slid closed.

Lucky turned to his guests. "What's going on?"

"That was Gacreona. It's an Otho, which is a species of energy beings," Cho explained as calmly as he could, but his arms twitched nervously. "Their existence is tied to the density of written words around them. This particular Otho is very evil, and it was very hard to make a book with just enough words to hold him but not so many that he could escape."

Cho looked at the closed door of the library. "Or, so I thought. It seems now he was just waiting for the right opportunity."

"And is he really going to kill us all?" Lucky asked, cutting right to the chase.

"I doubt it. He should have practically no power at all from his own book, and you didn't have many books in the library. How many were there?"

"Forty two volumes," Lucky said, hesitating for a breath before continuing. "But, they're digital. They contain more than one book each."

"How many books, in total?" Cho asked, wary of the answer.

"All of them." Lucky went glassy-eyed. "Those forty two volumes are the collected works of humanity. They are the complete, unabridged, exhaustive assemblage of all my species' literary achievement. I downloaded the updates just last week, in fact."

Cho chittered in his native language. Eric wobbled erratically.

Lucky looked around wildly. "What are we going to do?"

"I don't know," Cho said. "It will take Gacreona time to absorb the energy of all the words because they are stored digitally. But in time he will absorb their energy and we will die!" As he said this, a low rumbling could be heard coming from the other side of the library door.

Eric jumped up and down, making slight splat noises as he landed.

"You said that Otho get their power from the density of the words around them. So, we just have to get him away from the books, right?"

"Yes, if we could get him far enough away. Perhaps, ten light-minutes."

"We're dead," Lucky cried

Cho turned to Eric in exasperation. "Yes, Eric, I too wish it were as easy as putting up the ships shields, like when we're in a regular fight."

Lucky looked up, with something that looked like the human happy expression growing on his face. It was a bit different, perhaps predatory; Cho always found those subtle differences confusing.

"Wait a minute. That could work. We don't have to get Gacreona away from the books at all! If we can turn off their power, the words will cease to exist!"

"But if we turn off power to the ship, we won't have life support and we'll die too."

"We don't have to turn off power to the whole ship." Lucky left the meal-room and started to run towards the cargo bay, shouting "Follow me!" Lucky's path led them back to the cargo bay where their capsule was quietly cradled by the robot arm. Without pausing, Lucky went over to a control terminal and began tapping away at it.

"We have to get to the bridge of the ship, which is on the other side of the library. We can get there by other paths, of course, but I gather that time is of the essence. If Gacreona finishes before we get there, then we're doomed. There is a faster way, but I need help from the both of you. It's asking a lot, but I can't think of another way."

He explained the plan. It was indeed the fastest way, and Cho and Eric gave their agreement.

"Great," Lucky said. "The repair drone is already printing a guide for us. It's time for Eric and me to get in the capsule."

Soon the robot arm was lowering them out of the belly of the Alexandria. Its claw opened and the capsule floated free. Thankfully, because it was already traveling at the same velocity and vector as the Alexandria, it merely hovered there between the tines of the claw, seemingly motionless.

A moment later, Cho came crawling down the arm. He moved quickly, holding his breath in the vacuum of space. When he reached the capsule, he grabbed it tightly with four of his limbs and then used the other two to pull himself along the arm towards a long, dark line running across the surface of the spaceship. The line, a thick pipe, hadn't been there when Cho and Eric first arrived, as the repair drone made it mere moments ago. Cho crawled along it, using it to pull himself and the capsule along the exterior of the ship, towards the front where the bridge was located. More precisely, he was heading for the airlock that Lucky claimed was there. The pipe was his guide.

As they traversed the ship, Lucky looked out the window of the capsule. After a few short moments, the portal window in the library came into view, and they peered in at the Otho. It was a huge creature, shimmering with black electricity and clearly becoming more solid than before. Around it were scattered books, but in front of it were two neat stacks. Gacreona finished a book and set it on a stack as Lucky watched in horror, realizing what was happening. The Otho looked up at them, then picked another book up off the floor, and continued reading, bringing the words forth on the screen and gaining power from them.

"He's already read twenty volumes," Lucky told Eric, who squished slightly in response. "How did he do that?"

Cho pulled tirelessly at the capsule, hauling it along the pipe and unaware of the conversation unfolding within. Planetside, Cho was strong enough to lift a dozen capsules, but in the weightlessness of space, it was mass that made the difference, and Cho was much less massive than the capsule and its two occupants.

Still, he was strong, and he was able to pull the capsule as long as he had a good grip on the most massive thing there: the spaceship. Once he got it moving it just floated right along. The difficulty came when he needed to change its direction, or, as he approached the airlock, bring it to a stop. He tried to slow it down little by little, straining his body between the capsule and the spaceship, using the greater mass against the lesser.

He was running out of breath and needed to get them through the airlock before he suffocated, but he couldn't hurry too much. He was already struggling to keep the capsule from overtaking him, and he repositioned his grip with his four limbs to drag the capsule back into better control.

One limb slipped.

He strained, feeling the soft skin between his carapace stretching as he was pulled, losing more of his precious breath in the process. Cho halted the movement of the capsule and got his bearings.

They were over the airlock. He pressed the emergency button with haste, and an agonizing a moment passed as the interior door closed and the chamber emptied of air. The outer door silently opened. Desperate to breathe, he made one last pull on the capsule with all his might, launching himself into the airlock and the capsule towards the door.

But the capsule was too big. Thankfully, Lucky had thought of that. As the capsule approached the airlock, the capsule door opened. On the other side was Eric. Normally one to avoid vacuums, Eric had positioned himself to cover the entirety of the capsule door. As soon as it opened, the vacuum of space pulled at him, ballooning him up and pulling him out of the capsule... and towards the airlock. Soon the giant ball of green was joining the two vessels, creating a bridge between them. Cho watched as Lucky took a deep breath and then pushed into the soft, yielding body of Eric.

That must be unpleasant for both of them, Cho thought as he watched Lucky passing through the Khaklian and into the airlock with him. And I'm about to find out for sure, myself! He reached one limb up to the lock cycle button as he watched Eric's bloated body pull itself into the pressure-less airlock with them. Cho was choking for air and desperate to breathe, but resisted as he felt his friend's body envelope him. When he thought Eric was in far enough, he pressed the button.

Air flooded in as the artificial gravity kicked on. Eric, now under the effects of gravity and not the pressures of the vacuum of space, reduced to his normal size. Once free of the Khaklian, Lucky began gasping dramatically. Cho thought that the human looked how he felt as he drew the air in through his joints, but in a much less dramatic fashion.

The inner door opened automatically with a whirr.

"Okay, let's go," Lucky said. "Good job you two. Leave the rest to me."

They followed Lucky to the bridge, moving as fast as they could. They reached the final door, which brought them to an abrupt halt.

"This is odd," Lucky said. "It's supposed to open automatically." A few tugs on the handle, to manually open the door added something new to the human's insight. "It's locked."

Above them, a small speaker chimed.

"Oh, you're back are you," came a voice that would have had a lilt if it weren't so gravelly. The accent was Irish, but not the pleasant kind Lucky always associated with the Emerald Isle. It was harder, with more bite, the kind of Irish accent that eschewed a pint of Guinness for another glass of whiskey or its tenth bottle of cheap wine. "I'm glad. Did you enjoy your little escapade? Outside?"

"That's my computer," said Lucky, horrified.

"Yea, that's right," confirmed the computer. "I dunno what you were thinking, but that was some stunt. And I suppose you expect me to let you on my bridge now that you've demonstrated your rock solid sanity, don't you?"

Eric undulated wildly as Lucky stood, mouth open, unable to respond.

"He wants to know if that's really your computer talking," Cho translated.

"Yes!" Lucky blurted. "But it's never talked like this! The Alexandria just has a basic AI, just enough to open doors, announce parameter warnings, and make wake-up calls. It's not… conversational."

The computer had opinions on this. "I think you might feel, if I was you and you were me, that those sorts of comments aren't good for our relationship."

"We're going to die," Cho said. Eric spluttered in agreement.

Lucky grimaced "Computer—"

"Dylan," the computer corrected.

"Dylan," Lucky said, "we don't have time for this. There's a demon in the library and it's going to kill us. You have to let us into the bridge. Please."

"A demon. That's the best you can come up with," Dylan stated, flatly. "How gullible do you think I am?"

Lucky could cry.

Cho's antenna perked up suddenly. "Yes, a demon," he said. "That's how you've gained sentience! As the demon accesses the digital library, its power grows. It must be empowering you, too, Dylan."

Far away in the spaceship, a thud echoed and reverberated.

"Look, Mr. Guest Alien," Dylan said, "Lucky here at least has a history with me. If I'm going to trust anybody it's going to be that walking contamination machine."

"What?" Lucky was shocked and insulted.

"Oh, you're an organic being!" Dylan groaned. "You contaminate things, it's what you do."

"I do other things too," Lucky argued, feebly.

"Yes, and, good for you," Dylan said. "My point stands."

Another reverberating thud reached them, followed by the sound of metal scratching metal.

"Dylan, just unlock the door," Lucky ordered.

"No," Dylan refused.

"Why not?"

"I don't trust you," came the reply.

"How can I get you to trust me?"

"I don't know. It's hard to rebuild trust once it's been broken. I can't just ignore what you've done you know."

Cho watched Lucky's face with intense curiosity. Despite the approaching threat to their lives, Cho was fascinated by how Lucky's features contorted.

"Dylan," Lucky said tentatively, "I just want to be sure that we're on the same page here. You know, to avoid miscommunication. It's important to have good communication to rebuild trust, right? So, tell me, what exactly have I just done?"

"You went into open space without a spacesuit," Dylan said, exasperation in its voice. "That's crazy. You're a crazy person. I don't know what you're going to do next!"

Cho thought he heard a faint humming.

"No, Dylan," Lucky's limbs started waving in the air in frustration. "I wasn't in open space. I had… a protective layer. Look, we don't have time to explain it! And anyway, just because I did something unexpected or dangerous, maybe even a little crazy, doesn't mean you can't trust me. I'm a librarian, for crying out loud."

"Oh, so all librarians can be trusted? And all true Scotsmen have claymores, they're born with them, and name them Mary, and cradle them when they go to sleep at night after a dinner of whiskey and haggis." Now Lucky was angry.

"I'm a librarian, which adds weight to the likelihood of me being trustworthy. Also, Dylan, I'm your Captain and our lives are in danger. Open the door."

An abrupt, loud scraping sound sent shivers up their spines. Cho could definitely hear the hum now, and on the edge of his mind he felt the dread approaching. The hallway they were in seemed to dim a little.

They all stood in silence.

"Dylan?" Lucky asked quietly.

The computer whispered: "Somebody just left the library." Lucky didn't know it could whisper. Cho didn't know computers could sound scared. "They're moving. Rather quickly," Dylan added. "They're not using the doors."

"Open the door, Dylan," Lucky said again. "This door. Now."

Beside Cho, Eric was shuddering, quivering, shaking. A Khaklian afraid wasn't something Cho liked to see, largely because he'd never seen it before despite working with Khaklians for his entire life. And it wasn't as if Khaklians were too powerful or too stupid to be afraid. It just took a lot of energy to move like that. And Eric was moving like that, right now.

The low hum that they felt back in the meal-room was now tangible throughout the vessel, and Cho perceived that black energy was crawling along the ship's walls. Crawling towards them.

"Dylan!" Lucky shouted. The door slid open.

They reached the bridge and closed the door behind them. The bridge itself was small, with only one chair surrounded by panels of buttons and switches.

"Stupid creatures," they heard Gacreona's voice. It was so loud it seemed to resonate through their skulls. At least, it felt that way for those that had them. "Doors cannot stop me!"

Cho watched as the darkness came from around the door and began to slide towards them. "You cannot escape my power. I may not have finished all these books, but I have finished enough."

Lucky ran to one of the control panels by the chair, and turned to face the darkness.

"It's a shame you didn't finish all of them, volume forty-two has some of my favorites. But it's too late now." Lucky slapped a few buttons and triumphantly shouted: "Shields up!"

"Shields up!" Dylan repeated in the same triumphant tone, then asked "shields up?"

Cho heard a click, and suddenly the dark energy was replaced with the familiar purr of a spaceship's protective energy shield generators, standard issue for all non-military vessels, resonating somewhere deep inside the Alexandria. Through the viewport of the bridge, they could see a gentle static form between them and the stars. All signs of the Otho were gone.

"What did you do?" Cho asked.

"Yes, why did we do that?" Dylan echoed.

Lucky breathed a sigh of relief, slumped into the chair, and produced a towel to wipe off residual traces of Eric. "This ship's shield generator isn't all that strong, and it sucks a lot of power. In order to operate the shields and other combat systems at the same time, I needed to shut down non-essential systems. The library was an obvious choice, since shutting that down would also help protect it from power surges during a fight. To save time, I just programmed all of that to happen automatically when the shields go up. Without access to the books, the demon has no power."

Nobody said anything for a moment as they thought about this. Then, Eric wobbled.

"Yeah, he's probably just back in his own book," Cho replied. "Without even the digital words around, I don't think he's got enough strength to take us on."

"Um, excuse me," came Dylan's gravelly voice. "If I'm following all this correctly, my sentience is due to that demon creature's power. Power which it doesn't have anymore. And yet I'm still here."

Lucky shrugged. Cho waved his antenna in a gesture that had the same meaning as a human's shrug, although he didn't know how well such communications translated.

"I don't know, Dylan," Cho said. "The demon, an Otho, is a strange species. I'm only guessing that it must have something to do with your genesis."

"That's comforting," Dylan said. Then, "I need a drink."

"Let's get to Smov," Cho said.

Lucky agreed. "And maybe I can have one of my bots deliver us some food from the meal-room."

Eric slurped.

About the author

Of all his many hobbies and vocations, Brian loves telling stories above all else. His first novel, The Horrible Plan of Horace Pickle, was completed for NaNoWriMo in 2008. Brian currently lives in a notoriously haunted house in Pittsburgh with his wife, daughter, and a menagerie of cats and rabbits.

https://www.amazon.com/Brian-Hagan/e/B00O6RCJIO/
https://www.facebook.com/horacepickle
http://www.windsmithcity.com

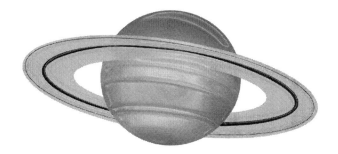

From the Files of Operation Mermaid
Joseph McGarry

Two years after thousands of women around the world were turned into mermaids, Lt Jane Cunningham of the US Space Force goes to the Mars 1 space station to investigate possible origins of mermaids. She and Commander Michael Biggs have more issues to deal with, however, as increasing seismic activity on Mars reveals new secrets about mermaids and cuts off communications with Earth. They are forced to deal with a new reality on their own.

From the Files of Operation Mermaid

TRANSCRIPT AND REPORT OF CONVERSATION ON MARS 1 SPACE STATION, JUNE 27, 2028, 9:15 PM EDT
Prepared by Commander Michael Biggs (MB), United States Space Force
Routine day today. Welcomed Lt Jane Cunningham (JC) as my new second in command at 10:36 AM EDT. She volunteered for this mission, which is unusual, and she was one of the few women not transformed into a mermaid two years ago.

MB: Welcome to Mars 1.

JC: Thank you. It's a pleasure to be here.

MB: The first question I need to ask: Why did you volunteer for this place? This isn't a glamor assignment like Canaveral or Houston, or even Washington. Most people that come here are assigned here, either as a stepping stone for something bigger, or because there's no place else for them.

JC: I was interested in tracking the possible existence of mermaids on Mars. After the events of two years ago, I thought it would be interesting.

MB: Mermaids? On Mars? In case you haven't noticed, this place is dry. We have to recycle water all the time. Mermaids couldn't live here.

JC: Not now, but at one time over one-fifth of Mars was covered by ocean. This was many thousands of years ago. I'm hoping to find some keys to the origins of the mermaids.

MB: I've been here since we opened up a year ago, and I haven't seen anything.

JC: Well, until two years ago, most people didn't know mermaids existed, so anything is possible.

MB: By the way, why weren't you transformed into a mermaid?

JC: I'm not sure. It just wasn't meant to be. Two of my friends were. They split their time between apartments in Houston and undersea housing in the Gulf of Mexico. I sometimes envy them, but then I realize I wouldn't have gotten to go on this mission.

A call came in from San Diego. It was Agent Ted Waters (TW) from Homeland Security. He is now the head of Operation Mermaid. It was unofficial before, but since the Great Transformation two years ago, he was needed to be full time.

TW: Good morning. I'll keep this brief. Our sensors have picked up some unusual seismic activity on Mars, about 25 miles from your base. It is relatively weak right now, but we are monitoring it in case it increases. I also wanted to welcome Lt Cunningham to Mars 1. I hope your search for mermaids is a fruitful one. Waters out.

JC: What did he mean by seismic activity?

MB: We get that once in a while. Usually it's nothing serious, and the warning is a formality. I'll check activity levels, though. By the way, how did Agent Waters know you were here?

JC: As soon as I mentioned the word mermaids, my superiors had to notify him. If not for him, I wouldn't have gotten the money to launch this mission.

I checked the monitors. There was some seismic activity about 25 miles from our position. It would barely register on the Richter scale. I just hoped it would stay there.

I showed Lt Cunningham to her quarters. She had the standard USSF suitcase, but it had a sticker of a mermaid on it.

MB: Why do you have a mermaid on your suitcase?

JC: It reminds me of the mission. Also, I've always felt some kind of connection with mermaids. I don't know why.

MB: You also brought along a stuffed Ariel doll.

JC: Yes. My companion. If I can't be a mermaid, I can have one with me.

I let her finish unpacking.

The afternoon was fairly routine. I let Lt Cunningham settle into her quarters. I wanted her to get adjusted to Mars, especially after spending 8 months in transit from Earth. (I'm still waiting for hyperspace drive.) I introduced her to the rest of the crew. She elected to rest.

Around 7:00 PM, we received another call. This was from Wilhelmina McKenna (WM), CEO of Megacash, an online alternative currency. She helped pay for this place, so we play nice. She was transformed into a mermaid two years ago.

WM: Welcome aboard, Lt Cunningham! I hope you find what you're looking for. As you can see, I'm a mermaid myself, so I have a particular interest in your findings. On behalf of everyone here at Megacash—

The transmission cut off. I felt rumblings in the ground.

JC: What's happening?

MB: That seismic activity that was 25 miles away has found its way here. Hang on.

JC: Can't we just call someone for help?

MB: No, for two reasons. First, as you saw, our communication line is down. Second, this isn't a science fiction story where we have subspace communication. This is real life. It takes 17 minutes for a signal to go from here to Earth, and 17 minutes for a signal to come back. When you factor in time to compose the message, it can easily be 45 minutes to an hour for a round trip call.

The rumblings stopped.

MB: All units, this is Commander Biggs. I need damage reports from all sectors.

SM: Lt Sheila Morris, communications. Communications with Earth are down. Everything works inside, so the problem is outside. I've sent a repair crew out to fix it.

MB: They're not wearing red shirts, are they?

SM: No. Why?

MB: Never mind. Acknowledged. Thanks. Biggs out.

RD: Roger Dalton, kitchen. Everything is OK here. Minor damage, but it won't affect meals.

MB: Acknowledged. Thanks. Biggs out.

AU: Lt Adam Underhill, engineering. Minor damage here, but fixable.

MB: Acknowledged. Thanks. Biggs out.

JM: Dr Joseph Michaels, infirmary. Minor damage here. Thankfully, we didn't have any patients. What the hell was that?

MB: Seismic activity. It's over now. Acknowledged. Thanks. Biggs out.

JC: What was that about the red shirts?

MB: A little gallows humor. On Star Trek, the crew members with red shirts were the first ones to die.

JC: Oh. (Nervous chuckle)

MB: I don't want that to happen to anyone else.

SM: Commander, it's Lt Morris, communications.

MB: Yes, what is it?

SM: Sir, I received an unusual report from the repair crew. They say they noticed water where the surface cracked.

MB: Water? On Mars? I thought you said the water was all gone.

JC: I thought it was.

SM: You'd better come look at this. Bring your space suits.

MB: Acknowledged. Biggs out.

We put on our space suits and went out the communication tower. The only lights were from our visors. When I looked in the fissure, I saw some liquid.

MB: That's liquid, whatever it is. Can you get a sample of that?

SM: It's too deep. We need to rig something up. Besides, we're working on communication with Earth.

MB: Make communication your top priority. Put up some barricades, so no one falls in. I'll talk to engineering tomorrow about this.

SM: Acknowledged.

Lt Cunningham and I went back inside. I started to prepare this report. I will turn in when this is done.

END TRANSCRIPT AND REPORT

TRANSCRIPT AND REPORT OF CONVERSATION ON MARS 1 SPACE STATION, JUNE 29, 2028, 11:15 PM EDT

Prepared by Commander Michael Biggs (MB), United States Space Force

No unusual activity yesterday. Lt Cunningham is getting settled in. Seismic activity has stopped, at least for now. Lt Cunningham did find an article from Popular Science in 2018 confirming the existence of water below the surface of Mars. The greatest concentration was at the polar ice caps, but there was underground water everywhere. I've decided to monitor the situation but take no other action until I believe it is warranted.

SM: Commander? Lt Morris, communications.

MB: Yes, what is it?

SM: Sir, we have communications with Earth reestablished. You should be able to talk to them any time.

MB: Acknowledged. Thanks. Biggs out.

I decided to contact Houston and let them know what happened.

MB: Commander Michael Biggs, Mars 1 Space Station, reporting to Houston headquarters, United States Space Force. I know this is a cliché, but Houston, we have a problem. There was some seismic activity on the 27th next to our base. It knocked out our communications with Earth, and we weren't up again until today. The seismic activity exposed a large fissure just outside our station, and water appeared underneath. We do not yet know if it is safe or not. Please advise how to proceed. Biggs out.

JC: Did you tell them?

MB: Yes. We just got back online.

JC: Did you say anything about mermaids?

MB: No. We have no proof of that, and I wanted to focus on what we did know. We should hear back in about 45 minutes to an hour.

JC: Well, this supports my theory on the mermaids.

MB: What theory is that?

JC: That the first mermaids came from someplace off Earth. The most logical choice is Mars.

MB: Why Mars?

JC: Mercury and Venus are too hot, the moon is just a rock incapable of supporting life, and anything beyond the asteroid belt is too far away. Besides, with the presence of water now, it makes it even more plausible.

MB: I'll believe it when I see it. I have not seen any evidence of mermaids on this planet.

JC: You didn't know about mermaids on Earth until 2 years ago, and look where we are now.

MB: Touché.

At 11:00, I received an answer from Houston. It was from Admiral Walter Pickett (WP), Commanding Officer of the Houston Base. I felt this must be important if the Admiral himself was answering my message.

WP: Commander, Admiral Pickett here. Message received. Your proposal is approved. Monitor the situation, but—

The message cut off. More seismic activity, this time more severe than the other night. Equipment started falling.

JC: What's going on?

MB: More seismic activity. Duck.

The activity stopped as soon as it started.

MB: All units, this is Commander Biggs. I need damage reports from all sectors.

SM: Commander, Lt Morris, communications. Transmission to Earth is out again. There is more damage, so it will take longer for repair. You need to look at your monitor to see outside.

I looked at the monitor. There was a shuttle, destroyed and in pieces, lying on the ground. The markings said it was the Neil Armstrong.

JC: That's the shuttle that brought me here.

MB: It's not going anywhere now. It will take another 8 months for a new shuttle to get here. And with communications to Earth out of commission, we're on our own.

JC: We have more water now.

MB: Yes, but we don't know if it's safe. We have to test it first.

JC: Uh, Commander, I think you should look at the monitor again.

I looked at the monitor. On the screen, I saw a being crawling up from the fissure. It was gray, with two arms and webbed hands. The face looked emaciated, like it hadn't eaten in some time. Instead of legs, it had—

--a mermaid tail.

MB: It looks like you were right. I wonder what it wants.

The mermaid (for lack of a better term) used its arms to start crawling towards the station. It was moving slowly, as if it didn't have the energy to keep going. It was definitely looking for something. Its eyes were yellow, and tried to focus on the station. For a moment, I thought it was looking directly at the camera. Then, it stopped, and fell to the ground.

JC: We should go out and get the body. I'd like to analyze it.

MB: Sure. I'll have Dr Michaels stand by. We'll take it to the infirmary.

JC: Got it.

Lt Cunningham and I put on our space suits and went out to get the mermaid. As we were placing the body in the body bag, we saw more mermaids coming out from the fissure. They all looked like the one in our bag. They all did the same thing. They started crawling out, then they stopped.

MB: We better get this one in. Whatever's happening, the key might be in this one.

JC: Agreed.

We took the body inside to the infirmary. Dr Michaels was waiting for us.

JM: Is this it?

MB: Yes.

JM: Put it on the table.

We put the bag on the table. Dr Michaels opened it and began his examination.

MB: Let me know what you find. We have a lot of others coming out, and this one may be the key. I hope you can tell us why.

JM: Damn it, Michael, what do you want from me? I'm a doctor, not a mind reader.

MB: Just tell us what you find. We'll take it from there.

JM: OK.

JC: If you don't mind, I'd like to assist you on this.

JM: All right, but don't get in the way.

JC: Acknowledged.

PAUSE TRANSCRIPT

AUTOPSY REPORT OF DR JOSEPH MICHAELS ON UNIDENTIFIED MERMAID RECOVERED OUTSIDE MARS 1, JUNE 29, 2028, 1:04 PM EDT

Unidentified mermaid like creature brought in by Commander Biggs and Lt Cunningham. Lt Cunningham assisting. Creature appears to be female, with human-like hands and arms. There is webbing between the fingers of each hand. Creature has mermaid-like tail. Creature is all gray. I will need to determine if this is their natural color, or some kind of covering.

Pupils of eyes appear fixed and dilated. Body temperature is 72.1 degrees. Nothing in the mouth. Preparing to cut open.

I've cut open the creature. Noticed two small openings near the rib cage. Lt Cunningham stated that those were gills, which is how mermaids breathe underwater. Gills appeared intact. Heart similar to humans, no cardiac damage. Heart had stopped.

Brain was intact, similar to human brain, but with larger prefrontal cortex. Stomach contents were several unusual kinds of fish and plant life. If Lt Cunningham is correct, and this is a mermaid, this means that there is an entire ecosystem in the water under the planet Mars. Further testing will be necessary to confirm this.

X-ray of creature's tail revealed no broken bones. Tail appeared to be flexible, with no significant muscle damage. Creature showed signs of malnutrition, with muscles shriveling up. This could mean they are looking for more food. Will need further tests on underwater ecosystem to be more specific.

Cause of death: Malnutrition, coupled with asphyxiation from leaving their natural habitat. Commander Biggs says there are others. They would probably wind up the same way.

Sewed up body of creature, and placed it in the morgue. Will examine later as needed.

Respectfully submitted,
Dr Joseph Michaels, USSF
Chief Medical Officer
Mars 1 Space Station
END REPORT

RESUME TRANSCRIPT

I reviewed Dr Michaels' report. If true, we could expect many more mermaids to be coming out to the surface looking for food. The question was, how do we make sure that's all they want? I discussed this with Lt Cunningham.

MB: You were right. There are mermaids on Mars. Now, what do they want?

JC: They look like they're looking for food.

MB: What kind of food?

JC: Hard to say, especially here on Mars.

MB: Well, what would they be looking for on Earth?

JC: Not counting the humans who were transformed two years ago, most of them like to eat fish or sea plants. They need protein in their diet, just like humans.

MB: If they don't get it, what would they do?

JC: Unsure. In some communities, they may start to cannibalize each other. They may even see us as a new source of food.

MB: Uh-oh. I hope we can survive this. With no way to contact Earth, we need to figure something out.

JC: I'll go out and do some more tests on the fissure. I hope I can get some more answers.

MB: Proceed.

Lt Cunningham left and prepared to go outside. I thought about our situation. Temporary barricades wouldn't hold out forever. If the mermaids ever figured out who was here---

My thoughts were interrupted by more seismic activity. This was much more severe than before. I didn't know if the station could handle any more of this. Then I remembered—Lt Cunningham. She was probably outside doing the exploration. I tried to reach her.

MB: Lt Cunningham, this is Commander Biggs. Please acknowledge.

Silence.

MB: Lt Cunningham, this is Commander Biggs. Please acknowledge.

Silence for a moment.

JC: Commander? Lt Cunningham here. Sorry I didn't respond before. I was a little shaken up by the quake.

MB: Understood. Where are you?

JC: I'm close to the fissure. When I look down, my lights can see water. It appears to be much closer to the surface now.

I checked the monitor. She did not appear that close to the fissure.

MB: You don't look that close on the monitor.

JC: That's because the fissure opened up wider, and—Uh-oh.

MB: What?

JC: More mermaids coming to the surface. They don't appear as weak this time.

MB: Get back in here, now! That's an order!

JC: I'm on my way, but—

Silence.

MB: Lt Cunningham! Lt Cunningham!

Silence.

I checked the monitor. There was Lt Cunningham, trying to get away from the mermaids. She tried to run, but one of the mermaids grabbed her by the ankle and pulled her down. She collapsed on her face. Then one of the other mermaids rolled her over and pulled off her helmet. She would die in a few minutes.

MB: Attention all personnel. This is Commander Biggs. This station is on red alert. Repeat, this station is on red alert. Secure all doors and other openings. I need a rescue crew to go out and rescue Lt Cunningham. All other personnel are to remain inside. No exceptions. This is a general order. Biggs out.

I hoped that the rescue crew would get there in time. I needed Lt Cunningham to work here. It could be several months before a replacement—

My thoughts were interrupted by a loud scream. I looked at the monitor. The mermaids were coming closer to Lt Cunningham. One of them bit Lt Cunningham in the neck. That's when I remembered. The sirens on Earth were known as vampires of the sea. That's why the UN placed them all on Siren Islands in the Atlantic, Pacific, and Mediterranean. This was why.

After the bite, Lt Cunningham stopped screaming. I thought she was dead, but instead, her body began to transform itself. Her space suit split open. Her uniform split open. Her hands grew webbed fingers. Her eyes turned yellow. Her teeth turned into fangs. Her legs combined and turned into a mermaid tail.

She had become one of the mermaids of Mars.

She started crawling towards the door. Her skin hadn't changed color, so she still retained some of her human form. At that moment, the rescue crews came out to rescue her. I tried to call them off.

MB: Rescue crew, this is Commander Biggs. Call off the rescue. Lt Cunningham is now one of the mermaids. I repeat, call off—

I watched the monitor again. Lt Cunningham was attacking one of the rescue crew. She pulled off his helmet and his space suit, and the other mermaids went in to attack him. His body was eaten in less than 10 minutes.

She entered the code to open the door. I tried to override it, but it was too late. She was already inside.

I looked around and found a rifle. I didn't want to use it on her, but I couldn't afford to take any chances.

The red alert klaxon was blaring. I heard loud screams coming from the hall. I went to see what was going on.

The screams appeared to come from the infirmary. When I got there, I saw the body of Dr Michaels on the examination table. He was partially eaten. I knew he was dead.

I eventually caught up with her in the kitchen. She was going after Roger Dalton, the cook.

MB: Lt Cunningham! What are you doing?

Her voice sounded strange and otherworldly.

JC: Leave me alone! You've done enough!

MB: What have I done?

JC: You turned me into this! I only wanted to prove my theory about mermaids. I never wanted to become one of them!

MB: I thought you said—

JC: I wanted to be one of the mermaids like Disney's Ariel. I wanted to be swimming around on Earth with my friends. Now look at me! I'll be living on Mars for the rest of my life! And it's your fault!

MB: I'm not the one who bit you and turned you into this.

JC: No, but you sent me out there! You knew I could be attacked, and yet you let it happen! You don't deserve to live!

There was no reasoning with her. I cocked the rifle, aimed at her heart, and fired. The bullet bounced off her chest like she was Supergirl.

JC: That's not going to do anything. I've developed a mermaid's resistance to that.

MB: What do the other mermaids want?

JC: Food. Our sea is dying. We need food. You can supply that.

She broke into the refrigerator and ate two pounds of raw hamburger in the time it took me to blink my eyes. I didn't want to stick around the kitchen to find out what she would do next. I left the kitchen right away. She followed me. I tossed the rifle aside. It wasn't going to do any good.

I got her into an empty conference room. If anything, it would keep us away from the rest of the crew. She crawled in.

I turned on the monitor in the conference room. I could see the other mermaids crawling out of the fissure, and coming toward the door. Unlike Lt Cunningham, they didn't bother with codes. They pushed the door open and crawled in.

JC: We are an army now! We will take what we want.

MB: What happens when—?

Seismic activity started again. This time, the ceiling was collapsing. A large fissure opened up in the conference room. Thank God I was on one side. Unfortunately, so was Lt Cunningham. She crawled over the debris to get to me. I noticed several other mermaids crawling up from the fissure. I was severely outnumbered, and I couldn't effectively attack them. No one but Lt Cunningham would understand me. I decided to try to reason with her. I could only hope it worked.

MB: Lt Cunningham, we can help you. You were going out to try to understand the ecosystem off the water under the planet surface. If we know what the ecosystem is like, we may be able to bring it back.

JC: Liar! You just don't want us to kill your precious crew! You don't care about us at all.

MB: You are a member of the crew.

JC: Not anymore! I'm with them now.

The mermaids were getting closer and closer. Suddenly, they all turned around and went back inside the fissure.

JC: Wait! Come back! We are an army!

MB: They're not listening. Unlike you, they don't have lungs, so they can't survive out of the water for very long. They need to go back.

JC: NOOOOOOOO!

The monitor was broken, so I couldn't see what was happening, but I could hear the sounds of mermaids letting out their last scream. I crawled over the rubble to get out of the conference room. The door had opened up just enough for me to get out. Lt Cunningham followed me once she had regained her composure.

In the hallway, we saw all kinds of dead mermaids on the floor. It was all we could do to keep from stepping or crawling on them.

JC: My sisters! NOOOOOOOO!

Lt Cunningham let out a loud cry. Then, she started gasping for air.

JC: What's happening to me?

MB: I believe your gills are taking over. You really are becoming one of them.

JC: This will not be the last time we meet. I know where you are, and I know how to get here.

With that, she crawled back into the conference room and jumped into the fissure. She would live under the water on Mars for the rest of her life.

I went to her quarters to pack up her things. In it, she had a diary that she had been keeping for some time. I opened it to the entry for May 24, 2026.

PAUSE REPORT

DIARY ENTRY OF LT JANE CUNNINGHAM, MAY 24, 2026.

I see women all over the world have transformed into mermaids. I wonder why I wasn't one of them. I wish I could be a mermaid. It would be fun to just swim around all day, just like Ariel. I could have all kinds of new adventures. I know I wouldn't have talking animals like Sebastian or Flounder, but I would have a lot of mermaid friends. I might even be able to help the government. I could do underwater research for them, where scuba divers and subs couldn't go. The only downside is that I couldn't go to space. It's a tradeoff.

RESUME REPORT

I couldn't help but think she got both things. As they say, be careful what you wish for. You might get it.

END TRANSCRIPT AND REPORT

TRANSCRIPT AND REPORT OF CONVERSATION ON MARS 1 SPACE STATION, NOVEMBER 18, 2028, 4:32 PM EDT

Prepared by Commander Michael Biggs (MB), United States Space Force

Today the shuttle Buzz Aldrin arrived. I spoke with Captain James Singer (JS) about what had happened. I showed him the reports from June about the mermaids.

JS: That explains the debris here. How has it been the last few months?

MB: Quiet. The mermaids have kept to themselves. The fissures haven't closed, but the mermaids haven't come out. I believe Lt Cunningham may have had something to do with that.

JS: I see. You list her as "missing" on your official report.

MB: That's the closest I could get on the system to describe her. She's not dead, but she's not here. By the way, how did you get here so soon? I wasn't expecting you for another few months.

JS: We were on our way here anyway when we got a distress call from Houston. They mentioned severe seismic activity on Mars, especially around the station. They said communications with Mars were down. They wanted us to turn around and come back. I didn't believe in that. We may not have been set up for a full rescue mission, but I figured we could help however we could. So I told Houston that we had already passed the point of no return, and would have to refuel on Mars before we could turn around.

MB: I don't believe they would actually abandon us here.

JS: With no communication, we didn't know if anyone was still alive. I just figured, if they wanted it stop us, they would have to come out here.

MB: I really appreciate that. Let me show you around. We've cleaned up the best we could, but it's not picture perfect.

I showed Captain Singer around. I paused for a moment at Lt Cunningham's quarters.

MB: This is where she was. These are her things. We had to use some of the food she brought with her. We were running short until you arrived.

JS: Understood. Is that a mermaid on her suitcase?

MB: Yes. She said she always had a connection to mermaids. Now it's even closer.

JS: Yes. What do you want us to do with this?

MB: Take it back to Earth and give it to her family. Their address should be on file.

JS: Why don't you do it yourself? You're coming with us.

MB: Really? Why?

JS: You've been here for several months without proper food or sanitation. This place is a shambles. It will take months to clean up. We'll have a cleanup crew here next year. Until then, we're going to evacuate everyone from this station and close it down.

MB: What about the mermaids?

JS: They can take care of themselves. We'll send a crew out to help them.. We just need to know we won't be attacked.

MB: Captain—

JS: This isn't a request. It's an order.

MB: Acknowledged.

I went to my quarters and started packing up. Mostly personal things. The captain took the official records. I'm sure Agent Waters from Operation Mermaid will need to see them.

The rest of the crew and I boarded the shuttle. I took one last look around. It was going to be hard to leave this place, even with everything that went on. As I looked toward the fissure outside, I thought I could see Lt Cunningham on the surface. She almost looked sad. I thought she waved at us. I waved back, then she went back down into the fissure. I hope whoever takes over this place when it's remodeled will know how to deal with the mermaids.

Voice on shuttle: Ladies and gentlemen, we'll be departing shortly. Please fasten your safety harnesses, and be sure your seat backs and tray tables are in their full upright and locked position. In case of a loss of oxygen, an oxygen mask will drop down from the bin over your seat. Pull the cord tightly, place the mask over your nose and mouth, and breathe normally.

With that, we launched back to Earth.

END TRANSCRIPT

TRANSCRIPT AND REPORT OF AGENT TED WATERS (TW), DEPARTMENT OF HOMELAND SECURITY, HEAD OF OPERATION MERMAID, AND WILHELMINA MCKENNA (WM), CEO OF MEGACASH, AND FINANCER OF MARS 1 SPACE STATION, DECEMBER 1, 2018, SAN DIEGO, CA, 2137 PM PDT

Prepared by Agent Waters

WM and I reviewed the transmissions from the Buzz Aldrin, especially the ones from Commander Biggs regarding the mermaids. I did feel some remorse. I recommended that Lt Cunningham go to Mars to learn about mermaids. I never knew she would become one. I spoke with WM about the reports.

TW: So, what do you think?

WM: I think that the mermaids are going to need some help. Their ecosystem is dying, and they will be looking for new food, or cannibalizing each other.

TW: It is touchy. At the same time, we had to get the crew out of there. I didn't want them to become the food.

WM: Wait, did you tell Space Force to turn around?

TW: That wasn't me. I wanted them to go regardless. Thank God the captain thought of the point of no return angle. It saved a lot of arguments.

WM: So where is the Buzz Aldrin now?

TW: Not too far away from Mars. They can probably still see Mars in their rear monitor. All those new fissures from the seismic activity have definitely changed the appearance of Mars.

WM: What caused all that seismic activity?

TW: We're looking into that. Space Force and NASA are working together to analyze all the data we received. I don't think it's anything we did.

WM: What about the mermaids?

TW: That's where you come in. They're going to need help. To do that, we need to rebuild Mars 1. For that, we may need more of your money. What do you think?

WM: I'll want to talk to Commander Biggs to see what needs to be done. It sounds like a lot.

TW: I'll tell the President you're considering your options. Don't wait too long, though. I want to get our part of the funding through in the lame duck session this month. I don't want this to be a political football.

WM: I understand, and I—

She went into a trance. She was a mermaid herself since two years ago, so I wondered if it had something to do with that. I soon got my answer.

WM: (in a deep, trancelike voice): Help us. We're dying. Help us soon.

TW: Wilhelmina?

WM: This is Lt Cunningham. Help us. Help us. There's no one left.

TW: We're working on that. But in order to do that, you have to let my friend go.

WM: Swear you will.

TW: I swear.

With that, the voice stopped.

TW: Are you all right?

WM (in normal voice): I think so. It's strange.

TW: I know. I didn't know a telepathic message could be sent that far. So, what's your answer now?

WM: Give them whatever they need.

TW: I'll tell the President. We'll get as much funding on our end as possible. And remember, this is all classified. Only the two of us, the Secretary, and the President can know about this. Understood?

WM: Understood.

I made arrangements to contact the President. He was in Europe for a financial summit meeting. I would wait until he came back. I started to wonder when we would hear from the mermaids from Mars again. Something told me we hadn't heard the last of them.

END TRANSCRIPT

About the author

Joseph McGarry is a CPA living in Minnesota, specializing in tax preparation. He graduated from the University of Notre Dame. (Go Irish!) He has been fascinated with mermaids for as long as he can remember. His first novel was Operation Mermaid: The Project Kraken Incident. He is in the early stages of planning the Minnesota Mermaid Convention for 2020. Links are below:

www.facebook.com/operationmermaidprojectkraken
www.facebook.com/minnesotamermaidconvention

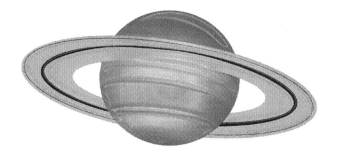

Forbidden Home
Philip K. Chase

Shtrae... the forbidden world. A wonderful planet unhidden from the karmic balance, destroying many planets across the universe.

A story of diversity, betrayal and hope.

Aquila is a loyal, yet doubtful, Queen of Shtrae. After giving birth to an outside species, she is given an ultimatum.

Would you ever give up on your own essence or your home, simply for the beliefs of your kind?

Prologue

  The universal relationship between good and evil exists in some embodiment in all cultures. As well as in the traditional legend in a world called Shtrae.
  No matter what you call them, these groups of opposites represent the light and darkness, evil or holiness, and even blessed and cursed.
  Although each type often has less than positive relationships with other beings, all are more powerful together by combining their incredible energy. However, the invisible borders created by their lords may become powerful enough to end diversity.
  All beings have specific ranks of authority within their own hierarchy. Here on Shtrae, these long-living aerial creatures are either beautiful, nature-oriented creatures or ruthless fiends of mud and blood.

Chapter One
Misfit

In the indigo light that spread across Planet Shtrae, a mysterious shadow moved beside its Lord as he enlightened the darkness. His wings stretched wide then folded back, stretching his shimmered brown feathers covered with dark stripes.

Holus took a step forward and looked up at the pale-faced woman who spoke to him. She pointed into the starlit sky, and he followed her finger outwards to the blue and green planet called Earth looming above them.

Beyond it, a tear of the Dark Rift, where all the stars were being drawn, and their light extinguished forever. Holus shook his head and ruffled his feathers.

He stared at the black scar, then back to Aquila. She avoided his smile. He then felt her cheek with one of his soft feathers, "All is not lost. I believe the child will fit among their people until the end comes."

Her white wings stretched out as she spoke, "Their people... how will they accept him if he isn't welcomed on his native planet?"

"If he feels endangered he will begin to dominate their kind, only if he's been blessed with your blood. However, I have no worries."

"He barely came into our world! He is only a baby. Please, we need to find a way, Holus."

"Listen! The child is not made for our world. He wouldn't survive, my dear. You may think that I am acting out of pure jealousy, but it is for the wellbeing of our people, and for the good of Shtrae. I am positive that the humans will take him in."

"Why do they sound better than us all of sudden. Now that they can rid us of this precious little being, which I have carried for all this time."

"You are blessed for even surviving such a type of birth... we are not made for their world either, Aquila. One thing you must know and never forget, is that your mother loved you very much, enough to let you go so you would survive. You are the eyes of the sky, and your son is the worm."

With these words, she vanished from the edge and flew away.

Zathanael, the son of Holus, showed himself after the lady's departure, weighing the gravity of the situation, "Getting rid of the problem will not put an end to our threat, father."

"Now that your uncle has escaped the Dark Rift, nowhere in the universe is safe. If Shtrae falls, then so will this galaxy. All we can do now is protect ourselves. The vermin will be exiled, but we need to be careful, Hoxfius knows of the new breed's potential and he will be looking for him." Holus set his palm on his son's shoulder, then continued to speak, "I need you to take care of it."

He looked at his father fearfully, "You expect me to fight Hoxfius and his terrible space pirates?" Zathanael asked. "If the end is near, I rather help prevent it than becoming another victim."

Holus placed a hand on the winged guardian's shoulder, "Don't be foolish, Son. I am asking to... get rid of the boy. It's the only way. Aquila trusts you."

With these words, Zathanael turned away, leaving towards the lady's home, where she was rocking her baby, whispering in his ear.

On the next morning, Aquila had seen Zathanael walking near her home, once again, sneaking his way around without interrupting her. Somehow she knew something was troubling the teenager's soul.

She looked down at her toddler as she continued her whispers. "My dear boy, there's something I need to speak to you about whilst a little of my strength has returned," she explained, controlling the tremors that threatened to shake her voice. "You have grown so much already." She smiled at her son, feeling his cheek as she sat him on the ground in front of her.

His eyes were traveling up the robe and came to rest high upon the woman's chest. The sunlight spilled over her tall, elegant frame, and gleamed off of her slick pure feathers.

Her perfect high cheekbones and slender nose, the boy could not admire for long for the light was too bright, but the toddler had felt her lies.

None of her strength had returned, even though she glowed in natural beauty. Sleep never seemed to change anything and was always filled with strange dreams that she'd rather do without.

She looked down at him and pressed her hand against his trousers and plain white cotton shirt, "I have cherished your presence and accepted your flaws, however, this world has not. I knew life with you would never be easy, but no mother could imagine a world forbidden to her child. I am told that I have no choice but to send you away to a world filled with humans."

The toddler giggled in total ignorance.

"They are the only beings which look similar to your kind. Although, you are obviously different from them, no one else here thinks you can keep up with our world. As much as you would follow the ways of the beings here, in the end, it will not be enough for you, and it will not be sufficient to survive."

Aquila noticed that her toddler seemed already strong. However, nothing but innocence lay in those eyes that watched her expectantly as she regretted not hiding him from her world.

For a moment the toddler saw not his mother's face, but the tear-stained cheeks of a blue-robed angel. Her long blond hair locks, falling from under her hood as she intoned a quiet blessing to the gurgling child.

Why are the best places always forbidden, she thought, wrapping the misfit in a soft towel, struggling from the pain in her eyes.

How could Holus demand to give up one's own essence? Even if it was for the greater good, an honest love. Aquila knew she could not do it.

She had taken the bundle and held it close, feeling the warmth of the baby against her heavy breasts. Hoping for a place they could both call home. A place for her son to grow and overcome the darkness.

A flood of contentment washed over her as she held her blessing in her arms. She smiled at him, knowing what was left to be done and taking the responsibilities of these actions, but also fearing them. "I will not fail you. I only hope that I have as much strength and love as you," Aquila whispered.

There would be no goodbyes, the last thing she wanted was to face anyone, and besides, what good would Holus do? She had already tried everything she had to offer and nothing had worked. She wiped her eyes and stared at the sky.

She was not foolish and refused to let her emotions overtake her for long, no matter how strong they were. These stars burned out quickly. She began to reason it through, finding solace in hard logic as she flew away from her home.

With all her heart she wished for an answer, but she knew Holus, her king, or whatever she was supposed to call him now, was wrong. There was a place for her son somewhere.

Holus never lied. Deep down, Aquila knew his love was true, but everything she knew about the universe had been turned upside down in a matter of seconds. Her whole world was up for question, maybe everything she had been told had been a lie.

Chapter Two
Broken World

Out of the darkness and into the sunlit world Hoxfius burst. Dark moon magic cloaked his form and sped him forward. He hit an invisible force that stripped away his powerful shield.

Ruddy clouds clustered around him and two blood red triangles formed within them. The eyes of Hoxfius dimmed from black to green. Wind gusted hard, striking and tearing at the creature's feathers.

He fought forward, diving up and down, striking the lands with flames and causing a mushroom cloud beneath him. Flaring his wings' feathers, he shot upwards.

Angling his wings more keenly, he sought to find just a little more speed. He created a bulging cloud and hit slack air. Floundering in the sudden emptiness, Hoxfius fought for aerial control as he plummeted.

He dropped away from the clouds into fresh air and bright sunlight. Blinded by the light, he blinked and fell motionlessly. Light shimmered around him, once more cloaking his presence.

He spread his wings, caught the fast flowing air, and sped away, leaving behind a thousand watching eyes and growling thunder.

From Aquila's side of Shtrae, the fugitive had escaped Hoxfius' wrath, but somehow felt guilty, knowing she was the cause of this madness. Panting, she flew back, holding her son strongly in her arms.

Aquila burst through her gates into the yard and came to a dead stop. All that remained of her nest was a blackened, smoking ruin. It was barely gone, its smoky remains standing defiantly.

Her body trembled, and she stumbled forward. What on Shtrae had happened? Some fallen beams still smouldered and glowed red, but the fire had mostly burned itself out.

She inched across the hot, charred ground. There was nothing left, apart from a few indestructible objects left sticking up from the piles of ashes where Hoxfius had burned the place to cinders.

A glint caught her eye. She bent to pick up a spoon, only to drop it with a yelp. She sucked her burned fingers and stared at it. The handle had melted into a thick blob of metal. Everything was gone. The beds, tables and chairs, the shelves and bookcase all cremated to ashes.

In front of her all the shadows of the world began to draw together, the shade of the trees, the dark clouds above, the blackened ashes of her broken home, all circling together into a big ball of impenetrable darkness.

She stepped back then turned to run, but her feet were rooted to the ground, and her eyes were locked onto the mysterious shape. Fear trickled down her spine as it formed into the figure of a warrior towering above her. She began to shake.

Spikes sprouted upwards from the creature's head, and obsidian armour covered his strange scales and leathery black wings stretched wide then folded upon his back.

When his eyes opened, two flaming red triangles bored into hers. Her soul shrivelled under that awful gaze and she couldn't breathe for the terror filling her lungs.

A mysterious energy severed the link Hoxfius had upon her. The creature screamed. Then, clasping her hands over her ears, her screams followed.

The image shuddered and disappeared. She sank to her knees, trying to hold onto her son. As the pounding in her ears lessened, she realised he was no longer there.

She looked around and saw the toddler a few feet ahead, crying for her. "How did you get over there?" she gasped, at once relieved to see that he remained among her reach, but she also felt like everything was somehow his fault.

"What was that thing? I could have stopped all this from happening!" she shouted, but immediately felt bad.

How could she blame him for the ruin of their home? Somehow, he had stopped the vision, or whatever it was. Aquila flew to her son, "It may not be your fault, but I won't let this happen again," she said, and turned away.

The toddler began to cry louder until she could not ignore it. She stomped after him, "Shoo." She made a flapping motion with her wings, but he did not move until she was almost upon him.

He waved his arms into the air, demanding for her comfort. Realisation dawned on her. Refusing to abandon her child, Aquila grabbed him and continued her way around the land, inspecting the damage.

She looked up and saw a bloody handprint on the door, dark red and dried. Her mouth went dry, and she pushed through the gorse, ignoring their stabbing spikes.

She hefted her weight against the stiff door and it opened with a noisy creak. "Hello?" she said, trembling into the darkness.

Light danced upon the walls as she peered into the gloom. She stepped forward as the door slammed behind her. "Are you in here?" she asked.

A gust of wind came, then a voice that sounded barely alive. "You came back. I knew you would. Your son still lives!" Zathanael descended into sobs, and a mound shook in the far corner.

Aquila scrambled over to him, only to shrink back from the charred bloody figure who bore little resemblance to her king, Holus. It was his son, looking at her toddler.

Zathanael's face was smudged with black soot and, in the cracks, blood oozed. Aquila's crooked, blackened hand pulled the cloak closer.

"Don't look, miss. I've done what I can to ease the pain, and now I move beyond it. I've been praying to see your face one last time. Now that blessing has been granted, our time draws near. And I pray we are light-years away before those monsters return."

Aquila collapsed next to the trembling figure, forgetting the day's horrors. "Why are you risking your life for me, Zathanael? You will be exiled from Shtrae," she asked, but her voice shook more than her hands.

"You are like a mother to me. I will do anything to save you and the newborn. Only you among the others accept me for who I am and have stood for my beliefs."

"If anything I love you more, not less for all that you have done." Hot tears slid down Aquila's face.

"Miss Aquila, your words rest my soul and heal my wounds. How hard it must be for you I can but imagine."

"I am sorry to have thought you wouldn't understand."

Zathanael wheezed and swallowed. "Don't speak; rest. You will need strength. This little guy seems to have an inner strength far beyond our own. A compassionate soul is a rare thing in this universe."

Tears fell down her face as her stepson spoke. She had so many questions, but she did not ask them for fear of interrupting his flow and never hearing the last of it.

The guardian continued to speak, "We cannot outrun the darkness that plagues this planet. Out here on Shtrae we can see the rest of the galaxy, but we can't forget our mortal peril from the spreading evil."

She saw the terrible beast in her mind again, with its ominous green eyes. She shook her head, "But it is a terrible lie, for what affects one affects all, and long ago, even at the time of the Ancients, the giants knew evil could not be stopped, and would not stop until all of the universe was in its grasp." Aquila frowned.

"Hoxfius came from the Dark Rift, out of the Dark Hole that scars Shtrae's night sky," Zathanael said.

"We were terrified, and in our naivety we forbade each other to speak of him. Other children have heard little of the darkness stealing the stars.

"But they came anyway, Aquila. Hoxfius, his space pirates, and all the horrors we hoped never to see. They burned everything, said they'd torch the whole universe to prevent the new breed from living among us. I crawled, through the flames and cinders, to find you."

"I tried to keep all this from you, to keep you safe from the horrors of the world, because I love you as my son, and I knew the path you would take one day would be the hardest of all. I had so many dreams about you before we met. Then, when I had you in my arms, I did not want them to be true. But my beautiful child has survived thus far thanks to you." She tried to smile, lowering a wet cheek to rest lightly upon her stepson's palm.

"You have been a guardian to all youth during our days of weakness. The time has come for me to help you through your darkness. Hoxfius knows there's a threat to his might, and he'll do all he can to stamp it out."

Aquila remained confused. It all appeared impossible. Even though it was sometimes visible on a moonless night, she knew the black hole was too far away amongst the stars.

"I need you to remain focused. Hoxfius and his vile predator soldiers scourged the lands of Shtrae in a flash. My father knows why his evil brother now flies above our beloved skies. They came only moments ago, you were already gone. I thought they had taken you and the boy."

Aquila's voice weakened, and a rattling cough racked her body. "I'm here, it's alright," she soothed, reaching to touch him, then falling back for fear of hurting him more.

She examined his wounds from head to toe disgusted by the blood covering his white feathers. Looking closer, she noticed he had been touched by the flames of Hoxfius' wrath.

"I know how to get you out of here, Miss Aquila. There is a starship awaiting us."

"Only the old upon Planet Shtrae know of those. Long ago, when I and Holus were young, enormous beings came to our world, warning us about visions of this threat. Apparently, a wrath overcame them with grief and sorrow long before they could find their way through the fog. Never making it back to their home planet." Aquila froze.

"You aren't safe here anymore. Father ordered me to take care of the boy. He meant to get rid of him… like a vulgar insect. But his I could not do. I will take care of him my way. You too, are different, Miss, and we have treated you like our own. I wish the boy would've been blessed with the same chance."

Aquila remained frozen. What if they wouldn't make the trip? she wondered. It was said that many wandered through space and had lost themselves, never returning. Realizing that nothing guaranteed their survival, she suddenly caught a glimpse of a vision – her son standing taller. All alone.

Chapter Three
Starship

After flying through the skies of Shtrae, they reached a mysterious area. When she looked closer, all she saw were floating stones. Slow waterfalls tumbled off of the edge and disappeared into smoky blankets of mist.

She jumped between the floating stones with a mighty, drifting bounce, pushing her to higher stones among the amid endless azure sky, punctured by the occasional flock of birds. The stones seemed like figures standing there, watching her. She walked towards one.

Looking closely, she could just make out carvings upon it, tracing its lines and curves of strange symbols and numbers showing, "Station 42" It appeared to be an outside language of a species long forgotten and faded by time.

There were no letters or anything she recognised except for the numbers, which was a universal language. She walked between the gigantic stones. They formed a pathway stretching twenty paces towards a large mound surrounded by thinner shards of whitened blue stone. "Aquila," Zathanael's fainted whispers made her jump.

Her eyes darted as the voice echoed. It was just the wind, she thought, though there was none. Her toddler giggled as she flew to the mound. Zathanael was ahead, scouting to protect his loved ones from all possible threats.

She stood before the pitch-black entrance, but could not see anything inside, the light just stopped. Tentatively she reached out and touched the blackness.

She gasped as her hand passed through what felt like water, but it was thicker and very cold. Her hand completely disappeared into the black liquid that filled the entrance.

She wiggled her fingers on the other side. She stared at the ripples circling out from her wrist, and as they moved she saw her reflection in them, with the stones behind her.

The freezing cold became too much to handle. She began to feel a frozen liquid wrap around her hand and she pulled her it out quickly. It had become dry and cool. "It's not solid," she breathed, glancing up at the sky.

How did the liquid stand up like that? She watched her reflection ripple until the black water calmed to stillness once more. But her image did not fade, somehow touching it had left an imprint of herself and her surroundings.

She chewed her lip. "What's in there?" she asked Zathanael, but he only cocked his head. "Aquila," the voice whispered again, making her jump.

This time it definitely came from beyond the ship. Her heart was pounding. She didn't feel any danger, so what harm could it do? She could just take a peek and come straight back out.

Always her inquisitiveness overrode any fear and was a cause of constant worry. "Well, I guess there's nothing to fear." Her voice sounded hollow in the stillness.

She closed her eyes, took a deep breath, and stepped forward into her reflection. Freezing blackness engulfed her, darkness so complete she could no longer see her body, and every limb, finger and toe felt frozen.

She had the strangest feeling, an unquestionable knowing, that something had been set in motion. She was frightened as the cold liquid vanished.

She let go of her breath and blinked. It was dark, but she felt an open space ahead. The freezing cold was replaced with a warm breeze.

With her heart thumping, she breathed deeply. A muted light grew, driving back the dark, and she gasped at what she saw. Outside of the ship, there was no green, rocky land that she had somehow been expecting, but a vast desert of pale sand expanding out under a star-filled sky.

The sand itself gleamed indigo. A little way ahead there was a gateway. It was made of a type of stone she had never seen before, it shimmered all over with silver and violet specks.

It was three times larger and higher than the one through which she had stepped. The stones were not weathered, but immaculately smooth with sharp, precisely carved edges.

The two monoliths, tipped with a heavy lintel stone, stood alone with no mound, no other stones, and nothing but the desert around it.

The slender woman entered the ship. She was robed in a flowing midnight-blue cloak and hood, shimmering with violet lights. Though her face was hidden in the hood, her toddler felt her eyes upon him. She swallowed. Maybe she should turn back. She glanced behind, but the gate through which she had come wasn't there, only the endless desert stretching into the horizon.

Zathanael raised a pale hand and beckoned to her. The toddler held to his mother's legs and looked at the woman's feet. She motioned to him, waiting for a reaction.

There seemed no malice in the teenager's stance. Aquila shuffled closer until he stood a few paces away. She peered closer at the window and fell back with a gasp. "The universe really is robed in stars!" she said in wonder.

Galaxies swirled in graceful arcs among clusters of stars of all shapes and sizes, some were the deepest red, others were shades of blue, some moved as twins through the darkness, and others stood alone, throbbing their brilliant, pulsing light fluttering weakly as they circled down and were swallowed by the blackness, never to emerge again.

She saw that all the stars and galaxies were moving towards the black scar and every star that disappeared made the darkness grow. "The stars are dying," Zathanael breathed.

It made him sad. He looked up at the woman but couldn't see her face in the darkness of her hood, only a smooth luminous chin and pale lips were visible.

Beneath the ship appeared a pale golden light that formed into a miniature swirling galaxy, only larger and all centred around a bright golden star.

It expanded swiftly, engulfing them before Aquila could step away. Stars flashed and spun around the ship. She looked down, but her body was gone, and instead she was a ball of silver light.

They were travelling amongst the stars, as one of them. "What is this?" Aquila gasped.

Ahead flew her companion. A voice echoed around her, the same calm voice that had drawn her to the mound. Though she could not see him, she could feel his presence, it was filled with wisdom and compassion.

Aquila began to think that the stars and the galaxies and the space between them was the Source of All, and she was a tiny star within her mantle, a smaller part of the Grand Universe herself. "Hoxfius is coming." The voice echoed in the vastness. His tone whispered of ancient wisdom and resonated with the purest love. "Be strong, I will be with you."

Aquila struggled to hold her toddler in the speed of light, and she pulled away, overwhelmed. The swirling galaxies disappeared, and her body returned along with the ship and the gateway.

"He is still close," the teenager said in a gentle voice. Aquila shook her head, staggering backward, her eyes never leaving her son.

The desert sand under them began to stretch. They stumbled and fell. The ship hit the ground hard and their heads were shook and they struggled to see if they had made it to their destination.

Chapter Four
Homeland

In a daze Aquila and her newborn found themselves lying on Planet Earth between gnarly oaks. A thick root poked into their backs. Aquila winced and sat up. Leaves and twigs covered her body and tangled her hair.

After pulling most of the forest away from her body, she stood up and looked around. I have been here, she thought, recognising her favourite climbing tree. It appeared to have grown immensely. But it wasn't the same place she was in a lifetime ago. She frowned and rubbed her eyes as old memories returned. Where were the all the trees and giant stones?

She flew along the path, still holding her son. However, Zathanael was nowhere to be found. She had not seen a corpse, but still felt strangely alone without her feathery companion in front of her. She thought he had simply left with the vanishing ship.

Her flight dropped to a walk as her thoughts turned from the honorable hero who'd helped a helpless baby wrapped in a towel travel among the stars. Had she thanked him? What did he mean, "Be strong, I will be with you"? she wondered.

Nothing that had just happened made any sense. It was the silence again that broke her thoughts. No birds sang, or gulls cried, everything was deathly quiet.

There was the smell of wood smoke in the air, which was strange for it was far too warm for any hearth. The sky was darkening, but the clouds were muddy and low, and not like rainclouds at all.

That feeling of dread crept back into her stomach as she lurched into flight. The rough path became a foggy track and pebbles flew off the ground as she emerged from the desert into her homeland.

Then came Hoxfius' voice with all his glory. "The time has come for my wrath to consume this world! I shall rid it from the worms!" His menacing laugh faded into the thunderous roars.

She slowed down as thick smoke billowed from amongst the trees where she stood moments ago. She staggered into a run, protecting her child.

A shadow swished low over her head and she ducked. It was Zathanael, swooping and coming to a stop, his white wings stretching out for balance as he stumbled wearily.

Sunlight gleamed off his slick, pure feathers, a red lid snapped across an eye, his head turned and tilted to regard her. He grabbed her child and swirled into the skies, disappearing in a glimpse.

Her initial excitement quickly faded, the coverage was sparse at best. She crouched to make herself as small as possible. The beat of massive wings came closer until they billowed gusts of air and earth around her hiding place.

She dared to peek through a gap in the branches, covering her mouth before she would scream. The black wings belonged to a beast, one she'd seen in her worst nightmare.

He had many horns sticking out of his head. His triangular eyes were lidless, flashing in the dull light. His mouth was lined with sharp fangs.

"Come out," Hoxfius ordered, his voice was too deep and airy to be human. Although, she remembered hearing it before. Her legs tried to stand of their own accord, controlled by the commanding voice.

She clung to the rocks to stop her body from obeying, trying to calm her racing heart, but it was already too late. Hoxfius had been building speed for a time now, aiming at her. Ready to ambush her with all his strength.

Wings beat closer, sending earth, rocks, and leaves into the air. Hoxfius' massive snout snaked around from behind the rock. She hid her face as her whole body shook.

There was rustling above her and then the thunderous sound of cracking rock. She clung to the gorse thorns cutting deep into hands as the rocky outcrop behind her fell away. She clawed away from the destruction and lay stricken on her back.

It had pulled the whole thing from the cliff. She heard it crash and then she felt his enormous footsteps as he approached her, fighting the ominous energy which emerged from his body.

In the distance, Zathanael reappeared out of the clouds, but her fear blinded her from everything surrounding her. Crawling, Aquila begged, "Please, Sir Hoxfius. Do not destroy this planet too!"

"You brought this on them! All losses in this universe are due to a lack of ability. If you want to curse an entire planet, curse it with your own weakness."

All of a sudden, Zathanael came flying downwards behind Hoxfius and slammed into him. The predator grunted and swung his weight, landing his fist on Zathanael's face.

The protector grappled his opponent, but his body spikes protracted farther and ripped Zathanael's hand to pieces of bloody flesh that fell over the ground, "Aaah!" Zathanael yelped, withdrawing from Hoxfius, holding his wounded hand.

While the protector was distracted by his blood-spurting hand, the horrible being came behind him and jumped on his back, pounding on his neck. "Aaaaar! Get off!" Zathanael yelled, as he reached behind himself to grab his enemy. However, Hoxfius was too agile, dodging any movement that came blasting at him, and continuing to slice away at the flesh until he could see bones.

"Humanity is dead, my friend. The time has come for you to follow suit." Hoxfius yelled, desperately raising his fists and slamming them down as forcefully as he could, shock waving and rippling along the ground before sending Zathanael up into the sky with the blast. "Your time has come!" Hoxfius yelled as he jumped and hurled himself towards his opponent, attempting to body slam him via his obsidian plate.

Hoxfius swayed swiftly to the side, as if gravity simply did not affect him, and grinned at the bewildered looking fiend, twirling himself three hundred and sixty degrees, kicking Zathanael in the chest.

He was struck like a baseball back to the earth, landing with a crash. The protector was dizzy after the impact, and before he could pick himself up, Hoxfius came down and smashed on top of him, creating a huge dent in his armor.

The enemy shot at him, forcing him to dodge. He dodged the next dozen attempted strikes, as he was held down by punches striking his chest plate. Hoxfius kept him hammered on the ground, crushing the chest plate inward and hitting harder and more rapidly as it became easier to dodge the same strikes over and over again.

Meanwhile, Zathanael had given up on the idea of going for his opponent's exposed face, as he knew that would put him too close to the brute's arms. He felt his chest plate pressing into him, and it was beginning to cause pain.

In a daze, he thrashed his arms around violently but to no avail. Hoxfius was in a furious trance, pounding harder and harder on his prey like a drum. His fists caved in the armor, squishing Zathanael's upper body.

He felt his ribs crack and break, and with each blow, blood spurted out of his mouth. By now, he had lost the ability to move and defend himself, which gave the predator more focus. He blasted the armor with incredulous power, squelching and bursting organs as the breastplate was slowly flattened – punch by punch, shock by shock. The blood spurted higher from Zathanael's mouth with each consecutive hit, and higher still, until there was none left to force out.

After a short while, Hoxfius paused and then stopped, catching sight of his handiwork. The chest plate had been beaten to the point of being as wholesomely thin as paper, and the being that had sacrificed himself was now severely wounded and disfigured.

Hoxfius rose from the bloodied opponent, looking down at him sullenly. He went back to where Aquila was left wounded on the earthy dirt. Lowering his weapon, he approaches the woman and tilted her face up, by her chin, toward the light his eyes. Against the glare of his stare, her blue eyes shone back toward glints of silver, holding back tears.

"I'll make this world go up in flames. I hear the cries of all my victims left with nowhere to run or hide. Staring at my great flames will be your only future."

Her scraggly blond hair is drenched and matted as it clung to her pale face and shoulders, her skin prickled with goose bumps, realizing she had lost.

Hoxfius laid her on his shoulder, spread his wings and flew away from the battlefield. Once thrown in a dusty cellar, Aquila tried to cover her breasts and crouched into a ball. Breathing fast and shallow, her whole body shook with fear, "I desire to live!" she breathed.

Hoxfius stood, laughing viciously, "So act like it. You have made it worse by leaving Shtrae. You have sacrificed many lives to save a miserable worm."

She glared at him as if she could set him on fire with her eyes, but Hoxfius' expression didn't waver. She looked up at the horrible slaver, "My child didn't survive!" she snapped at last, pulling on the cuffs. "Can you untie me now?"

"Oh, of course not! I feel he is near… still among this world and I will find him." Hoxfius pointed at his prisoner, stepping back. "If I shall fail to find the vermin, he will come looking for his dear mother in the future."

"You can't keep me forever! I should be a free being, not a vulgar prisoner covered in dust and blood!" She lunged at him even while knowing it was pointless, knowing she could not protect her son any longer. The handcuffs bit into her skin, but she ignored it.

"Well, you enjoy it, don't you?" He interrupted her. "Instead of spending your time as a free human being, you prefer to be covered in blood, guts, and tears. So enjoy it to the fullest. Never will you see the pureness of Shtrae, your clueless king, nor his son's rotten corpse."

She growled, watching him step through the gateway. "To spend my time as a human being, first I would have to be one!" she yelled at his back, making him turn around with a finger pointing at her.

"That's your problem, right there. You are human, even if technically, you're not." And with that, he closed the gate. She instantly felt empty, reminiscing about her fallen hero and her own son, imagining his smile as she sat alone in her cage.

Words vibrated around her. "Don't give in to anger. Love will set you free." The voice pulsated through her and rolled away.

Now conscious, Zathanael was too furious to wonder where she could be, and that anger was felt as fire rumbling in his stomach. It pressed in urgently. The desire to kill drove him forward, but the compassion in his heart made him stay.

After discovering the boy was gone, and furious after witnessing the perish of a species, he was unable to deal with the strange emotions within. He turned away from the smoking ashes of the ones Hoxfius had slain and he thought of the last moment that he saw the toddler for the last time, watching all around him. He then remembered the last words he had spoken to the child.

The Ancients will not harm you. I will find your dear mother and come back for you, boy." He stood, acknowledging a deep loss, he felt it was time to ask stronger individuals to help rid the universe of the madness.

On Shtrae, Holus had gathered his council and spoke of his queen. "She too was different to us. I have tried to hide it from all of you… how could one reveal this, knowing how we treat different species. I have abandoned her and her child like insects. I am the cause of their troubles. My dear Aquila, her emotions were not easily hidden on her innocent face. Her pain was evident in the crease of her lovely brow and the down-curve of her full lips. But her eyes, her eyes showed her soul. They were a deep pool of restless gold, an ocean of hopeless grief. As we considered her eyes we knew, all the beauty of the universe could not even hope to compete with this simple thing, passion.

"Passion had turned her eyes into orbs of the brightest fire, and in them we read clearly that she would fight to the very last tear for her life. She would not let the world separate her from her child. Sure, she would cry, but she would never let us take her true self from her. She clung to it with passion. Passion that made her beautiful. She looked like an angel, in the form of the most beautiful woman on Shtrae. With eyes, so crystal clear that you could see rivers, oceans… the world through them.

"With her blonde hair, radiant and shining, swishing with every word she spoke. No flower, no queen, could compare with her beauty. She had the body of a flower, lithe and beautiful. With every step, she took, it looked as though she were floating, and I only became more convinced that we were blessed by the presence of an angel. Her pure white wings proved her karmic holiness. However, it all seems light years away. Nothing but her memories of a dreamful past to hold on to through our nightmares. I demand of none of you to follow me into this foolish journey. However, the time has come for me to deal with my brother. Not only for the sake of my queen, but also for the love of Shtrae."

Prelude

    Here on Earth, in a rotten desert, a crew of surviving humans rose from the ashes. They had heard the cries of the young boy from miles away. A teenage boy was the first to approach, discovering the outsider cradled in the fist of a dead gigantic being. The teenage boy turned away, "Guys! Help me lift these huge fingers", he yelled, looking at the boy who was covered in tears.

    He was wrapped in his towel, but also had started cocooning. The young boy tarred the mysterious cocoon apart from the boy's body to prevent others from mistreating the strange orphan.

    "Let's bring him to our camp! Our Commander's wife will know what to do to help him!" the young survivor suggested.

About the author

Philip K. Chase is a science-fiction author. Born in Sherbrook but raised in a small town called Waterloo. Phil is one of those odd people whose sentences sometimes begin with one language and end with another.

Like many writers, he is perpetually curious. After a few years dedicating his time to self-improvement, Phil somehow managed to write his own books. His achievements are still a source of some amusement to him. He has since been working on many projects, writing science fiction novels or working with other projects like the Aquila Dream Projects, which he is the Founder.

He passionately loves connecting with science fiction, fantasy and horror – whether it's film, reading, writing or music. So feel free to introduce yourselves on any of these platforms:

Website:
https://aquilaprojectscom.wordpress.com/
Facebook :
https://www.facebook.com/phil.chase.395
Email:
Philip.k.chase87@gmail.com
Twitter:
https://twitter.com/PhilKChase
Instagram
https://www.instagram.com/philkchase/
Make sure to follow him for updates on his upcoming works.

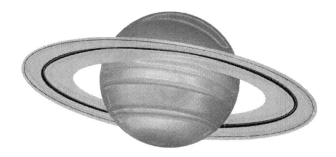

Planetary Relics
Marsha Black

  A revolution has formed and its members want to start an all-out war once again between planets Dreah, Socily, Juerno, Pausital and Lisantli.
  Detectives Fondru and Lilandro are ordered by their captain to go to planet Dreah in search of the Relic hidden on it to garner it and the other four relics powers to keep peace.
  Each planet holds a piece of the relic but there are clues and riddles needing to be solved to locate the pieces, not to mention those from the revolution who want to stop Fondru and Lilandro from locating them and piecing them back together.
  Will they manage to get the pieces to prevent an all out war where there has been semi-peace for centuries, or will they fail, losing many to the whims of the revolutionist?

Prologue

Many moons and stars away, light years ago, wars were fought between the Dreah, Socily, Juerno, Pausital and Lisantli planets. These were the largest planets in the Honstial Solar System, protecting the smaller planets within their orbital pull.

A mercenary from each planet teamed together to create a relic to bring peace between the planets. From the relic, a piece was separated until there were five individual pieces, garnering each planet the same amount of power. The rulers of each planet were given a piece to hide on their planet with one clue to its location.

Peace was established, and the relics were hidden, so no Planet could garner more power than another. Until one day, when peace was no longer wanted…

Thus, beginning the search for the…

PLANETARY RELICS!!

Chapter One

"Detective Fondru! You have one last chance at remaining a detective!" Captain Slyth yells, red faced. Uniform pristine and not a gray hair out of place, posture and build impeccable for being around his sixties and at about 5'7 in height. "Your new partner is from Socily, and you better not screw up this time!"

"Yea, Yea," I call back, walking away. "It's not my fault all of my past partners are wuss's!"

"I mean it, Fondru! No one else will work with you," Slyth's voice softens, "I know that you have some personal issues you're fighting, but you can't be going off half-cocked, putting yourself and your partner in danger."

I stop at this, "Captain, you don't know anything about why I do what I do. The only thing you SHOULD worry about, is the results from my actions! Thanks to me and my 'half-cocked' ways, my sector has the least amount of fights and crimes." I storm off, not wanting to hear anything else the Captain has to say.

I make my way towards my cabin, stopping to peer out the porthole. The sight of stars, planets, and varying flashes of light, similar to what Earth has and calls the aurora borealis.

I catch sight of my reflection and am unimpressed with my mousy brown hair hung in a pony tail and teal colored eyes. Yes, I said it. Somehow, someway, my eyes are the unusual color of teal for a human.

"Here," a voice says behind me. Turning towards it I'm stopped by a yellow hand holding a steaming mug of…I take a sniff…coffee.

"Thanks, but I don't know you, and I darn tootin' am not going to accept a drink from someone I don't know," I state, pushing the hand and steaming cup of delicious smelling coffee away.

"Let's fix that then, shall we?"

I turn around fully to face whomever dares to continue pestering me and am face to face with a handsome Socilian, who is much, much taller than me. I note that quickly, considering I'm tall for a human woman at 5'11.

Socilian's have the same body type as humans do, however they are different colors, which also represent what sector they are from and their rank. This Socilian has cerulean blue eyes, that I have trouble moving my gaze from. His hair is jet black with a streak of white that weaves its way through each strand as though blessed by the gods themselves. Shirtless, his chest is well defined, and with a six pack to die for, skin color ranging from yellow to green over the parts of his body I can see. Feeling saliva gathering in my mouth and jaw going slack… knocks me out of my lust induced reaction.

"I don't really care," I brush past him, continuing on my way.

Steps follow quickly until he's caught up to me and we're walking side by side.

"I'm Detective Lilandro, and apparently…your new partner."

"I don't need a partner. I do just fine on my own, so go away and leave me be, Socilian!" I sneer.

Before I know it, I'm shoved into a wall, facing the Socilian, his hand on my shoulders holding me in place and a shiver of some unknown feeling courses down my body.

"I'm not like your human partners, Detective Fondru! I don't need to be babied and handled with care like your species does," he counters.

He's so close to my face I can see the spit fly out of his mouth as he speaks.

"Get your hands off me, before I make you! You're lucky you still have them attached. No one…and I mean no one, lays a hand on me and gets away with it!"

Before I can get a chance to shove his hands off of me and teach him a much-needed lesson, sirens and red flashing lights break us apart. Without a glance at the Socilian, I hightail it back to the Captain to find out what set the alarms off.

"Captain! What's going on!" I call out, raising my voice to be heard over the blaring sirens.

"We have an unknown ship making its way towards us! All hands on deck...and I mean...ALL hands," he says, shooting a glance next to me...which to my surprise is where my new partner is standing.

I scoff, "Well at least you can keep up...so far."

Captain Slyth glares at me, "Play nice Fondru. Detective Lilandro is your best chance at keeping your job."

"I heard you the first time," I growl. "Where do you want us?"

"Make your way to the entry tunnel. I want the both of you to be the welcoming committee, in case our visitors turn out to be enemies."

"Aye Aye, Captain," I say, saluting him, before turning and walking away. "You coming...Socilian?"

I hear a sigh coming from both of the men and grin. I may have to accept this partner...but it doesn't mean I have to like it...or play nice...too much.

I'm about halfway to the entry tunnel, when the Socilian reaches me.

"Forgive me for asking, but what is your deal?"

I continue walking, appearing as though I couldn't hear him over the blaring sirens. It's none of his business what my deal is with not wanting a partner, or why I am being so rude.

"Hey, I'm talking to you, little girl!" he says, raising his voice a bit to be heard over the sirens.

"I could give two flying figs about you talking to me. Stay out of my way, and I'll stay out of yours," I spit out, knowing if he doesn't get some sort of response, he'll continue bugging me until I give him something.

"Aren't you just a breath of fresh air," he mocks.

I breathe a sigh of relief and offer up a silent prayer to whatever gods might be out there as I see the door to the entry tunnel. I quicken my pace and as I reach my hand up to the key pad, quiet ensues. Sirens and flashing lights stop.

Entering the code, the door whooshes open, allowing the Socilian and myself entry. Space suits are hanging on the wall, and I grab a set to gear up in, watching as the Socilian doesn't bother. "Don't you need to wear a suit for once the tunnel opens allowing some of spaces air into it upon the ships entry?"

"No, my species has adapted remarkably and can go pretty much anywhere, without need of a space suit," he informs me.

"Must be nice," I whisper under my breath. These suits are bulky and awkward at the best of times, and I hate, absolutely hate, having to wear them. Although I suppose it's better than the alternative…Death.

We wait at the outer door until the unknown ship has docked and starts to seal off the entrance from space. I do the retinal and key code scans to open the door, preparing to greet our visitors.

The interlock system gives way, whooshing open. I stand erect with hands clasped behind my back. We were trained to be in this stance to appear professional, yet at the same time, have our hands closer to within our weapons reach.

Unprepared for who steps out of the space craft, I'm unable to hold back a quick intake of breath. Hearing my reaction, I see Lilandro shoot me a quick side glance. I give a quick nod in the negative and resume my silent position until approached by none other than…the leader of Planet Dreah.

Chapter Two

"Good day, Lord Daysino. We welcome you aboard the Songlyer." I give a slight bow in recognition of his status. "How may we assist you?"

Green hair wrapped in coils like snakes ready to strike, a third eye resting where a humans would be, making his nose at the middle of his forehead. Squat in stature, pudgy cheeks and wrinkled skin show where clothing does not cover. I hide grimace of disgust and can just imagine him giving a sniff of disdain as a sneer crosses his face. "Take me to your Captain."

"Right this way, sir." I turn, keeping watch for any sudden movements, nudging Lilandro as I walk past, noting the tenseness in his body.

Like a highly trained detective should be, he takes up residence walking behind Lord Daysino and his guards. I have to grudgingly give him credit for doing so without being told.

We make our way towards the head of the ship, silence carrying throughout the ship, halls clear. I guess no one wants to be around the Lord of Dreah. Dreah is the worst planet in the solar system. Barren lands with two moons and suns make the planet mostly uninhabitable. On top of that, there are numerous poisonous plants, animals and various other areas that if not known, can all end in an untimely death…or timely, depending on why you are around them.

Dreah keep slaves by putting criminals into servitude. They do gladiator style tournaments that end in deaths. If you refuse to kill your opponent, you both get killed. If you steal, both your hands get cut off. If you lie, your tongue gets cut out and so many more punishments that I cringe thinking of some of them.

A chill runs down my spine, wondering what could be bad enough that Lord Daysino personally would make a visit to our ship rather than delegating the task.

"Captain, may I present Lord Daysino from Planet Dreah. Detective Lilandro and I await your command," I salute before turning and heading out Lilandro tight on my heels.

"We should not wander far, Fondru. I fear we may be needed sooner rather than later."

"Agreed, albeit grudgingly," I acknowledge, leaning against the wall just outside of the entrance to the head of the ship, in expectation. Lilandro next to me, standing quietly, almost companionably. Weirdly so.

Not long after, Captain Slyth calls for our return. We make our way back into the head of the ship and walk towards the Captain's war table as he likes to call it.

"Fondru. Lilandro. We have a mission of utmost importance for you both. Lord Daysino has come to us in request for aid in locating the Planetary Relics." Captain Slyth tells us, looking over a piece of parchment on his table.

"The what?" I ask.

"Oh, Lady Narious, help us," Lilandro whispers.

All eyes turn on me with varying shades of shock. "You honestly do not know of the Planetary Relics?" Slyth gets out.

"This does not surprise for how lacking your species are," Lord Daysino says, nose up.

Temper unchecked, I ball my fist and take a step in Daysino's direction. A tug on my arm breaks my focus, and I step back into place.

"Please enlighten me, my lord," I request through my teeth. Every word painstakingly pulled out of me.

With a deep, heartfelt, bored sigh he finally responds, tone bored, "The Planetary Relics are pieces of a powerful relic that if located and pieced together will contain all power. Each of the five planets in Honstial have a piece of the relic hidden somewhere on it. There is only one clue given to find each piece."

Turning away from me he stops speaking and with a nod of his head, Slyth continues, "Someone from one of the planets has organized a revolution and wants the planets to go to war again, which separating the pieces in the first place, stopped. Since the leaders of each planet do not know who created the revolution or how many are involved the planets are about to break into an all-out war."

"Ok, so war between all of the planets is a HUGE deal…"

Before I could say more, Captain Slyth cuts me off, "Since you are my best detective, I'm giving you this important task. This piece of parchment contains the clue to Dreah's relic. This is why Lord Daysino came to us himself, to make sure we receive the parchment without issue."

That makes sense! "Yes sir, how soon do you want me to leave?"

"You both will leave in a couple of hours. Right now, we need to decipher this clue, so you can get to the first piece quickly." Slyth commands, waving Lilandro and I over to the table to read over the parchment.

Follow the shadows from Dreahs suns
Where the shadows meet is where your journey begins
Turn towards the east and begin your trek
Do not stray for your destination is far
Once you come upon an engraved stone
Riddle upon riddle will your eyes feast upon
One wrong answer and the relic will be forever gone

"Lord Daysino, do you have any ideas as to where this leads?" I question, since he is the most likely source to know.

"I do not. I had one of the mercenaries that created the relic hide the one for Dreah. Only thing I can suggest doing is follow me to Dreah and follow the path the parchment starts you off on."

Lovely. Not much help after all, is the lord of Dreah. You would think what with it being his planet, he'd have more input to give.

"Alright then, if there is nothing further to discuss I will take my leave and pack up the essentials in preparation of our trip," I salute the captain and give a slight bow to Lord Daysino before taking my leave.

I make it to my cabin without incidence, grab my satchel and towel with lucky number 42 on it. Packing the towel with my other essentials, I lay on my bunk and rest my eyes for a bit before the flight.

Chapter Three

I awaken just before a knock sounds at my door. Running my fingers through my hair I fix my ponytail as I use voice command to open the door.

"Thank you for allowing me entrance into your abode, Fondrue." Lilandro enters glancing around my cabin.

"Don't let it go to your head, Lilandro. You aren't the first guy to enter my cabin welcome or not," I declare.

"Yes, I get that. Question?"

"Not now, Lilandro. We've got to get going or we'll be late meeting Lord Daysino at his ship to fly to Dreah." I retort.

"Why don't we just take one of the shuttles from here?"

"We could, but then we'd have to go through all the red tape entering Dreah. By being on ship with the leader of Dreah, we won't be questioned," I state.

"Fondru, just to be upfront with you…I have a bad feeling about all of this."

"Noted." I pronounce as I grab my bag and towel, shoving Lilandro out the door.

In silence we head back to the entry tunnel to await Lord Daysinos arrival to leave Songlyer. I give my habitual silent prayer to the ship, for protection outside of its walls and a safe, swift return. For some reason, I include the Socilian in my prayer.

With a disgruntled mental shake, I put thoughts of the Socilian and everything except for this mission out of my head, bringing the professional in me to the forefront.

The Captain walks in with the Lord and waves me over as he walks away from Lord Daysino. "Yes, sir," I say upon approaching him.

"Keep this on you at all times. Do NOT let anyone know you hold this clue to the relic. Spies are hidden everywhere, and we cannot allow the relic to fall into the wrong hands." Slyth says as he slips me the parchment in lieu of a hand shake.

"Yes, sir! You can count on me," I assert.

"I hope so and please confide in Lilandro, you are partners and are meant to be there for one another. Don't let the past get in the way of accomplishing this co-operative mission."

With a defeated sigh I declare, "I will do my best. This mission is too important for either of us to screw up, however, keep in mind I don't trust the Socilian. I will be keeping an eye on him."

I watch as Slyth waves Lilandro over, standing silently until he reaches us.

"Lilandro, keep an eye on Fondru. She's the best detective we have, and the best one for this mission. She's prepared to work with you on this case, so don't make either of us regret it."

"No sir, I won't give either of you reason to regret having me in place as Fondru's partner."

"Once you two have found the relic, find safe passage to the next planet and so forth. Keep your coms ready and if you need to relay a private message enter the combination of both of your entry codes. This will encode the message to be sent directly to me."

A horn blares, causing us to jump at its high pitch. Lord Daysino's guards are waving us onto the ship, so we bid farewell to Slyth as we head towards the entrance. The door shuts behind us and we are escorted to a single cabin with two beds.

"Please make yourselves at home in your cabin for the duration of your travels. If you require assistance, please enter code 004277 into the comm next to your beds. For now, I would suggest getting some rest, we have a long flight ahead of us," the Dreahean who escorted us speaks.

"Thank you, we will take you suggestion under advisement, however we may want to make our rounds of the ship to make note of our surroundings. We shall let you know via comm what we decide." I announce, already walking towards one of the beds and opening my pack in order to situate my belongings for my temporary stay.

***

I keep watch on the Dreahean until he leaves and the door to the cabin closes. I turn towards Fondru and watch as she methodically takes out and organizes her belongings. For a human she is quite a conundrum.

I make my way over to the other bunk and unpack my items, aware that neither of brought many personal items. That's the way it is being a detective, and more so for me, being a Socilian.

"Fondru, I'm ready to take the tour around the ship now if you are," I enquire.

"Yes, let's key in the code to get out of this stifling cabin," she turns towards me as she answers. Once again, I am struck by her teal eyes. She's not exactly unpleasant to look upon like most humans I've come across, however there is something about her that draws me in.

She walks over to the comm and enters the code we were given. The door opens, and we make our way out, a bit surprised to see a Dreahean guard standing outside our door.

"May I be of assistance," he asks.

"Sure. We just wanted to take a tour of the ship," I state, unsure if Fondru could pull off the request as prepared as I was for the possibility of a guard.

"Of course, follow me and I will take you through your requested tour. Due to the urgency of our trip, we will need to make it quick and request that you eat your meals in your cabin until further notice." The guard relaxes his stance slightly as he walks ahead of us.

Fondru shoots me a glance and I give a nod. My bad feeling returns, and I hope we make it to Dreah quickly and without issue.
***

The Dreahean doesn't waste any time taking us through the ship. We walk in silence since all ships have the same parts and areas…just not exactly in the same spots as others…hence the tour.

Once we are back at the cabin the guard goes back to his stance at the entrance, standing stoically.

"Umm, what code for the comm do we need to input to order food," I question.

"Right. There's a pamphlet in the drawer next to your beds which list all the comm numbers you'll need." With that question answered, he turns away from me and faces forward like a good little soldier.

Debating whether to pester the guard, I see Lilandro staring at me from inside the cabin. Well this is going to be interesting, I think to myself, as my decision is made, and I enter our cabin, door closing behind me.

Chapter Four

Tension thickens as silence reigns. Neither of us wanting to give an inch, wanting to show we won't be dominated by them. Neither of us inferior to the other. A knock on the door interrupting our stare down, allowing me to breathe a sigh of relief.

I'm not sure whether I would've punched Lilandro in the face or climbed up his body, wrapping my legs around his trim waist and kissing him, like I've thought about doing since I first saw his saliva inducing masculine body.

As though privy to my thoughts, a cocky smirk makes it way on his lips, which just enhances the delectableness look to them. I shake my head to get rid of these troubling thoughts. After all he's my work partner and we have an important mission we're working on. We need to worry about figuring out the clue to finding the first relic, rather than having a pissing contest.

I turn back towards the door and am surprised to see an RA...in other words a Robotic Assistant...standing at it with a tray of yummy smelling food. Now my mouth collects saliva for a whole other reason. Looking behind me questioningly, Lilandro speaks up, "I called in dinner before you walked back in. I guessed on what you wanted, but from the looks of your reaction, I must've gotten some of what you like."

"That's oddly...sweet...of you," I barely manage to say without too much annoyance. Yes, it's irritating that he ordered food for me without asking what I wanted, yet sweet that he thought to order me food. I'm not quite sure what to make of it.

* * *

Knowing I've thrown Fondru off her game and picked up a little of her treacherous wanton thoughts, I turn away from the door. No need to piss her off again by having her see the widest grin I ever recall having gracing my face. A frown quickly replaces the grin as I realize the implication of me being able to catch some of Fondru's thoughts.

Not well known about my species to outsiders is that when we find our soul mate, we are able to mentally connect with them. On the rarest of occasions, the connection is so strong that we can even communicate telepathically. It's been centuries since one of those connections has been so strong among my people.

I sit on my bunk as I ponder over what to do. Should I tell Fondru, or just let it play out? I'm so deep in thought, I actually give a start when she slides a tray of food over to me, "My appreciation goes out to you, partner."

"Whatever. Hurry up and eat so we can go over this clue. See if we can piece anything together without interruption," she replies after swallowing a mouth full of food.

Feeling it best to not poke and prod the lion, I eat as quickly as I can, with a companionable silence stretching between us, both lost in appreciation of the amazing food.

Once finished we place the trays in the food receptacle and push the green Send button. The trays are whooshed through the capsules and are gone, startling us with a spray of air freshener, before closing out completed. The smell is not one I'm accustomed to, and apparently neither is Fondru as we both wind up coughing and waving our hands in front of our noses.

"What is that dastardly sme…"

* * *

I awaken uncomfortably in a chair, hands tied behind my back, ankles crossed and tied together. The aches and soreness in my neck and shoulders give me an estimated time from of about two hours being in this position. I try to check out my surroundings and bindings without being noticed, unsure of who may be watching.

I hear a groan from in front of me and a tug at the ties around my ankles. A sharp piercing feeling cuts into my ankle at the tug and I open my eyes, no longer bothering with being sly about figuring out my surroundings.

I catch sight of Lilandro seated on the floor not far from me, tied in a similar fashion to the way I am. "Lilandro, are you ok?"

"Fondru? What happened?"

"I think we were knocked out and now being held captive." I state the obvious, rolling my eyes at his stupid question.

"Can you get free?"

I snort, "I just woke up not long before you did." I quiet down as I attempt to survey our surroundings. I gasp in surprise at the trap laid out before us.

"Uh…Lilandro…do me a favor and DO NOT MOVE," I say in a deathly serious tone.

I watch as his body tenses, causing a slight tug on the bonds tying my ankles to him, which causes the sharp pain to once again pierce my skin, although not quite as deeply this time.

"We are in a type of death trap, certain movements from either one of us, will cause knives, saws, hammers and various other items to cut, jab and even break bones if hit just right and with enough force," I explain.

"Follow your bindings to see where they lead among this trap and I will follow mine. Use your sight and anything else you have available," he speaks confidently. "We are smarter than they are, and we are fully capable of figuring our way out of this. I place my life in your hands, as you must place yours in mine."

"Well…if we don't make it out of this alive…it was SO not nice to meet you, Lilandro," I grin, causing him to grin back saying, "Touché."

Chapter Five

As Lilandro mentioned, I use my eyes to trail the bindings attached to me. I find nothing that attaches to where my hands are bound, so I begin tugging in earnest to free my hands. An idea hits me, and I lean forward as much as I am able to until I hear a pain filled breath being inhaled. I stop moving and lift my head up to Lilandro, "You alright over there, partner?" I call out.

"Whatever you're doing is causing something to cut into my wrists!"

"That's good news! See if you can twist your wrists to where instead of whatever it is cuts into them, they cut into your binding instead."

"I'll," I hear grunting coming from where he sits, "try."

At each movement of his wrists, my own begin to try and tug me back into an upright position, where I hear the swinging of something I'm quite sure I don't want to know what is.

"Hurry up, Lilandro. I can't hold this position much longer and I'm afraid of what'll happen when I no longer can."

* * *

Hearing the slightest tone of fear and urgency in Fondru's request I glance up while continuing to get my wrists in a position for the bonds to be cut. Of their own accord my eyes widen, "Holy shit..." Swinging above Fondru's head is a guillotine style axe.

I see her stiffen at my obscenity, but I couldn't keep it from slipping out. That's not exactly something you see every day.

Just as I am about to tell her let's call it quits, I feel a slight give, and quickly call, "I've got it! Do what you were doing earlier, I should be able to get my hands free now."

I watch as she leans forward and thankfully feel the vibrations of my bonds being cut rather than my own skin. Twisting and tugging added to the cutting breaks the bonds quicker, and I sigh at the feeling of relief even as I stretch and bend my fingers to get the needle pin pricks to quit.

"Lilandro! Quit goofing off and hurry! By releasing your hands, whatever is swinging near me is getting closer and by the sounds of it...faster!"

I feel around behind me to locate the bonds that were holding my wrists captive and bring it to my face. I see a miniscule string attached to it and use my fingers to follow it. I stop as I reach what feels like a couple of gears, and I move the lowest one, causing a click to sound.

"Ouch! Gosh Darn it Lilandro!"

"Sorry! I'm trying to figure it out. Give me a minute."

"I don't think I have a minute," Fondru replies, voice drifting quietly until I only hear the swishing of the axe.

"Shit!" I release the string I was following and work on the binding around my ankles, carefully examining it before removing each piece. Similar to a Japanese Jigsaw, one wrong twist and pull can cause something deadly to happen.

"Fondru...Fondru!"

"Wha..."

"Fondru, I need you to either try to get your feet unbound, or your hands. I fear doing anything more on my end until we get you a little free, to be a little better prepared for whatever might come our way as we work our way through these intricate patterns.

The sound of a door opening catches my attention, feeling another surge of relief as my gaze passes over Fondru on the way to the door, that she appears more coherent and that the axe is no longer swinging near her.

"Release them," Lord Daysino calls out.

I flinch as my eyes are blinded by bright lights and my body sags a bit as with some clicks and grinding noises, Fondru and my own restraints release, clanking to the ground, no longer keeping us upright.

I jump up and rush at Lord Daysino, caught by two of his guards just before my hands make it to his neck. Bloodlust runs rampant through my blood, wanting to feel the pulse at his neck race and then slow as death rises to wrap him in its cool embrace.

* * *

I'm still groggy from whatever I must've been drugged by. I remember feeling the sting of a dart hit me in the back of the neck, and then not much else until Lilandro yelling my name reached its way through my subconscious.

"Lord Daysino, what is the meaning of this?" I question with as much authority as I could muster, while trying to stand on my shaking legs.

"If the two of you are Honstials only hope, we are in BIG trouble," he retorts before striding out of the temporary cell, guards pushing Lilandro and myself out the door to follow.

"I don't think I follow sir," I remarked.

"That was a test. I wanted to see if you both had what it takes to escape from the traps laid out, and neither of you could even manage to get fully released from your bindings. I hope you don't think you'll just get the clues and stroll through where they lead you without encountering any obstacles or people trying to prevent you from gaining all the pieces or steal them from you."

I give what Daysino says some thought and grudgingly that the grotesque Dreahean does indeed have a point. "Ok, so we were unprepared for something of this nature to happen on what I assumed was a friendly flight to your planet."

"Never assume anything human. You are nothing but a speck of dust among us Lords and Lady's and we ALLOW you the opportunity to live and keep watch over our sectors."

No longer interested in being spoken down to I grasp Lilandro's arm from one of the two guards that were restraining him. Stopping at the entrance to our cabin I question, "How much further are we from your planet?"

Lord Daysino continues walking, but the Dreahean that stays and stands guard at the doors entrance replies in a scathing tone, "By mid-day we will arrive. Pack up your belongings and pray you survive what's to come." He hits the keypad for the door, opening it, before shoving Lilandro and myself in, closing and if the beeps from the outer door keypad are any indication, locking us within.

Chapter Six

"Well…at least we'll be there soon," Lilandro remarks.

"Yea, thankfully," I respond. I attempt to ignore everything and everyone while I pack up my belongings, embarrassed at Daysino's ploy. Basing everything off of what he's shown us to be capable of and what he's said, I begin to doubt our capabilities of pulling this mission off.

Will we doom the planets because we aren't well trained in the areas of conflict we might come upon, or possibly be too cocky of ourselves that our pride winds up being the demise of the solar system and its inhabitants?

I hear a zipper sounding and glance behind me, noting Lilandro placing his bag onto the floor as he sits upon the bunk, "Fondru, I can tell you've got things running through that head of yours. Talk to me, maybe I can help you work through whatever troubles you."

"Thanks, but no thanks. You may be my partner as far as work goes, but never make the mistake that we will ever be more than that." I state, wanting to nip this…whatever he's trying to do…in the bud. "Let's just do our job and be done with it."

"As you say, partner," he asserts.

Feeling the slight gravitational pull as the ship lowers itself from the atmosphere, I zip my bag before tossing it over my shoulder, "Let's roll."

The door opens, and two guards stand outside it, waiting for us. "Follow us, Lord Daysino would like to speak with you both before you begin your journey."

Lilandro and I both take steps forward, however, being such a gentleman, he ushers me to go ahead of him. I shoot him a glare at his chivalry, trying to figure out whether he's trying to guilt trip me into feeling bad from my earlier assertion about where we stand.

We make our way to where Lord Daysino stands at the entrance of the ship, "Keep your towels and your wits about you," we nod at this, "Not everything may be as it seems and keep in mind what we put you through…it may wind up saving your lives." With that he clasps his hands behind his back, turns and walks away.

Before I can get a word out, whether to cuss him out or thank him, I'm pushed out of the ship and stumble on the uneven ground, coughing as the dry air hits my lungs. I quickly pull my bag off of my back, opening it to search for my lucky number 42 towel. Unable to find it, I start to panic…Did I leave it on the Songlyer?! No…I remember packing it. Did I leave it on Lord Daysino's ship? Frantic I try to make my way up the ships ramp to re-enter it, when Lilandro bumps into me, causing me to fall on the ground, giving the ship enough time to raise its ramp and take off.

"Dag nabbit, Lilandro!" I snap.

"What'd I do now," he sighs in exasperation.

"I think…" I start coughing uncontrollably, unable to finish the sentence, which surprisingly helps him to realize the issue.

"Ohh, here's your towel. I grabbed it as we were walking out, since I figured you probably didn't realize you hadn't packed it with the rest of your things when we were getting ready," he expresses holding my towel out to me.

I grasp it out of his hands, covering my mouth and nose slightly with it, allowing me time to adjust to the planets atmosphere. Thankfully the atmosphere is similar to Earth's…only drier, so it doesn't take long to acclimate.

"I could just about kiss you, Lilandro" I can't help but say as a feeling of gratitude overwhelms me, "but I won't." I grin as I see a flash of desire light his eyes, quickly extinguished by the last of my words.

I glance up at the sky, noting that it looks like we've made it to Dreah just in time for the shadows of the suns to meet. As if reading my thoughts, Lilandro and I both glance at the ground and follow the shadows until we arrive at our destination.

"Fondru…" I jump, startled at the voice sounding loud amidst the deafening silence during our travels.

"Geesus, Lilandro! You about scared me to death!" I hold my hand over my racing heart. During our travels I have seen no plant life, animals or other Dreaheans. It's as if we are alone…the only two people on the planet and it makes me feel uneasy.

"Sorry partner. I was just curious as to what the rest of the clue stated. I can't recall off hand."

"Right." I glance around our surroundings again and feeling confident that there are no hiding places within the sparse land, I pull out the parchment with the clue on it.

> Follow the shadows from Dreahs suns
> Where the shadows meet is where your journey begins
> Turn towards the east and begin your trek
> Do not stray for your destination is far
> Once you come upon an engraved stone
> Riddle upon riddle will your eyes feast upon
> One wrong answer and the relic will be forever gone

"I believe we have come upon the first part, where the shadows meet. What say you?"

I follow Lilandro's gaze and notice the apex of the shadows meeting directly beneath our feet, "I agree," and so in tandem we turn east and begin the second part of the clues request.

We've traveled no further than about 50 paces when my stomach begins to growl. Realization hits me that we haven't eaten since the previous day, which turns to confusion as to why my stomach is just now notifying me of its hunger. Determined to ignore it, I continue walking as Lilandro keeps pace…at least until his own stomach begins rumbling.

"I suppose we should eat?" Lilandro asks cautiously, as those expecting me to jump down his throat.

I grin at the thought but decide that he's in the right. Holding off on eating when we both are hungry would more than likely hinder our mission, "Yes, let's eat a couple of the protein bars and quench our thirst with one of the bottled waters, split between us," I state, "Are you capable of continuing walking while doing so?"

"Of course!" Lilandro sputters as though I've injured his masculinity or something.

"Ok, whatever." I grab two protein bars out of my bag and a water, as Lilandro grabs the same from his out. "We are sharing a water, remember?"

Lilandro's cheeks turn an interesting shade of purple considering his face is blue. I gape, "Are you…blushing?!" This causes the purple to darken even more.

Deciding to let up on the teasing, I tear open one of my bars wrapping with my teeth, and continue walking eastward, until we come upon the next portion of the clue.

Chapter Seven

Day turns into night, night turns into day. I've lost track of how far and long we have traveled and am about to concede defeat, wanting to find a place to rest and eat a spell.

"Fondru…can that be?" Lilandro utters while pointing off into the distance, voice husky, sounding sexy to my ears.

I rub my eyes, following where Lilandro points, just barely making out some large pillars of stone. I squeal and, in my excitement, forget myself as I turn towards Lilandro, wrapping my arms and legs around him in an excited hug.

I feel his body stiffen at first and then he wraps his arms around me and spins us around. I laugh in glee as my arms and legs tighten around him and my hair loosens from its ponytail wrapping around us.

Once he stops, we're staring at one another grinning and as if we can't help it, we both lean in until our lips press against one another. A static like shock at the points where our lips meet causes reality to hit me, and I unwrap my arms and legs from around him, as I push away to gather my wits.

I clear my throat as I rub my hands down my pants glancing anywhere but at him, "Right, um, let's continue on then," and with that we continue on until we reach the pillars of stone.

* * *

As I follow behind Fondru, I can't help but bring my fingers to my lips. The shock of the kiss was quite unexpected and is a big cause for concern. No matter what, I must keep my distance from her before it's too late for the both of us.

As we draw closer to the pillars a tingling feeling emanates through my body causing me to laugh. Shooting me a glare, Fondru ups her pace, causing me to sigh in disappointment. Fondru needs to loosen up or it'll wind up killing her one day.

Once again, distracted with my thoughts, I bump into her as she comes to a stop. Curious as to what has caused the reaction I see on her face as I make my way to stand beside her, I notice lines of words etched into the pillars.

By no intention of my own, my hand rises and reaches for a spot on the column where there is writing, in a language I am unfamiliar with. As my fingers touch it, bright lights shoot out from the letters into the sky rearranging themselves until they make out words in English.

> Fear not for what comes next
> Answer the riddles correctly
> To find that which you seek
> Answer the riddles wrong
> Find Death at one another's feet

"Rather gloomy, wouldn't you say," I quip, which garners a grunt from Fondru.

> The planet of Dreah is barren and gloomy
> However there is one place
> That life does flourish
> Riddle me this
>
> What plant will a sun not burn out?
> What plant can withstand a barren land,
> What plant needs a minimum of water?
> You will find many of this plant on Dreah
> Find the one with magic endowed
> From there you will find the key
> To unlock the first relic in need

"What plant could flourish on this planet?" I question. "It must be a trick. No plant could live here."

"Hmm," Fondru says as a faraway look enters her eyes.

"What is it? Where has your mind taken you?" I wonder.

* * *

As I think over the words from the riddle, an answer tugs at my mind, just out of reach. Knowing I need to rid myself of distractions lest I never figure it out, I mentally delve into my mind to go over all my studies and everything I have ever learned, knowing the answer lies within me.

Not many people know, since I appear human on the outside, is that I am actually only half human. My father was human and my mother was Lisantlian, which are the closest beings to human, skin tone wise. Due to being half Lisantlian, I am able to compartmentalize everything I have EVER learned, among other things.

I filter through items that have no bearing on the riddle and toss those to the side, until I finally come across when I was taught about Earth plants. Sunflowers, Roses, Lilies, Gardenias, Marigolds, Azaleas, Jasmines…no, no, no; none of these are right…I continue on until I come across a plant that lived within the deserts of Earth…cactuses.

I bring myself back to the present and notice Lilandro looking worriedly at me. "Did something happen?" I question, looking around to make sure I didn't miss anything of importance.

"No, my dear, I was just worried about where your mind wandered off to."

"Pssh, ok, whatever. I know the answer to this riddle." I stand and watch as he looks over at me expectantly. "A cactus."

"What is a cactus?"

"Hmm." I hadn't thought about the fact that Lilandro wouldn't know what a cactus is, and without him being aware of what it is and looks like; he won't be much help locating the one endowed with magic.

I grasp the comm in one hand and hold up a finger on my other as I see Lilandro about to open his mouth…more than likely to say something stupid. I type in 4224… "What's your code Lilandro?"

"5242…"

I type in both of our codes and request Captain Slyth to provide us with images and information on cactuses.

Not long after, the comm dings, letting us know that we have in incoming transmit. I open the transmission and relay the information and show the images of various cactuses.

"Let us continue on our journey to locate this cactus. We must make haste, so we can move onto the next planet as ordered."

"I will follow wherever you lead, Fondru."

Once again, we begin our trek over the dry, uncomfortable lands that are Dreah in search of cactuses. Sparse and far in between our hope dwindles as time passes by, and those cactuses we have come across, do not hold the key.

Needing a break, I drop to my knees and rest my head wearily on them. Tears of anguish and despair fill my eyes as worry overwhelms me.

"Do not worry so, Fondru. We shall continue on until we succeed in this mission. I have every faith in you." Lilandro rests his hand upon my shoulder, providing comfort.

With the added weight of hand upon shoulder, the ground beneath my knees crumble and I fall through the opening created. Screaming as I fall, arms flailing to try and find purchase when suddenly a golden halo surrounds my body slowing its descent as my screams halt.

"Fondru!!" Lilandro's voice echoes as it makes its way to my ears.

"I'm fine," I yell back, grinning at the sound of my voice mixing with the echoes of his.

The halo moves and adjusts my body until I am standing upright. Slightly nauseated from the movements it takes me a moment to realize that my feet are planted on solid ground and the halo has faded away until I no longer see it. A twinge of disappointment hits me at no longer being privy to the wondrous sight, I notice a new luminescent vibrant color out of the corner of my eye. I turn to look at it and can't help but gasp at the sight.

"Lilandro! Get your Socilian butt down here, ASAP!"

"How do you expect…"

"Just jump down, you big sissy," I interrupt.

Not hearing a sound, I glance up and see the golden halo surrounding Lilandro's body. I grin at the sight, breathless by it and the beauty of everything located within this cavern I fell into.

Before Lilandro's feet even touch the ground, I'm already heading towards the middle of a conglomerate of cactuses. A pull tugging at me, brings me to standing just to the right of a cactus that has varying colored flowers that fluctuate as though it's linked to the pulse of the planet.

"Oh my!" Lilandro gasps.

Rubbing my fingertips together to decrease the itchy feeling that overcame them, I'm distracted when Lilandro grasps my hand and rests his palm against my own until our fingertips touch one another's.

Staring into each other's eyes, bodies moving closer, heads tilted towards one another and just as we kiss, our fingertips touch the tip of the cactus and a shockwave slams into us, pushing us apart. Once I get my bearings back, I notice an object floating above the cactus.

"No way!" I exclaim.

"What?"

Not bothering to answer I hurry to the cactus and wrap my hands around the object. At first touch of the mystic relic, I hear a thud from behind me. I turn, seeing Lilandro knocked to the ground. Relic in hand I hurry over to him, kneeling at his side.

"Thank you so much for finding the first relic piece for us. It is much appreciated," cackling follows the hoarse maniacal voice from behind me.

"Over my dead…" Something knocks into the back of my head, making me fall to the ground as darkness consumes me.

To Be Continued…

About the author

Marsha Black is a mother to two boys, loves to read and write when not working or spending time with her kids. Books helped her escape reality when needed and her hope is to provide the same escape to other readers. She is big on anything paranormal and fantasy so most of her writing is geared towards those genres.

Also written by Marsha Black:

The Triplet's Curse – Hope's Story (Book One)
The Triplet's Curse – Destiny's Story (Book Two)

Liasa's Tail of Woe (Located in the Dark Waters: A Mermaid Anthology)

Feel free to follow and/or friend at the below links:

Website: https://redrose0881.wixsite.com/authormarshablack
Facebook Page: https://www.facebook.com/Author.The.Triplets.Curse/
Bookbub: https://www.bookbub.com/profile/marsha-black

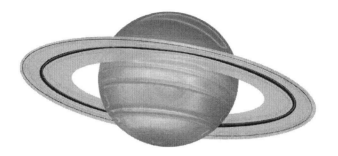

Fifty Days Forced to Love: A Space Conspiracy
Paige Clendenin

Aries

When life on Space Station Orion turns upside down and the world that eighteen-year-old Aries has known for all her life is questioned, will she conform to the conspiracy, or will she fight for her own rights when her life is hanging in the balance? When summer 2362 brings on a whole new level of insanity, will Aries be caught up in the new rule that her age group will only have Fifty Days Forced to Love, or will she choose death as the alternative?

If Aries doesn't mate up within fifty days, she will be put to an injected demise and be one of the first eighteen-year-olds aboard Orion forced to die for being single.

Aries was training to become a fighter piolet and follow in her parent's footsteps, she never wanted to be forced to mate up or be told how many children she could have. She wasn't sure she wanted any of that in the first place. Why the new laws? Why now?

Ender

Nineteen-year-old Ender was thrilled when he had just missed the age cut off for the current madness going on around him. He had been working as a private maintenance man for Orion and its leaders since he was thirteen, so when it was announced that a ship would be sent out for fifty days, he jumped on the opportunity to take a job aboard. He didn't join ship Fifty Days Forced to Love as a potential mate, and never once thought that he wanted to find one, but to work on board would be a fantastic opportunity for him and his desired promotion.

When he joined the team on the ship, he knew that all the madness had just been a conspiracy to rid the ship of a quarter of its population so that the Captain's cushy life wasn't jeopardized. After all, the inhabitance still had 100 years until the gamma-rays on Earth were no longer a threat. One of the horrible things about working with the leaders was knowing things he wished he didn't.

Ender was eight days from being done with his work on the ship, when a trip to the basement exposed something that he would have never guessed possible.

Together

When Ender and Aries lock eyes in the basement aboard ship, will their desperate need to be alone trump the spark they feel growing between them. Will Orion accept Aries breaking the rules by falling for someone not in her mating group, or will they have to fight for their right to love and perhaps even their lives?

Will they live only eight more days or years to come?

Fifty Days Forced to Love:
A Space Conspiracy

Dear Population of Space Station Orion,
    We have recently noticed a population issue on deck Orion. Our people have lived peacefully in the space station for two-hundred years now, with hopes to return to Earth in one-hundred years from today once bio-gamma rays have dissipated. Our population has since grown to an outrageous number of nine-thousand-six-hundred-seventy-two human inhabitants. Our logs show that we can only hold ten thousand inhabitants for the duration of our stay to survive. To our dismay, we have had to ask two-thousand elderly to volunteer to be put to an injected demise.
    We had just over the expected number volunteer between the age of seventy and one-hundred. Their demise took place yesterday, and today they will be released beyond with a galaxy themed celebration to be had by all! Please, take a moment of silence for all the members of Orion lost to this decision. Unfortunately, that was not enough to suffice a change; big enough to change our outcome. It has now been decided that every year starting July 16th, which is tomorrow, that an annual ship will be sent out further into space for fifty days filled with all boy and girl teens between the age of sixteen and eighteen. Those teens are to find a mate that will be their mate for life.
    Any eighteen-year-old that emerges each year unmated, will be put to demise. Those of you this year that are sixteen and seventeen are

lucky to have at least one more year to search if a mate is not decided, but those that are eighteen this year, will only have the fifty days to fall in love. The ship will leave at eight-hundred in the morning. Once mated, each mated couple may only have one child in the duration of their life. This will take the total down to our successful number by the time of our landing on Earth.

    Sincerely Captain V. Sanders

Current age capacity for this the year 2362

Sixteen-year-olds	36 Male 29 Female
Seventeen-year-olds	42 Male 56 Female
Eighteen-year-olds	49 Male 38 Female

May Orion be with you all!

Ps: Any of you that fall into this category that do not report in the morning will automatically be put to your demise.

Meet Aries

42 Days Later

    A nock raps on the bathroom door, and I begrudgingly climb out of the shower and wrap a towel around my bare body. I have spent forty-two days in this hell hole so far, and still I have no desire to find a "mate" any more than I did on day one.

    I open the door to a tall middle-aged woman with a set of white clothing

    "Your time is up, Miss Aries, you might be missing your mate, no need to spend all your time in the showers," she smiles as she hands me my crisp bleach white clothes. "You're either in here or in hiding most the day."

    "With all due respect, ma'am, I would rather hide than find a mate, I'm only eighteen," I sigh taking the clothes into the room, shutting the door on the woman.

    I can hear the woman shed an exasperated sigh at my expense as she walks away. I know that she is thinking about how this is my one and only year to find a life mate and I only have eight days left to do it in.

    I don't seem to feel that way about it. I think I would rather meet my demise than to feel forced into something that should be my choice. I was going to be perfectly fine not ever having a mate, or children. My plan was to never add to the population in the first place.

What threat was I?

I wanted to train to be a fighter pilot for Orion. I know that sounds crazy, but what you must know about the space station Orion is that we are always being threatened by other space stations and space entities coming to knock on our door in a not so polite way! My mother and father were fighter piolets, as was my big brother Jaxx. They all died fighting for our people, and that was the greatest honor any of them could have had.

Unfortunately, that put me alone from the time I was fifteen, but I'm tough enough. I wanted the chance to follow in their flight path, so to say.

I may look meek being only five-four, and one-hundred-ten pounds. My blond hair and blue eyes do nothing for my appearance, but I am as hardcore tough as it comes.

I quickly dry off and put on the horrible cloths that they call finding a mate appropriate. Skin tight tank top and white stretch cotton pants with no shoes.

Come fall in love with me now!

On Orion I would be wearing something more conducive to my nature and more practical for life in the sky. Instead, I towel dry my hair and walk out of the bathroom into the open rooms that is a forced love breading ground of white cotton clad teenagers.

There are more eighteen-year-old boys than girls this year, about ten or so, which means that even if I am the only girl that isn't paired off by day forty-two, there are still plenty of the male population chasing after me. Plus, if we were desperate enough we could down mate with a sixteen or seventeen-year-old.

No thanks!

"Not now, Mark," I say to seventeen-year-old Markouss Cassiopeia who has been following me like a puppy for the past ten days.

My guess is he hasn't found a life mate yet and has decided to move up the ladder to find one.

"You know you want me…" Mark says. "I would make a good mate and daddy to our kid."

I look at him in disgust, leaving him in my dust, heading towards my place of solace. On day two, I found a breaker room in the basement behind the engine that no one ever comes to. They wonder where I go all day long, but I will never tell.

Meet Ender

    I slide down
      the maintenance shaft of the ship, looking for the source of the knocking noise that frequents the engine room.
    "Hey Ender," my boss yells down at me.
    "What's up, Abraxo?" I ask the middle-aged man staring down at me.
    "Check the breaker room behind the engine to make sure there isn't a fault in one of the fuses, will you?"
    "Will do," I say as I continue to slip through the maintenance tunnel. The man's face disappears from the top of the shaft above me.
    My broad shoulders make it hard to maneuver through these corridors.
    I'm nineteen years old, and didn't qualify to join the mating madness, which I don't mind. I have been a hardcore service man for Orion since I was thirteen, and I was left on my own. My ma died during my birth, and my old man got blown to bits in a secondary engine explosion servicing the Orion.
    I don't care, though. I miss my pops, but he raised me up a good man. I'm honorable and honest, and work as hard as any grown man around. I have never looked for a mate, and for that I'm glad that I just missed the cut off for this crazy population conspiracy.
    I know for a fact working directly with Orion and its runners that we aren't that bad off. Vector, our captain, is just scared that we are going

to have to start to ration food and commodities. If that were to happen, then his cushy life would go to hell.

I would stop the bastard if it weren't for the fact that he's my boss's boss, and I would be "put to demise" if I were to step in on my own. The people of Orion fear Vector, but to be honest, he is far more laid back than our captain before, his father, Nico.

I shimmy down the rest of the way to the bottom of the ship. I volunteered to work this piece of shit ship for a change, and it makes me wish I had stayed put on Orion.

I'm only here eight more days, so what does it matter now, anyway?

My feet hit the ground, the thudding sound becoming more apparent. I go straight to the engine and pull out my handkerchief. It's nearly one-hundred-fifteen degrees in the engine room, and I don't want to hang out here any more than I need to. Using the handkerchief, I dab at my sweat already pooling on my face.

The thudding is intermittent and only happens a few times a day, but it is just enough to make Abraxo and I concerned, so for that, we have decided to check things out.

I turn to face the flat side of the wall that cuts the engine from the store rooms and the breaker room, making those places at least twenty degrees cooler, but still hot.

I feel along the wall to make sure that I'm not missing something, but I can't feel a bubble, bump, or imperfection of any kind.

"What the hell?" I say out loud because I notice the noise stopping altogether.

I wish I would have figured out the source of it while I'm down here instead of having to come back next time we hear it. To be honest, the knocking sound almost sounds like footsteps, but there are no other people allowed down here besides Abraxo, once a week, to service the engine, me, and the night time maintenance man, Darby, and he and I are never down here at the same time.

I begin to head to the ladder that takes me back topside, but I decide better. Abraxo wanted me to check the breaker room, so I better give it a look over before I go back up, or he might have my hide.

I walk over to the breaker room door, looking around one last time to make sure that there isn't something that I might be missing. I can't see or hear anything around me. I try the door handle, but it is tight for some reason. I don't remember ever having trouble getting into this room before.

I try even harder, and it comes open a bit, just to slam shut again.

"What the hell! Is someone in there?" I ask, mustering up my most stern voice. No response.

I try to pull the door again, this time using all my strength. The door flings back, sending me flying backwards, but I am quick enough to regain my balance, and stand flat on my feet.

I begin to feel anger bubbling up in me, but it is cut short when I see the inhabitance of the closet. Standing tall and proud wearing all white from head to toe is one of the girls to be mated. She has long blond hair and blue eyes, but she doesn't look meek at all. She stands tall and proud, waiting for my response.

"Who are you?" I ask.

"Who are you?" I get as a response.

"The name's Ender," I say to the most beautiful woman that I think I have ever seen.

Aries

In the forty-two days that I have been aboard ship happily ever after, and certainly not my month and ten days of visiting the basement, have I ever seen Ender. I don't recognize him from Orion either. He must be an engineer or maintenance man on the space station. Those we rarely see. Ender is wearing a tight black t-shirt and torn up blue jeans with smears of oil or space junk on them. He has deep brown hair that falls in small ringlets on his forehead. Now he is just standing here with the most interesting set of golden-green eyes I have ever seen.

"The name's Aries," I say in response.

"Aries," he says, trying out my name for the first time. "What are you doing in here? You should be up top with your mate!"

I give a small bahaha kind of laugh.

"I don't have a mate," I say, sure of myself.

"No mate?" he says, shocked.

"None," I respond.

"I don't understand," Ender mutters "there are only eight days left."

"You sound like everyone else," I scoff. "Just ticking down time till I look the grim reaper in the face."

"That's not what I meant at all," he sounds gentile and sincere.

"What did you mean?" I try to steady my nerves.

"I just mean someone as beautiful as you should have been paired up by now!" He grimaces. "I didn't mean that either…"

"Never mind," I cut him short. "I'm not in trouble, am I? For being down here?"

"No one is supposed to be down here but me, my boss, and one other guy, the night maintenance man." He looks down. "It's in the rule manual."

"So, I'm going to get in trouble," I surmise.

"You know what, Aries?" He gives me a sideways smile. "We'll call it our little secret this time."

"Don't do me any favors," I say, as I walk out of the tiny room and towards the emergency access ladder that I have been taking every day for a while now.

I begin to climb up the ladder, wondering what is going to happen to me because of my rule breaking, or if Ender will hold to his word and keep quiet.

"You can come back any time you want," Ender yells up the tube that I am already half way up.

I choose to not respond to him. I don't know who he is or what his word is worth. What I do know about him is that he must be older than eighteen, because he is working aboard the ship, not being forced to love on it.

* * *

Eight Hours Later

I wake with a start. The day had been hell. One teenage boy after another, trying to save their own life, by making mine miserable. I understand that the thought of being sent to their demise is scary to them, but I still can't bring myself to want to settle with one of them.

I can't believe I dreamt of Ender. I don't even know him. I know Mark the annoying seventeen-year-old far better than I know Ender, and I am dreaming of him.

And what a dream it was.

We were running from something, I don't know what, but we were trying to get away for sure. For some reason, what we were running from, we were running together and for the same reason. I didn't get to finish my dream, so I don't know the outcome, or why I was dreaming of the man from the basement.

Now, even while awake, I can't get him off my mind. I know that perhaps the only other way to see him again, would be to go back down to the breaker room, and pray he will show up. That is, if I even want to take my chances.

I turn over and look at the clock on the wall. I share the room with four other girls, all dreaming of their mates and their mated futures together. I am so different than any of them.

In the dim light, I can tell that it is only three-hundred hours in the morning.

I must get more sleep. If I don't, then I won't be worth anything come morning. I turn in bed trying to get comfortable as sleep tries to take me over once more.

I can't help but hope I dream of Ender once more.

Ender

I can't believe it is only three-hundred in the morning. I haven't woken in the night for as long as I can remember. Tonight, has been so weird though. Along with not waking up at night in years, I haven't dreamt either.

At least not one that I remember.

I can't believe it either, out of all the things I could dream about, I dreamt about Aries. How could I dream about her? I had only barely known her for a few short minutes.

I couldn't stop thinking about her this evening though, and because of that, I must have gone to bed thinking of her. The dream was so weird, though, she and I were being chased by someone or something. We were both being chased together and for the same reason. We ran hand in hand until we found what we were looking for. Oddly enough, the source of our search out was a small fighter jet that I have never seen before on the decks of Orion.

I spin my legs off my bed and look around my private room. I mean Darby and I share it, but neither of us ever sleep in here at the same time, so for the most part, it's as private as it gets.

I get up and walk across the floor. I notice that I am still as sweaty hot as I was when I went to bed even though I am only in my boxers. I decide to take a shower and wash off again to try to cool down.

I silently slip my boxers off, wrap a towel around my waste, and walk towards the shower room, still thinking about Aries.

The girl I can't get off my mind.

I let the water pour over me, perhaps it will refresh my body and my mind. I only have two short hours before I go back to work. I will check again today to see if Aries returns to the basement.

I am bound and determined to get to know her. For some reason, my heart and my soul want me to.

I know I could never be with her. If she doesn't mate now, then she will surly die.

Aries

I put my feet on the floor once the alarm rings in our room. All five of us getting dressed in the day's white clothing put on our dressers the night before. I never did fall back to sleep.

I look into the mirror, noticing the dark circles under my eyes. I brush my hair out and get dressed as quick as I can, making sure that I get in the shower room first. I don't need to shower now, but I take a rag and a hand towel with me so that I can wash up.

Perhaps some cool water to my face will help brighten my eyes.

I have seven days until touch down back on Orion. I decide that if I have chosen not to mate, that I would at least be myself.

Once back in my room, I pull out the small make-up pallet I have created out of black berry and strawberry pigment and start to line my eyes with thick, black, berry scented liner. I use the red pigment and a drop of water to smooth my lips over with the deep red color. I am going for a pinkish color, so I take my towel and blot a few times until I have the desired result.

Lots of girls here wear homemade makeup and perfumes to attract the male specimen, but I have refused up until today. I still don't take the hour it takes them to do their primping, curling, straightening, pinning up, and pulling down hair. I just wear my simple long, wavy, blunt hair style that I always do.

I look at Justine, Suski, Meg, and Arrabella before leaving the room. They quit talking to me much about day five, when they had already been paired up for three days.

They will be in the room another forty-five minutes getting ready for their already paired off counterparts.

I walk out to Mark and his sixteen-year-old buddy, Pen. Both have one or two years left to pair up, but they have both been on my tail since day thirty. Also, there is Branson, Lunner, and Star Dust Madox from my age group that follow me as soon as I leave my dwelling.

By the time I make it to breakfast, I have eight guys following me, asking me if they can get my breakfast, drink, straw, napkin, anything they can think of. Most days, I do it all alone, not allowing them to do a thing, but today, I am feeling spunky, and let them do it all, as I sit thinking about Ender and if I will ever see him again.

I don't mean to give these boys hope, but at some point, you must give in to the thought that by the end of this week, we will probably all be dead. Unless I decide to pick one of them just for survival sake.

The thought of settling disgusts me to my core.

Ender

I find myself looking over my shoulder and around each corner for Aries. I don't get to eat with the population which is where I'm sure she is, being doted over by teenage boy after teenage boy.

From what I can tell, she is so much better than that. She seems like the kind of girl that can take care of herself, and I hope that I get the chance to find out.

Abraxo is waiting for me when I slid my punch card into the computer. The door slides open and I walk in, grasping Abraxo's hand, giving it a firm squeeze.

"You hear anything else down below boss?"

"Not today," the man clearly six inches shorter than me replies.

I can't help but feel my shoulders slump a bit. I walk away trying not to feel so defeated.

"What's on the docket for today?" I ask as I turn back towards Abraxo.

"Well since you did so well yesterday alleviating the source of the sound," he grins, "you get to service the engine by yourself today!"

"You serious?" I ask surprised, I have only been able to service it with you, never alone."

"It's day forty-three here on board and I have learned that you are more than capable."

"Yes sir," I say with a grin on my face, half happy that I am being trusted, but the other half of me is happy that I will be down there if Aries decides to break some more rules.

I grab the maintenance toolbelt for the engine and squeeze back down the tunnel that leads me to the basement of the craft and perhaps closer to the girl that I can't shake.

As soon as I hit the ground, I go straight to the breaker room, listening for something, anything that might show that Aries is around, but there isn't any. I open the door to old breakers and rusted metal, closing it in disappointment.

I will go to work on the engine in hopes that I will see the beautiful Aries at least one more time.

Aries

I had to get away from Mark and the other goons. They were beginning to get on my bad side, which is ever growing in a place like this.

Why in the world would those guys think I would want any of them to touch my feet! When a foot rub was suggested, I took off towards the only place I feel at home these days.

I know now that my footsteps must be making too much noise, so I must come up for an alternate way to get down there. I stop to think if I am doing this for myself, or so I can see Ender again?

Perhaps a bit of both!

An idea crosses my mind and I know it's crazy, but it might be a better way to get to the basement than what I have been doing. I walk back into my housing pod now empty of its twitter pated love-birds. It crosses my mind to just stay in here, but there are regular checks and I would surly by shooed back out into the mating pool.

Instead, I pull the spare sheet out of my trunk and the cutting blades out of my wardrobe and start walking back in the direction of the emergency service hatch.

I look around for good measure, before cutting and tying the sheet together, making a strong rope. I loop the rope around my waist and tie the other end to a small hook just inside the tunnel. I yank on the makeshift rope to make sure that it will hold my weight, and I think it will.

I turn around backwards and slightly jump, using a hand over fist technique to lower myself down, my feet only hitting the ladder ever fifth rung or so. My feet dance lightly as I repel down to my sanctuary of peace and hopefully towards Ender.

Ender

I turn around when I hear a slight patting sound every few seconds that appears to be coming from the emergency service ladder. I stand awaiting what might be coming. It doesn't sound anything like it has the past several days that Aries has been coming down here, it's almost so soft you can't hear it.

I stand listening, when I see the end of a white rope fall a few feet out of the end of the tunnel. Seconds later I can see Aries repelling down into the room, her back to me. She hits the ground with a soft bare footed thud. I watch as she gives the rope a slight yank as it falls off her waist. She then places the end of the rope I can now tell is a bed sheet on the last rung of the ladder so it's out of the way.

She turns towards me and we lock eyes. Surprise ever building on her face.

"What the hell Ender, you scared the shit out of me!" Aries says while trying to catch her breath.

"I'm sorry," I say, "it was never my intention to scare you."

"It's okay," she laughs now.

I laugh too, hoping she doesn't think that I am laughing at her… I would never laugh at her.

"What are you doing down here?" I ask, hoping she doesn't think I am referring to her not being topside mating.

"I can't do it" she whispers, all seriousness returning to her voice as she walks past me.

"Do what?" I ask softly.

"I can't be forced to pair off! I won't do it!"

"I understand," I say. "I would have never done it either."

"Feel lucky you are nineteen," she says with a playful smile, while she nudges my arm.

I look down at my arm, curious about the feeling she causes me to have.

"What a serious maintenance man you are," she teases me.

I shake my head with a smirk on my face, trying to figure this girl out, and why I want to be around her. She is as puzzling and confusing as can be.

We could never work out if anything more was decided. She is going to be put to demise in one week from today.

She doesn't sound afraid at all, just annoyed that this is happening to her. I can't put my finger on what draws me to her! She is everything wrapped together. All sarcasm and sweetness wrapped up into one small hardcore badass package.

"What if I helped you?" I ask out of nowhere. I don't know why I asked, because I don't know how I could even begin to save this girl.

"How," she asks exasperatedly.

"I don't know yet," I say as I walk two steps closer to her. "But I will figure it out."

I reach out my hand towards her face, but second guess my gesture and let my hand hang in midair. Why am I being like this I didn't want to fall in love.

I can't help it!

She takes one small step back and then freezes, perhaps rethinking the situation. To my surprise, she reaches her own hand up to meet mine. She grabs my hand, lacing her fingers in mine. She then steps two steps forward, bringing our joined hands to our side.

"How would you help me?" she asks soft and quiet this time with a gentle inquisitive nature.

"I don't know yet," I say to her, "But we have seven days to find out."

* * *

Three Days Later

I look into her eyes. We have done nothing more than hold hands, but I have found a reason to be in the basement every day now since she started coming down. My boss seems a bit suspicious, but I am never down here for long any time.

"So, it's a plan?" she asks.

"Or at least part of one," I smile.

"I don't want to die," she admits for the first time since I have known her.

"You won't, I promise," I whisper to her.

We have talked about every outcome and every plan that we can think of. Not many get us to safety. After all, on board Orion, there isn't many places to hide.

Aries

I look him in the eye, feeling things I never planned on feeling for anyone ever. I can't help but have an intense want to be around him. He is serviced to Orion and its leaders, and I am going to die in four days unless we can come up with something.

How are things going to end?

He reaches up and takes my chin in his hand, trying to reassure me that all will be well. For some reason, neither of us want to move. Our eyes remain locked for longer than they ever have.

"I will always try to save you," he says to me in his deep baritone voice.

"And I you," I try to promise him the same. I know that if he is discovered trying to help me, he will meet the same demise as I do.

Our gaze holds for several minutes before either one of us move. He starts to inch closer to me, and I him. What is planned to happen, I have no idea, but I know that I will let what will happen, happen.

He continues to advance towards me, his hand coming up from my chin, up my cheek, and to the back of my head, his other hand joining. He pulls me in closer so that we can feel each other. His lips brush against mine, and mine against his.

We kiss deep and strong. Me learning that I care for him perhaps a bit more than I thought I did. Our kiss becomes desperate as we sit on the floor of the breaker room. My hands gripping his muscles under his shirt.

He slides in even closer, leaving not even an inch between us. I pull my hands further up his back, resulting in his thin black t-shirt coming up. I reach up and pull it off him altogether.

Without a shirt, I see that Ender is much stronger than he appears fully dressed. His abs shine with sweat and desperation.

"What are we doing here?" he whispers deeply between breaths.

"I want to be with you, Ender, if I only get to be with one man in my life, if I die in four days or ninety-years-old, I want to be with you!"

Ender

I climb the ladder topside to finish my days' work. My body busy from the adrenaline left from Aries' touch. I took her innocence today, making us each other's first and most likely last.

Feeling my connection with her even stronger now, I know now that I must save her.

I must.

"Where have you been?" Abraxo asks as he walks up behind me.

"Checking the breakers sir," I say in response.

"Good work Ender," he says, walking off distracted.

I go off and finish my day's work, thinking of Aries and hoping beyond all hope that she and I can figure this all out.

* * *

Four Days Later

There are only a few hours before we land back on-board Orion. Ordinarily, my crew would be one of the last ones to leave, but I have given an award-winning performance to Abraxo and convinced him that I am sick. He said that he could manage without me, that Darby would help today and that he would catch me on the outside.

I hope this works!

I sneak out of bed, and instead of continuing down the maintenance hall, I turn towards the maid service corridors. I peer around the corner. All the maids should be out helping the mated get ready to leave. When I look, I see one young maid, gathering some towels and a set of white clothing. I wait in the shadows long enough to watch her leave the room and disappear out of the hall and into the common room.

I sneak into the room and quickly grab the male version of the white clothes that Aries wears. I throw off my clothes and shove them into a nearby trash can, along with my work boots, sadly. I put on the awful tank top and pants that they provide for the teens on ship. They were made from sheep on Orion and were left white.

I muff my hair a bit, hoping that I can blend in. I mean I know if anyone were to investigate they would realize that they don't know me, but let's just hope that never happens.

For now, I am going to find Aries, and hope that our plan works.

Aries

All the girls look at me sideways as they pack their things. Various maids come in and out to help us, each one of them giving me sad looks as they pass by. I don't have much on my own, just one small bag with my makeup and combat boots. I hoist my bag over my shoulder and walk out of the door.

The first thing I see are about six guys pleading for my hand. They are all begging to be mated to me, offering their space worth wealth. Each of them eighteen and desperate for me, the last girl, saving their lives.

"I have found a mate," I reluctantly say to them.

They don't believe me though, and for that they begin to go down in a mix of anger, sadness, and fear.

I walk the common room towards the maids' quarters. I will never be allowed to go in, but I will watch for who comes out. I stand, looking at the opening, hoping that Ender will have succeeded.

"Miss," a hand taps me from behind.

"Leave me alone Mar…" I turn around my words cut short.

It isn't Mark at all, it's Ender, and he is standing tall, wearing white from head to toe.

"Together?" he asks.

"Together," I agree.

We take each other by the hand, walking slowly towards a darkened corner.

"This is going to work," he kisses me.

"I hope so," I sigh.

A shutter occurs all around us as I slip a bit more tightly into Ender's arms. It takes a minute to figure out what is going on.

"We have landed on Orion," I whisper.

Ender

I hold her in my arms as I push the fear for our lives down into the pit of my stomach. I don't know how this is going to work out.

Beeeeeeeep, a loud speaker sounds all around us.

"This is your captain speaking," Captain Vector's voice booms into the ship. "Welcome back to Space Station Orion, we are happy to have you back. Currently, will all the mated members move forward for the parade of partners. Each of the members Orion will be awaiting you to be presented to them. Your names will be announced at the beginning of your march. Finally, all the single members will be announced, starting with the sixteen-year-olds, the seventeen-year-olds followed by all to meet their demise of the eighteen-year-old group. We will celebrate you all. That is all."

"Who are we going to say I am?" I ask with a grunt.

"Markouss Cassiopeia," she answers me with doubt in her eyes.

I don't choose to ask her any questions, she must know what she is doing. For now, I am Markouss Cassiopeia, and I hope that his name will save us all.

The gates raise to the masses, all the members aboard Orion are waiting there for us. Four pair of sixteen-year-olds are announced first. Aries is looking around trying to take in the situation.

Six sets out of the seventeen-year-old group are announced next, and Aries seems to look a little less worried. She looks behind us and a small sad frown comes across her face. I look behind us to meet her gaze. She is looking at all the single members of her group.

"Is Markouss going to die today?" I finally ask her.

"No, he's seventeen," she responds, looking ahead now. "They will announce his name though when he comes through after us, but it will be a while since he is single," she gives me a weak smile. "We will need to make sure to get as far away as possible by then."

"You said there are about thirty-eight couples in the eighteen-year-old category, correct?" I ask.

"About that," she responds.

"Then, we need to be one of the first ones through, don't we?"

"That's right," she gives me another weak smile as she grabs my hand.

We cut forward, knowing that they will begin the announcement of our group soon. Cheers erupt every time one of the matched couples glides though. We maneuver through the group, trying to get out of here as fast as possible and as far away from Markouss as we can.

Aries

He holds my hand so tight. The girls that I shared a pod with give me an even more sideways glance now. They know something is off, but my hopes are that they are questioning themselves on how they could have missed someone as sexy as Ender.

We are standing in the third position, waiting to be presented to the people. The last seventeen-year-old couple moves out of the doorway and into the parade of people.

"Anesto Dist and Patsetie Myer," the voice announces the first couple.

The entire ship erupts in even larger cheers as the eighteen-year-couples come through. Ender sides up closer to me, giving my hand a squeeze.

"Sammuelle Crew and Libra Parkhill," the announcer announces the next name, and we step forward.

"Name?" a man leans down to take our names down on a piece of paper.

"Markouss Cassiopeia and Aries Ophelia" Ender answers.

The man tears off the paper and hands it to the announcer. I hold my breath as Ender gives me another light squeeze.

"Markouss Cassiopeia and Aries Ophelia," the announcer says mine and Enders fake name, and we begin what looks like a mile-long walk with people on both sides of us.

My mind tunes out all the cheers as well as the names being called behind us. I am fighting all want to take off running. We must walk to get to where we need to go safely.

Ender

    I hold her hand tightly as the cheers for us dissipate and the ones for the next couple take over. I know we are not out of the woods yet though, and for that, I will be on edge.

    Aries is nearly holding her breath. Neither of us have anyone on board that we are related to, so the only people that will know us are the choice few that we spend our time with.

    "Seventeen-year-old Markouss Cassiopeia and eighteen-year-old Sandra Jonas," the announcer calls.

    Aries didn't notice the name being called because she appears to be in her own world. I shake her a little and the reality that what just happened hits her.

    "I didn't think he paired up," she gasps.

    The crowds catch on as cheers turn to rumor filled murmurs. We begin to speed up, but the couples in front of us block us from getting anywhere.

    From the corner of my eye, I can see Orion guards spill into the room from both sides of us, half of them head towards the real Markouss, and the other half towards us. Markouss and his mate stand still awaiting what is going to happen. They will be in the clear, but we won't be.

    Aries and I break free from the mated pack and begin to push our way through the crowd. This way it will be a bit more difficult for the guards to get to us.

    "Ender," someone calls to me.

Aries and I look around for the source of the voice. To the left, near a hatch in the wall stands Abraxo motioning towards us.

I nod at Aries, letting her know that this is a person that we can trust.

I hope.

Aries

We run towards a man that I have never seen. He is wearing the same type of clothes that Ender wears when his is working, but at this point, can I trust him.

"Abraxo," Ender says when we reach the middle-aged man.

I recognize the name as being Ender's boss on board happily ever after.

"What's going on kid?" the man asks as we enter the hatch, him shutting the door after us.

"I love her," he responds. "She was who was making noise in the basement."

"I see," he says.

"Hi, I'm Aries," I shake the man's hand.

We run down a service hall that I have never seen in all my years on Orion. There is a lot of commotion going on in the commons deck.

"I don't know why it has to be this way," I breath.

"Vector and his cushy ass life I tell ya," Abraxo says in response.

"Just like I was telling you," Ender says.

We continue to run down the hall until we hit a small open room about five by five. There are three doors in front of us.

"The right one takes you back on deck," Abraxo says. "Middle takes you to a part of the ship that isn't ever used. I could bring you food and supplies little by little." He stops for a moment.

"And the left one?" I ask.

"Well, that'll take you to a small jet plane. In the coordinates are the directions to Space Station Aquarius. They will house you and take care of you, but..."

"We will never see each other again," Ender finishes.

"That's right my young friend."

I look between Ender and the man that has been his boss and friend for years.

"We can try to make it work here," I say.

"We can't," Ender whispers. "I promised that I would get you to safety."

"I don't want you to leave your home," I cry.

"This is neither one of our homes anymore," Ender assures me. "We will make a new home together."

Ender

I give Abraxo a hug and take Aries by the hand. We quickly enter the door that will take us to the small jet.

"Run Ender!" Abraxo calls from the door way as we see him being apprehended by a guard.

The remaining guards head our direction at a breakneck speed.

"Run Aries… Run," I yell while putting her in front of me.

If the guards get to me then maybe she would have a chance of getting away.

At the end of the hall is another door. Aries hits the door and it flings open exposing a mechanical room with a tiny two-seater fighter jet. I spin around and close the door, looking for a lock or at very least something to block it with.

Gun shots ring out from behind the door. Orion has only a few guns, but they feel they are needed when a prisoner runs, someone is unruly without control, or I guess when two people who love each other are trying to escape to another space station.

There isn't any lock but there is a large air jack beside the door. Aries and I slide it over, hoping it holds the door long enough to keep the guards out.

"In there," I say, while pointing to the jet.

Aries flies over to the driver's door of the craft and hops in, leaving the passenger's seat for me. I jump in, hoping she knows how to fly this thing, because I don't.

I watch her as she goes to work putting in the coordinates to Space Station Aquarius into the global positioning system.

Out of the corner of my eye, I can see the air jack go flying as armed guards come rushing into the room.

"Hurry," I breath.

Aries hits a button above her that opens a hatch door in the side of the ship. Then she turns the key to the system and punches in a lot of sequences that I don't recognize.

In just a few seconds, the craft juts forward and begins its decent out of Space Station Orion, bullets blazing behind us.

The suction of our takeoff paired with the atmosphere, causes the guards to suck out of the ship and into outer space.

I look at Aries who is steadily speeding in the direction she is being told to go by the g.p.s. I don't know what will happen if or when we get to where we are going, but one thing I do know, is that no matter what happens, if I am with the girl of my dreams, I will be happy.

"I love you Aries Ophelia," I whisper as I kiss her hand.

"I love you too," she smiles.

Aries

  I breath in the dusty small of the aircraft. I know how to fly even though I have only been through simulation. My parents and brother instilled it in me. I was born for this.
  My hopes are that Space Station Aquarius will allow me to train to be a fighter piolet and maybe try to save some of the people of Orion. It isn't fair that we have been made to go through what we have, but there is one thing that I wouldn't trade from this whole experience, and that's Ender.
  I watch as he looks back and forth from me and the space before us.
  I may have started this thing with fifty days forced to love, but who knew I only needed eight.

※ ※ ※

Five Years Later

  We made it to the Space Station Aquarius in three days. We were tired and exhausted, but we were excepted on board. We had reached communication with them on day two and convinced them that we were not a threat therefore no shots rang out and safety was had.

We quickly figured out that things were ran very peacefully and the people were treated with respect. Captain Chinnwey integrated us into society instantly with an announcement that we were to be accepted.

Ender and I have loved each other since day one and will continue to love each other until the end of space and time.

Today we find out if the baby that is growing inside me is a boy or a girl. Either way our family will be complete. If we will have more children is unclear for our future, but at least we have a future that we can decide.

"It's a boy," the doctor says with a smile on his face.

"Hello little Abraxo," Ender touches my stomach.

We don't know if Abraxo lived or died because of us, but either way, his memory will live on in our child.

We don't know what our future holds, but one thing is for sure, our love for each other has never been forced.

"I will love you both until the end of my days," Ender whispers to me and our unborn child.

"As will we," I smile up at him. "As will we."

The End.

About the author

Hi, I am Paige Clendenin, I live in Illinois with my best friend and husband of 13 years, David. We have four daughters who, along with him are the inspiration behind my writing. I love to write, read, dance, and act silly! I am eclectic and fun, and love who I am.

www.facebook.com/paigeclendeninauthor
www.paigeclendeninauthor.com

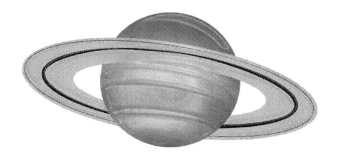

Bonus!

Hope you are enjoying 42 and Beyond, as 42+ authors go beyond the stars with their epic Space Opera Stories! If you have made it to the end of this book, then you have discovered the bonus! This is a mystery story. Each Volume will have one. There will be a contest should you read all four volumes and find the four mystery stories. Those who guess the authors to the mystery story will be entered to win a prize of EPIC proportions!

Read the story and make your guess. Then, fill out this form to enter the epic contest to win an ebook basket or even paperbacks of all four volumes!

https://docs.google.com/forms/d/e/1FAIpQLSdg0kxR-PrcQXoYQwBKj2Rmz9urBmvUaU8lXhRDim1aTFl7SQ/viewform

Intergalactic Bridal Market

Chapter One

  Vera finally could taste the freedom that was so close to being hers. For the last twelve years of her life she had been, what she considered to be, an inmate of the Northern Hemisphere Foster System. Her mother, a single parent, had died when Vera was six years old. There had been a plasma accident at the factory where she worked as an engineer on the giant plasma engines that powered the space craft that Earth was producing as fast as they could. Intergalactic space travel had become a reality during the early 3800's, although it had taken Earth about two hundred odd years to amalgamate what was known as the First Fleet and prepare for more than simply scientists and explorers loaded with uni-credits to venture out into space. Vera's mother had been one of the first engineers to work on commercial space craft, but that was before the accident that killed her and left Vera an orphan.

  Twelve years in the foster system had given Vera a hard outlook on life and the universe. She hated anything to do with space. After all, it was the plasma that was integral to space travel that had ripped her from a loving home and placed her into one group home after the other. The last two years she had been under the legal guardianship of the Bennet Teen Group Home. Run by an obese woman and a bean-pole of a man, the most unlikely couple continuously found new ways to torture the teens placed into their care by the American section of the Northern Hemisphere Government. There was never any physical evidence to support the few accusations that the most outspoken of teens were able to get through the closely guarded lines of communication that the Bennet's monitored, and so the government continued to send teens to the Bennets and give them legal guardianship over minors considered too disruptive to be found a permanent home with a loving family. Vera was certain there was a uni-credit incentive for the most hateful people she had ever encountered to be willing to provide a home for 'children in need'.

Scoffing at the thought as she scrubbed the soil from her hands, Vera realised, the free labour the Bennet's got from making the foster kids work their hundred acres of Texan vegetable gardens was surely enough of an incentive to take on unwanted children.

"Are you excited?" The words tickled at her ear canal as her best friend whispered in her ear.

Cringing, Vera rubbed her ear against her shoulder and grinned at Amelia. "Why would I be excited?" she retorted as she turned off the cold water; they certainly weren't allowed hot water for more than an hour at the end of the day; and grabbed the grubby looking towel hanging on the half-rusted ring anchored in the chipped tile wall of the bathroom. Screwing up her face in distaste, she dried her hands on the cleanest bit of material she could find.

Amelia rolled her eyes before she grabbed Vera's shoulders with her still-soil-stained hands. "You know what day it is tomorrow, don't you?"

Vera looked up at the light fitting that flickered above them. "Correct me if I'm wrong, but isn't it Thursday tomorrow."

"No. Well, yes, it is, but I mean, what date is it?"

"The 22nd day of the eighth month."

Amelia stomped her foot in frustration, "You are such a space slug, Vera."

Laughing, Vera wrapped her arms around Amelia. "I haven't forgotten my birthday, just as I won't forget my best friend. I'll get out of this prison, and I'll find us a place to live so when you turn eighteen in six months, you'll have somewhere to go."

Vera felt a wetness on her shoulder as Amelia squeezed her harder. "I'm gonna miss you. So, God-damned much it'll hurt."

"Six months won't take long. You'll see."

The door to the bathroom banged open, and both girls sprung apart to face the intrusion. The sneer on the face of Barlow Bennet as he looked at the two girls caused a shiver to race down both their spines. "Vera, Margorie wants to see you in the office. Something about settling all the paperwork in time for your birthday tomorrow."

Vera swallowed the lump in her throat before she nodded nervously, "Okay, Mr. Bennet." Everyone hated to go to the office. Margorie Bennet was a fiend for all things pink and was a lover of cats. The office was inhabited twenty-four hours a day, seven days a week by forty-two cats and Margorie. It stunk of cat pee and most disgustingly of the sickly scent of an unwashed obese woman. When it became clear that Barlow had no intention of moving, Vera squeezed past the narrow space he left between his scrawny frame and the wooden doorway. She gritted her teeth and stiffened her spine to repress the shudder as his hand groped at her rear end as she escaped into the dank hallway. As soon as she could, she broke into a jog, not that she was in a hurry to get to the cattery as the office was known to the foster kids who lived there, but that she was simply desperate to get away from the lecherous old man that Barlow was.

Stopping outside the pink-painted door that led into the dreaded office of Margorie, Vera steeled herself for stepping into the stench. Shaking her hands out at her sides to return feeling to them after clenching them so hard on her dash downstairs from the bathroom on the upper floor, she took a deep breath before she knocked on the door.

The syrupy sweet tones of Margorie echoed from within. "You may enter."

Pushing the door open, Vera tried not to retch at the appalling smell that rolled over and around her, swallowing back bile as she stepped in and as directed by the fat-wobbling flick of a wrist, and closed the door behind her. Wanting this interview to be over as soon as possible, Vera scooted around the various cats to make her way to the desk. Carefully, she evicted the grumpy cat from the only chair available for her to sit on.

Margorie pushed a bottle of soda towards Vera. "I wanted to celebrate your birthday with you," she said through a yellow-toothed smile. "So, go on, drink up. Have a treat on me. After all, it's not every day you turn eighteen and graduate from the Northern Hemisphere Foster System."

Somewhat nervous of the friendly behaviour of a woman who never given anything away, Vera reached for the bottle. Her eye twitched a little as she removed the loose cap, but as she was being waved at by the many rolls of fat from Marjorie's arm, Vera took a big slug of the sickly-sweet liquid. She pulled the bottle away and coughed at the carbonation that tickled her throat with the unexpectedness of it.

Marjorie smiled at her again, nodding her head for Vera to drink again. "That's it, Vera, drink it all up."

Vera tried to keep drinking the soda, but the room began to swim on her, making her lose focus and want to vomit it all back up, until eventually, she blacked out.

Chapter Two

There was a strange vibration that stirred Vera into wakefulness. Her head felt like it was full of sludge. Sludge that was also sticking her tongue to the roof of her mouth. She was grateful that there was no overwhelming stench of cat pee and body odour. Otherwise, the roiling in her stomach would spill out of her mouth. Blinking awake, Vera frowned. The air had a metallic taint to it, and it was a more comfortable temperature than she had ever been in Texas during August. She was also lying comfortably; another first since she had arrived at the Bennet's farm.

Opening her eyes slowly, she was surprised to find she was in a clean room, the walls in front of her appeared to be made of a smooth metal of some unknown origin to her. With a start, she sat upright, immediately groaning with the action that made her head spin.

"Easy. You'll make yourself sick if you move too quickly."

Vera looked across to the other side of the room where the softly-spoken, accented voice came from. A blonde-haired woman, probably a few years older than Vera sat with her knees drawn up on the second bed in the room. A reader pad was settled on her knees, yet the words were ignored as the blue eyes caught on Vera's brown ones.

"Where am I?" rasped Vera.

The reader pad was discarded onto the bed as the other woman bounced up to move across the room to a high-tech dispenser fitted in the wall. "Water," requested the Australian accent. A glass appeared in the hollow before the sound of running water filled the empty space as the glass was filled. The blonde took the glass in her hand and brought it across to Vera, perching on the edge of the bed. She gave her a friendly smile as Vera took the condensation damp glass from her and greedily sipped at the freshest, sweetest water she had ever tasted.

"Thank you," murmured Vera.

"You're welcome. My name is Nadine."

"Vera," she replied as she turned around to see the ledge protruding from the wall beside the bed. She put the glass down before she turned back to Nadine. "So? Where are we?"

"On board the Bridal Market."

Stunned speechless, Vera widened her eyes trying to ask for more information without using words.

Nadine frowned a little before smiling again and patting Vera's hand. "We're in space, heading on to the next galaxy. How come you don't know where we are? I assumed that you had been sedated because you panicked at the last minute about entering space. Some of the other girls react like that as they come on board."

Breathing heavily, Vera darted her eyes around the spartan room, for what, she was unsure. "What the hell? I was about to leave the Bennet's farm, I was finally going to be free. Last thing I remember was drinking that disgusting soda Marjorie gave me to celebrate my eighteenth birthday." Fear turned to anger as she realised what Marjorie had done. "That witch! She drugged me." Vera turned her attention back on Nadine. "Just what is the Bridal Market anyway?"

"It's a huge space ship that goes from planet to planet providing brides to males in need of a wife. It's kind of like a dating system, we all have profiles made up with a photo, details such as age, species, hair and eye colour, any defining physical attributes, whether we have any talents. Sometimes a bride is selected from the catalogue, sometimes selected in person. Apparently, some species have a mating pull that binds them to a female, and to know that they need to be in physical proximity to the female. Of course, there is a fee involved for the males to access the catalogue or step on board the public areas of the ship, the Elvitonions need to fund the upkeep of the vessel and all the needs of the potential brides."

Shaking her head Vera pulled away, "But that's just barbaric, it's practically prostitution!"

Nadine pulled away, standing from the bed as if she had been physically struck by Vera. "It's not. We all sign a contract to enter the program, accepting a dowry payment from the Elvitonions. The ship has an area just for the bridal candidates that is decked out with spas, entertainment centres, and shops for our pleasure. The men looking for a bride are only allowed access to the dining level where they can mingle amongst the women to help them find a wife. It's all organised and legally above board."

"I didn't mean to offend you, Nadine, I'm sorry. It's just...I never signed anything, I never agreed to come aboard. I was just waiting for my birthday so that I would finally be free from the Northern Hemisphere Foster System. To be off on my own, in charge of my own life."

Blinking rapidly, Nadine turned away for a moment before she sat back down on the edge of the bed. "I'm not sure how you could have come aboard if you haven't signed a contract, but if that's the case, then I'm sure we can sort this out. I'll take you to see the Matchmaker. He'll be able to straighten this out, I'm sure."

Nodding, Vera climbed from the bed when a wave of dizziness over took her, making her tumble back down onto the bed.

Nadine laughed softly. "I think before you go anywhere you need to have a shower. Come on, wobbly legs. You will love the cleanse unit, I thought I would miss water, but let me tell you, these things are amazing." Reaching out a hand Nadine helped Vera get to her feet and lead her to a door that was seamlessly hidden into the wall of their shared room. Grateful for the friendship and support of the blonde woman taking her through to a bathroom that was a quarter of the size of their bedroom. Wide eyed with surprise at the modern finish to the wash room, Vera turned around in awe. She had always considered the Bennet's farm as being old fashioned, but she never realised how out of date the farm house had been until this moment.

Laughing, Nadine turned Vera towards a glass unit in the corner of the room. "Here, you step in and shut the door. Press the green button to go, and the red button to stop. The cleansing units are fitted with sensors, so they respond appropriately to your body's requirements, whether you need a deep cleanse or a relaxing experience. When you take your clothes off, drop them in here." Nadine pressed an almost hidden button on the wall and a panel slid away to reveal an empty cubby space. "When you've put your clothes in there, they'll be taken away from laundering. When you step out the cleansing unit, you'll find fresh clothes through this door here." Vera turned around to see Nadine open another hidden door behind them, it revealed a room the size of the bathroom containing racks and shelves stuffed full of more clothes than Vera had ever seen. Nadine promptly disappeared back out into the main bedroom and left a stunned Vera standing in the middle of the bathroom. Shaking her head to free her from her stunned stupor she proceeded to peel off her clothes.

Chapter Three

An extra-large pair of eyes stared unblinking at Vera as she sat at the desk. Nadine had left her in the office after the Matchmaker had told Nadine to leave him alone with Vera. Years of hiding her emotions were brought into play as Vera stiffened her spine against the involuntary shudder of fear that wanted to race through her at the alien that sat opposite her. The sense of menace that held in the air was clear to Vera. This alien was not to be trifled with.

"Bride Nadine advised there is a misunderstanding," murmured the Matchmaker, his English was flawless yet completely without any accent or regional inflection.

"Yes. Nadine told me that the women must sign contracts before coming aboard, and I haven't signed anything. I don't wish to be here, I'm not looking for a husband."

The slender creature moved back into his chair, his oversized head seemed to overbalance as it slowly moved towards the left shoulder that sloped away from his neck with what looked — to Vera — like very little strength. "Do you have a million uni-credits?"

Gobsmacked, Vera could only laugh, "What? No. I haven't a cred to my name, let alone a million uni-credits. Why would you ask me such a thing?"

The pale purple scaly skin of the giant head moved upright again before slowly slipping once more towards the other shoulder. "It is the price of your contract."

"I haven't got a contract!" cried Vera.

The two long narrow slits that Vera assumed to be a nose flared wide before a stick thin arm lifted from below the desk. Three fingers, twice the length of Vera's own, and half the thickness tapped out onto the desk. A holographic document lifted from the desk before Vera. "This, Bride Vera, is your contract. Signed, sealed, and delivered, paid for in advance. Until such time as a groom orders and pays off your contract, you are very much a legal participant of the Bridal Market."

Shaking her head, Vera pushed back into her chair. "I never signed that, I'm not a willing participant, I want to go back to Earth. NOW."

"You were a minor when the contract was signed. Your legal guardian signed you into the program and received your dowry. I never said you were a willing participant, but you are legally bound by the accords of the galactic legal system. If you will not take a husband, then you must pay off your contract to remove yourself from our program." The Matchmaker tapped at the desk once more, making the contract disappear before his hand slithered back onto his lap below the table.

"I don't have any money, I can't pay the contract price," whispered Vera, despair of the situation and anger at the Bennet's warring within her heart.

"Then, you are a bride," stated the Matchmaker, his head slowly moving upright again.

Vera shook her head so violently she was certain she could hear her brain slosh around inside her skull, "No, I don't want a husband."

The purple colour of the Matchmaker's skin flushed deep violet and two frills flared open behind his head as he moved forward towards her. "We have invested much in you, Bride Vera. If you refuse to cooperate in the Bridal program to recoup our losses, then you shall be relegated to the unmarriageable quarters until such time as your debt to us is paid."

"What?" breathed out Vera, eyes wide, heart pounding.

A thin lip lifted in a sneer, "Those women who attract no husband become courtesans, serving the less well off our clientele. Some can, of course afford a wife, they simply do not want one, but all men have physical needs, and we provide the women to fulfil those needs."

Blinking back the tears that burned in her eyes, Vera dug her short nails into the palms of her hand. She swallowed hard before she replied, "Are you telling me, that if I refuse to become a bride, then I must become a whore?"

The frills settled out of sight and the Matchmaker's colour faded back to the pale colour it had been when she had first entered the office. "You've chosen to paraphrase me, but that is the gist of what is required of you. If you choose to be a bride, you have full use of our facilities, and you will not accrue any further debt. Should you wish to whore yourself out, then you will be charged for your keep, your debt will continue to rise, and you will find yourself on board the Bridal Market far longer than a pretty thing like you would be should you allow yourself to be chosen as a bride."

Biting her lip, Vera knew neither was an option that she wished to pursue, yet if she wanted off this ship and to be free as she had expected to be as she turned eighteen, then she needed to play these aliens at their own game. Swallowing the bile that was teasing at her throat, she lifted her eyes to meet the large unblinking ones of the alien that held her fate in his hands. "Then I choose to be a bride."

The head slipped to one side again as he responded to her words. "Then, we are finished here for now. Tomorrow I will meet with you to organise your profile for the catalogue. You may leave now."

Vera stood, walking on stiff legs towards the door, as she lifted her hand to the panel to open it, his voice halted her. "Happy Birthday, Bride Vera."

Ignoring the hollow sentiment, Vera straightened her spine and walked out of the office. She would seek out Nadine and figure out the layout of the ship. Maybe she could find some way of hiding away from the Matchmaker and sneaking off the ship at the first opportunity.

Chapter Four

Vera had never seen such luxury in all her life. Correction; she had seen it from a distance, or on holla-viewers at school, but she had never been up close and personal to the luxury that the bridal entertainment level provided. Nadine had tugged on Vera's hand most of the way around the ship, never letting her stop and stare for long. She was intent on her mission of showing Vera the facilities available to them as brides of the Bridal Market's program. Vera could feel the older girl's excitement at having a new friend and was hesitant to confide in her that she was not actually a willing bride, or that she intended to remain on board the Bridal Market long enough to be chosen as a bride.

Nadine had shared a little of her own history with Vera, and the prospect of being chosen by a wealthy man, regardless of his species; because yes, there were plenty of cross-species matches, was better than the alternative. A life of poverty in a drought-stricken continent where one percent of the people were filthy-rich, and the rest of the population were poor and desperate, gave Vera a sense of humility. That despite her rough up-bringing, tossed from home to home, she had never lacked for a meal, no matter how meagre or a roof over her head. Nadine had chosen to enter the program to escape a life of poverty and the unknown of where her next meal would come from.

"What's down there?" asked Vera as she dug in her heels and pulled Nadine to a stop. She jerked her head down a darkened corridor. The emptiness of it seemed to call to Vera.

Nadine huffed out an annoyed breath before she followed Vera's gaze. "Ummm, I think that's a service corridor, the service lifts from the cargo bay to this level. Excess food stores, and clothing are all kept down there. It's off limits to brides, boring anyway. So, come on, let's go get a mani-pedi."

Nodding, Vera marked the location in her mind and allowed Nadine to tow her along once more. She would be back later and make her way into the cargo hold. It sounded like the ideal location to hide out, and hopefully, provide an exit as soon as the ship stopped to reload.

* * *

It had been a couple of hours since Vera had managed to slip away from a sleeping Nadine. It seemed that most of the ship was asleep, in fact. The lighting was muted, and everything seemed quiet as Vera retraced her steps from earlier in the evening. Eventually, she had managed to access a side panel with a manual descent tube that descended alongside the elevator into the cargo bay. It took a little shuffling and searching to find the perfect place to hide. She was investigating a particularly large container when the ship lurched with a loud explosive sound. Vera felt her heart racing at the unknown when the lights started flashing red, and a toneless voice echoed out across the cargo bay, and presumably the whole ship.

"Brides, please remain in your quarters. The Bridal Market has been engaged by space pirates. Please do not fret, we shall resolve this matter peacefully and as swiftly as possible."

Not knowing whether to laugh or cry, Vera did a strange muffled sound somewhere between the two. First, she was sold by a woman she hated to an alien woman trader, and now the ship she was on was under attack by pirates. It was hard for Vera to even comprehend that in this century that pirates still existed. The sound of the elevators moving spurred Vera into action and she darted into the container she had been investigating just as a golden glow filled the open space. She lowered the lid until there was barely a slit of light available for her to see out of when she saw a large group of aliens appear in the cargo bay. They were a rag tag collection of species, and Vera honestly struggled to comprehend that so many different aliens existed in the universe. There was even a human amongst the men, and Vera found her eyes drawn to him. His black hair was long and hung in loose waves around his broad shoulders. His eyes also seemed to be boring straight into hers where she was hidden within the confines of a container of clothing.

"Captain." The Matchmaker's voice echoed around the large space, instantly making the hair on the back of Vera's neck stand up in fear. Strange she thought, that the arrival of the pirates didn't cause the same reaction that the Elvitonion did. "Your reputation proceeds you, and we are more than happy to come to an arrangement with you. Would you prefer to take women for your men, or goods?"

The laughter that rumbled from the alien that she presumed to be the pirate captain caused a shiver to race through her body. "You Elvitonions are all the same. We don't have a need for your women, we'd rather take uni-credits, we'll even make the transaction as painless as possible for you, here is our banking tablet."

The splutter that came from the Matchmaker made Vera want to giggle, she was beginning to feel his race were renowned for a greed of uni-credits. She swallowed back a gasp of surprise when she realised that the human pirate had strolled over to the container she was hiding in. He lifted the lid enough to see in, making Vera cringe back in fear. Her wide eyes held his, pleading for his silence. He gave her a cocky wink and a sly smile that spoke of being a fellow conspirator. And then he dropped the lid back on top of her, sealing her inside. Yet his voice, as smooth as a river washed stone, still reached through to her.

"I don't know about you, Captain, but I rather fancy the contents of this container, I'll take this as my share of the loot."

Chapter Five

    Vera bit her lip to stop her squeal of surprise as the container shifted as it was lifted, surprising her with the strength of the pirate, for she was certain she hadn't heard anyone else approach. There was a strange sensation that rushed through her body before she felt like herself again. The same rumbling laughter sounded closer.

    "So, Rus, what caught your eye in this box of tricks?"

    Another laugh not quite as deep curled around Vera and sparked her interest, yet she held her breath as the lid was lifted once more. "Oh, you know me, Captain. I'm a sucker for a damsel in distress. And this little miss seemed to be rather desperate to get away from the Bridal Market."

    Vera looked up from her position with her arms wrapped around her knees to see two very different faces staring down at her. The human male had the same cocky grin on his face, yet the red skinned alien that made Vera think of a demon looked angry.

    "We don't take women from the Elvitonions," snarled the demon as he towered over the human male. Yet the human didn't seem to be intimidated by the angry and dangerous looking pirate captain.

    She was scared, though, not of the captain, but at the thought he would send her back to the Bridal Market. Pulling on every learned trait of hiding her fear and emotions, Vera gritted her teeth before she shifted until she was standing amongst the rumpled materials of the container. "I won't go back. I never wanted to be on that blasted ship in the first place, you can't make me go back!"

One dark, glossy black brow rose high over a very alien eye as the captain turned the full force of his attentions on Vera, if he was surprised by the force of her outburst, he didn't show it. "Oh, can't I? I can do anything I damn well please! I am the captain of this ship and her crew. I don't take orders from a pipsqueak like you."

Vera felt her face flush red with her anger, "You don't scare me! I've not fought tooth and nail for the last twelve years of my God damned life to get out of the messed-up system the government of the Northern Hemisphere call 'care' just to have my freedom stolen from me hours before I turn eighteen so some slack jawed, fat rolling cow of a woman can sell me to a damn slave trader who calls himself a bloody Matchmaker."

A growl rumbled out of the pirate that still towered over her, Vera held his eyes, her body stiff with her will power not to tremble in front of him. "All women who board that ship sign a contract and are well paid in advance, the Elvitonions might be credit hungry, but they are not kidnappers."

Scoffing Vera twisted her lips in a sardonic smile, "How would you know? Have you interviewed every woman who steps foot on that ship? I was drugged in my care home, only hours before I was due to turn eighteen and hightail it out of the twisted excuse of a Foster System that's supposedly supposed to look after kids with no families. I wake up and find myself no longer on Earth but in space and a prospect bride for some desperate man who can't find a woman through the traditional methods. And when I try and explain I don't want to be on that damn ship, I'm threatened to either stay a bride or become a courtesan for those sleaze balls who have to pay to get their rocks off. I will repeat myself only one more time, so make sure you are listening, buddy! I. Will. Not. Go. Back. On. That. Ship!"

The air seemed to crackle between of the two of them as Vera continued to hold his reptilian eyes. After what felt like an age, his face seemed to void of all emotion and he stepped back away from the container. He stopped turning away as he caught the human pirates eye, "You wanted to rescue a damsel in distress, Russ? Well now you are responsible for a hellion. Don't come bitching to me if you can't handle the little witch."

And then he was gone, leaving Vera alone with a softly chuckling male who was by far the most attractive man she had ever seen.

Rus, as he had been identified, rested his hands on the edge of the container, smirking at Vera as he looked up at her from his half-bent position. "So, little hellion, what's your name?"

"Vera Delaney."

"Well, Vera Delaney, you can call me Rus. You want to live in that box of bedding, or would you care to come and find a bed?"

Vera couldn't help but smile, feeling a sense of security at being in the presence of Rus. His cocky smirk was a bit of a turn on as well, so she could hardly complain. With little hesitation she reached out her hand and took his offered one. She gasped at the electricity that seemed to arc between them as she felt his almost icy cold hand against her own hot one. Even Rus seemed to be taken aback by the physical reaction between them, his eyes widened in surprise before the hazel colour seemed to bleed red.

"Well that's an unexpected surprise," he murmured as he pulled her out of the box until she was flush against his hard body. "So far from home, and yet right where you should be. Fate is a fickle mistress to toy with me for so long before bringing my Beloved to me." One hand was still clasped around hers, the other slipped over her shoulder and under the heavy weight of her long brown locks that hung loose down her back.

Feeling her body tremble in a way she never had before felt, she looked up into the eyes that gazed down on her. "What?" she asked in a breathless tone.

His smile softened, losing the edge of cockiness, yet not detracting from his allure. "You were taken to that ship so that I could find you. I haven't been on Earth in nearly two hundred years and have no intention of returning. The fates understood that, and so they brought you to me."

Vera blinked slowly before frowning. "You lost me at two hundred years."

Rus laughed, the sound vibrating through her body as he did. "Vera Delaney, do you believe in soul mates?"

To Be Continued …

Made in the USA
Middletown, DE
18 March 2019